HEAVEN'S RAY

—

Cheryle Coapstick

Series:
MY MAMA'S MAMA

Alaska's Firy

About Miss Ruth

Alaska's Mama

They Settled in Sitka

First paperback edition November 2024

Paperback: ISBN 978-1-7366706-7-5
eBook: ISBN 978-1-7366706-8-2

Cover design and interior formatting by Andy Towler
www.aplusscreative.com

Published by Biorka Books
chercoaps@gmail.com

Notes of Gratitude

Many people have supported and encouraged me on this journey. It would be difficult to list them all, but special thanks have to be given to Bodie Thoene, who challenged me to write my family story. Her cheerleading spurred me on when I was down and ready to sit on the bench.

My soul sister Denise Phillips listened to countless chapters and pressured me to keep going even when I insisted I was not a writer. She said, "Don't worry about the writing. It will come. Just tell the story. You are such an awesome story teller."

My faithful technical team of Patty Huey and Vicki Karlsson have been with me since my first feeble attempts and Maureen Harlan joined us shortly thereafter. Grammar, plot, punctuation, and character development are their forte.

The Pond and Parchment Writer's Guild listened to my scribbles every month and offered encouragement and unique suggestions. Jesse Jury, Olivia Jury, RJ Norton, Ron Jenkins, Linda Jenkins, and Patty Huey.

Andy Towler of Aplusscreative has formatted and uploaded all of my files. He's taken my vague ideas and turned them into distinctive covers. He's an incredible artist and technical expert.

My family gave me all the time I needed to research and write. It's a precious gift, and I appreciate it.

To my readers, thank you and bless you. Your feedback

through messages and social media has been incredible. It has been a joy to meet some of you in person. Please follow my Facebook author page.

I am eternally grateful to the Lord Jesus for putting a love for words in my heart. I have always been an insatiable reader, and now I want to write as much as I read! I'm so appreciative of the imagination and love of story God has given me.

Thank you all from the depths of my being.

It can't be
what it was,
but
it can still
be good.

—*Miss Ruth*

PROLOGUE
St. Paul, Pribilof Islands
1788

The weather, as always this time of year, was unbearable, with arctic winds bringing iced rain that pushed sideways out of the sky. They hit the few exposed parts of my face with a freezing burn; stinging scratches that caused fierce pain. I looked to the sea from above the rookery. The low clouds, swirled and pushed by the wind, merged with the foaming gray water. The dark water, heaving and surging, hit the cliff my grandfather and I stood on. Fifty-foot waves threatened to wash over the small island.

"Will the waves overtake us, Grandfather?" The salt spray etched itself into the scratches on my face, causing more pain.

"They will not."

"Maybe they should. Our lives in this place are without value."

"Life always has value, no matter where we are or what happens to us." He pulled a soft piece of sealskin from beneath his parka and wiped the wetness from my face.

Grandfather Atkak thought his words wise, but I was not sure. He often spoke of a time when these islands were uninhabited and unknown to the Russians. Millions of seals have returned yearly since before time. They wished only to mate and give birth. This place is no longer a haven for them.

We had always lived farther south. When the Russians first

came to our small islands, we did not expect their treacherous brutality. They gathered us on the beach and separated the men from the women and children. My father protested, and his life was taken by a Russian firestick. There was a loud boom and a puff of smoke. My father crumpled.

Seeing the power of that weapon cowed everyone, and we bowed to their superior strength. All the men of our village, even the elders, were forced into their large sailing ship.

"Hey, you, boy. What is your name?"

I did not understand the Russian's words, but I heard an evil authority in his tone. He gestured for me to go with the men. I had only reached twelve summers, but I was as tall as my grandfather, and so they took me.

We sailed north, and they planted us on these two barren rocks they called St. Paul and St. George, the Pribilof Islands, named for the sea captain who had discovered them.

To keep our women folk alive, we obeyed these brutal over-seers. We began clubbing the seals when the sun rose, and by the time it bid us a setting farewell, we were covered in blood and guts. The smell of dead, rotting flesh made many of us ill. There was no reprieve. Week after week, the Russians stood over us with their fierce faces and firesticks. We did not know why they forced us to kill the animals, preserve the fur, and fill their ship.

Chasing the shrieking seals, clubbing them, and leaving their bloody carcasses strewn across the beach was against everything we believed in. Grandfather said the Russians were disrespectful to the Creator. It was not right to kill and kill, but not for food. We could not accept that these Russians slaughtered without thought, but that was the reality they forced us to live in.

One night, when the others thought I was asleep, I heard Natak say, "We are valued only for our labor."

"Our Russian overlords see us not as men but as beasts used to kill other beasts," Kanak said, "We must try to escape."

Grandfather Atkak stirred the small driftwood fire the men huddled around. He let the stick fall into the flames. "You are brave but foolish. We do not know where we are. We have no weapons and no oomiak, not even a badarka or kayak. We do not know how to sail the Russian ship."

"We cannot live this way," Natak said.

"The unceasing overcast sky darkens my soul," Kanak muttered.

"The Russians force us to do their bidding, but they can not imprison our spirits," Grandfather said.

"I feel imprisoned, " Natak said.

"My soul is dead, and I long to escape." Kanak hung his head.

"Do not struggle against the futility of escape. Fight to keep your soul and spirit free. I will tell you the story of our people, and we will sing our songs." Grandfather Atkak pleaded with the young men to listen and be wise.

Natak kept grandfather up, night after night, asking questions. "I must learn everything in your mind, Atkak, and in your heart. You are old, and soon your spirit will depart. You must leave your wisdom behind."

Kanak became silent, morose. Day after day, he killed seals. At night he walked the black sand beaches. The fog shrouded him, and the roaring wind covered his cries. Early one morning, we found his clothes on the beach. Three days later, his naked body washed ashore. True to his word, he found a way to escape.

The following year, Grandfather Atkak died. Like a heavy fog, a pall hung over us, and we had difficulty forcing ourselves to keep up the pace the Russians demanded. No amount of punishment encouraged or coerced us.

Natak had listened closely to the Russians, and after a long while, two or three summers, I think, he could speak their language.

"The Russians said their priest is insisting they build a church here. They will bring our women, and we will have a village. This will be our life," Natak said.

A small village was built, and the women were delivered to us. I was once again held in the arms of my mother. She brought comfort and an expectation of hope. She told us the priest was a good man and had some power over the Russians. Over time, he was able to improve our living conditions.

Natak became our leader, but the words he spoke belonged to Grandfather Atkat. Every day, we killed. Always killing but without feeling. At night, in our little village, with our families close, we lived.

As Grandfather instructed, we kept our hearts intact and our spirits free.

Russia
Attu
Kiska
North Pac
Japan
Midway Atoll
Sou
Papua New
Guinea
Solomon
Islands
Vanuatu
New
Caledonia
Australia

Alaska
Dutch Harbor
Kodiak
Sitka
Ocean
Hawai'i
San Diego
Pacific Ocean
*Map not to scale.

CHAPTER ONE
Kodiak Island, Territory of Alaska
Summer 1942

"Who was that?" Ensign Mark Lawson IV slapped a stack of reports on the battered metal desk, but his eyes were on the tall, slim woman who breezed past him without a glance. Her auburn hair peeked out from her nurse's cap and curled on the nape of her neck. Mark shrugged out of his jacket and set his cover—military cap—on the edge of the yeoman's desk. He wasn't used to being ignored. Women always gave him a second look and usually a third. Older women, younger women. Pretty ones and those not-so-pretty. It didn't matter. They all looked. What was wrong with this one?

"She's not for you."

"What's her name? And why haven't I seen her before? I've been on this blasted rock for over a year."

The short, thin, and non-descript clerk who arranged Commander Mark Lawson III's schedule and organized the multiple copies of the paperwork the Navy seemed to favor frowned. Nothing happened on the base that the yeoman couldn't sort out and control. Nothing except the commander's son and namesake. "Let it go, Ensign." He pulled a handkerchief from his back pocket and wiped his wire-rimmed glasses.

Mark Lawson IV sat on the edge of the paper-strewn desk. "Come on, Elly, what's her name?"

"In case you have forgotten my name—it's Elwood A. Richardson, Yeoman 1st Class, United States Navy. I'll thank you to remember that."

"I've known you as long as I can remember. You're my godfather. Of course, I know your name."

"The trouble with you is that you are too pretty for your own good."

Six-foot-two, Ensign Lawson had the grace to blush, "I'm handsome, not pretty. It's not my fault I was born with blue eyes and dark wavy hair."

"Hmmph! It is your fault when you flex your muscles and use those eyes to get what you want."

"Give me a break, Elly. I'm harmless."

"You're not, and this girl is different." The slightly balding yeoman tapped the Bible on the edge of his desk. "You need to do some serious thinking, young man."

"There's a war on Elly, and a lot of us aren't going to make it. We have to live it up while we can." The ensign glanced out the window for a fleeting look at the young woman. She flipped the hood of her jacket over her head, crushing her nurse's cap, and bent against the wind. He shifted his gaze to the thick clouds that looked ready to spill all the water they held.

"And if you don't make it, what then?" Yeoman Richardson tapped the book again, "Pay attention."

Ensign Lawson shrugged. "My mother dragged me to her church when Dad was stationed in Washington, D.C. People were concerned with their appearance, who was invited to which embassy affair, and who had the ear of the most powerful congressman. It was more like a country club than anything religious. And the church in Newport wasn't much better."

"Your mother's churches weren't like that, but I'm not talking about a church. I'm talking about the Creator of the universe. What would you say to Him if you didn't make it?"

Ensign Lawson shook the serious thought away. "All I'm thinking about right now is that girl. I need a diversion, someone different. I'm so tired of—of," Ensign Lawson's shoulders sagged, and he fiddled with the yeoman's stapler. "—just tired."

Elwood Richardson, feeling more like the young man's grandfather than godfather, studied Mark for a long minute. He saw a dull red creep up Mark's face. Richardson looked toward the commander's door, then whispered, "Her name is Heaven Ray Turner, but you didn't hear that from me."

"Heaven? The scrappy civilian nurse that took on the old man last month?" The ensign exchanged the stapler for a chocolate from the open box on Richardson's desk. "Not everyone has the guts to do that."

"A little respect for Captain Mark Lawson III, commander of this base. And more to the point, your father." Yeoman Richardson removed the candy box from Mark's reach. "Your Casanova attitude is not something he approves of."

"By the way, is the Old—the commander in?"

Hearing his son's voice, Commander Lawson came to the doorway of his office and frowned, "Stay away from that girl. She and her mother are the finest nurses I've ever seen. Until the Navy nurses arrive, I need these civilians. Don't distract them."

"It's not my intention to distract anyone, sir."

Commander Lawson snorted his disbelief and said, "They were recently part of the team assessing the station hospitals in

Cold Bay, Naknek, Adak, Unalaska, and Umnak. Nurse Turner doesn't need you filling her head with—whatever it is you fill women's heads with."

Ensign Mark Lawson stood at attention and gave his father a precise salute, although his eyes twinkled, "Yes! sir!"

The commander returned to his office as he muttered, "If I hadn't promised your mother—I'd transfer you to a battleship ASAP."

Ensign Lawson spoke aloud, "I wish he would."

"Your father would like to command a ship again," Yeoman Richardson looked thoughtfully after the commander, then turned his attention to Mark, "Just like he did in the Great War."

"He's always been behind a desk. He loves pushing papers around."

"You don't know him as well as you think. After World War I, the Navy discovered your father's organizational and logistical talents and restricted his time at sea."

"You said he commanded a ship? He's never talked about it. Tell me."

The yeoman shrugged, "That's his story, not mine."

Mark looked at his father's office door. He thought about bursting through and asking him about his career during WWI but knew he wouldn't get any answers. Instead, he gazed through the window. Bulldozers pushed dirt from one side of the compound to the other. He had heard his father curse Kodiak's lousy ground. It was either rock or muskeg, covered with a layer of volcanic ash ranging from three inches to eight feet in depth. Sometimes, crews encountered drifts up to twenty feet, stopping construction until it could be hauled away. Trucks loaded with volcanic ash drove everywhere on the unpaved roads, throwing up dust in Kodiak's fierce wind when it was dry and stalling in thick mud during rainy weather. Cranes hauled timbers into place. Men yelled orders to each other but couldn't be heard over the machines. However, they could see Commander Lawson swear in frustration whenever he drove his Jeep across the base.

"This base is chaotic, hardly functioning," Ensign Lawson sputtered.

"Your father had to start from scratch. Most of the locals working on construction are fishermen and only pound nails during the off-season. The civilian construction crews brought up from the States are overworked, and there are not enough of them. Your father first had to establish the seaplane and submarine bases. They needed to be on a war footing as soon as possible."

"It's a mess."

"The Commander is trying to get some Seabees posted here, but Europe and the Pacific have priority regarding personnel, artillery, and supplies." Yeoman Richardson moved constantly as he spoke, arranging and filing papers, stuffing and addressing envelopes, and signing requisitions while pushing chocolate after chocolate into his mouth.

"Europe's where the action is, and I am stuck on this rock," Ensign Lawson moaned.

Elly shuffled the papers on his desk and tried to keep the irritation out of his voice. The tight lines around his mouth betrayed him. "We were posted here a year sooner than our contract specified because intelligence said Japan's too interested in the North, but you didn't hear that from me." The Yeoman 1st Class closed his eyes and pursed his lips. He glanced at the commander's door and said, "It was just a SNAFU that you ended up here."

"I thought he arranged it." Mark nodded toward the commander's door.

Irritated that Mark did not get along with his father, Elly stared at the closed door with the gold lettering: CAPTAIN MARK LAWSON, III, COMMANDER USN KODIAK. He sighed and chose a dark chocolate cream. "When your mother heard about the attack at Pearl…"

"And my brother Brad's death on the Arizona." Mark swallowed the lump in his throat.

Yeoman Richardson swiped at his eyes. "Yes, well, she put the idea to keep you out of the Pacific into a visiting senator's ear at some social event in Newport."

"I can't believe Mom would do such a thing or that the commander would go along with it," Mark said.

"They had just received news that Brad died. Try to think like a parent, not a hotshot officer trying to win himself some glory."

Mark ignored the rebuke. It wasn't glory he longed for, but something more personal. "I'm glad Eugene was on the Hornet."

"I'm sure your mother was relieved the Hornet was off the coast of Virginia when Pearl was attacked. One son in the middle of battle was enough, especially when that son didn't make it," Elly said.

"Eugene's in the thick of it now, I bet." Mark wiped his hand across his eyes and thought of his brothers, one at the bottom of Pearl Harbor and the other at sea aboard the Yorktown Class aircraft carrier.

"I'm grateful you didn't lose both brothers at Pearl." Yeoman Richardson blew his nose and fished for another chocolate.

Ensign Lawson turned his eyes away, then frowned and asked, "What senator?"

"One that had influence with the Department of the Navy."

"She should have left well enough alone. I'll write to her and ask her to talk to the senator again—to get me on a ship," Mark groused.

"Cut her some slack, Mark. She's still grieving for Brad and worried about Eugene now that he's in the Pacific. She wanted her youngest boy safe." He glanced at the commander's door.

"Why so nervous, Elly? He can't hear you."

"I wouldn't be too sure," Yeoman Richardson shrugged, "but you didn't hear that from me."

"I don't hear a lot from you, and I love it." Mark stretched, snagged another chocolate, and wondered if he would have joined the Navy given a choice. Expectations ran high for the fourth-generation sons of a prominent naval family. His oldest brother, Brad, should have been christened **Mark Lawson IV,** but according to Elly, his mother objected, believing it was too much pressure. She felt the same when her second son was born two years later. She lost the naming battle when Mark was born.

With the long naval tradition of his father's family and the political influence of his mother's, Mark believed everyone's expectations of him soared. He felt the presence and pressure of their eyes even though he was stationed in faraway Alaska.

Yeoman Richardson shoved the candy box into a drawer, gave the ensign another long look, then whispered, "Heaven Ray's mother was supposed to pick her up but apparently has been delayed. It's a long walk to the girl's home."

"Thanks, Elly, you're the best." Grinning, Ensign Lawson opened the drawer, grabbed the box of chocolates, his jacket, and cover, and dashed out. A moment later, the commander's Jeep threw dusty little tornadoes from the back tires as it roared away.

Before the yeoman returned to his paperwork, he peered out of the window and stared after the vehicle. "Heaven Ray, you just might be the making of that boy—please God." He unlocked the metal filing cabinet and pulled out another box of chocolates while wondering what consequences the ensign would suffer for taking the old man's Jeep.

The Jeep slowed next to Heaven Ray. Eyes straight ahead, she kept walking.

"Hop in. I'll give you a ride."

"It's a nice day. I'll walk." She slid her eyes sideways to take a peek at him. *He is handsome.*

"It's cold, windy, and about to rain."

"For Kodiak at this time of year, it's positively balmy." She pulled her jacket tighter.

"It's a long way to wherever you are going."

"My legs are strong." *Such blue eyes, oh my!*

"And lovely."

"Move along, Ensign. I'm not interested." *I can see why all the girls say he's to die for.*

"In what? A ride?"

"In you. I've heard about your way with the ladies." *If only he hadn't dated every girl on the island.*

The ensign gunned the engine and sped away. A few yards ahead, he executed a perfect U-turn and blocked her way. She quietly waited for him to speak. He seemed to be at a loss for words. She tapped her foot. He focused on it.

"Didn't your mother tell you it's rude to stare?" she asked. *I wonder if he likes what he sees.*

"I have chocolate."

"No, thank you." *I haven't had chocolate in months.*

"How can you turn down chocolate?"

She threw a half-grin in his direction. "I admit it's harder to turn down the chocolate than you." *He is charming. Get a hold of yourself, Heaven. There is a war on.*

"I am deeply hurt." He placed his hand over his heart and sighed but couldn't keep the twinkle from his eyes.

"I imagine women succumb to your charms all the time." *I refuse to be a part of your harem.*

He removed his cover, ran his hand through his dark, wavy hair, and winked. "So, you admit I am charming. That's progress."

"I admit nothing," her green eyes flashed, but she couldn't keep from grinning. *Why does he have to be so likable?*

He looked toward the sky. "Those dark clouds rolling in tell me it's going to rain."

She glanced upwards. "And you think I won't get wet in an open Jeep?"

He patted the dashboard. "This baby will get you home much faster than your all too lovely legs."

"I'm not going home, and I don't think it will rain, but on the off chance you're right, I'll accept a ride." She climbed into the Jeep, sat at attention, and once again kept her face forward. "And only a ride." *I can't let him know I'm tempted.*

"Nothing else is on offer, ma'am."

"Not even the chocolate?" *Why didn't I accept the candy when he offered it. Stupid.*

"No, ma'am," He laughed and stuffed the box under his seat.

The green-eyed nurse with the classic profile remained silent as they crossed the base and headed toward the village of Kodiak. He asked about her parents, what had brought them to Alaska, why she became a nurse, what readiness the station hospitals were in, and what kind of music, movies, books, and food she liked. Her refusal to answer confused him, and he kept glancing her way. He drove slowly even though the dark clouds seemed ready to release their rain.

"You can drop me there." She pointed to a square white building at the end of the town's main road. Even though it was summer, three local girls clustered on the wooden sidewalk, bundled in jackets, hats, and scarves. He groaned. He had dated two out of the three. His mind was focused on the woman in the Jeep, and he didn't glance at the girl with Delores and Barbara.

"Thank you," Heaven Ray murmured politely. *Don't make eye contact. Don't succumb to his charm.*

"Wait, don't you want coffee, tea, a sandwich, something?" He spoke to her back. She was already halfway into the building.

A tall brunette leaned against the Jeep and laughed, "Torpedoed, Mark. You've been hit."

"What's with her anyway, Delores?"

"Mark, you're all fun and games, which is good since there is a war on, and we'll all probably die."

"Yeah?"

"She's not like that. In fact, Heaven is a good name for her. She talks about God and heaven all the time, even when we were kids. Despite that, we still like her."

Mark shook his head and wondered if Heaven Ray was a religious fanatic. She was pretty, no doubt about that. He decided she was worth the risk. "What are you all doing here?"

"In an hour, the mayor is giving a talk on civil defense at City Hall." Barbara pointed to a small building across the unpaved street.

"An hour? Why is everybody here so early?"

Delores laughed. "Mail plane flew over thirty minutes ago. Everybody stops by the post office sooner rather than later."

"Small towns," Mark muttered.

Delores slugged him on the arm. "Don't disparage our ways, city boy."

"At least you have electricity and indoor plumbing," he winked and waggled his eyebrows.

"We haven't had them long and are grateful for all the Navy has done, along with the Kodiak Electric Association." Delores laughed and kissed the air in his direction, "All four hundred inhabitants of Kodiak are thankful."

"I'm sure the outhouses in winter were a lot of fun." He grinned sheepishly and changed the subject. "I heard Heaven Ray barged into the commander's office last month, demanding to join the team touring the station hospitals. Elly—Yeoman Richardson—wouldn't give me any details."

Delores laughed and leaned against the Jeep. "She made an appointment and had an answer to all of his questions. Besides, her mother is a traveling nurse for the Territorial Government and has been taking Heaven to the Aleutians for years—unofficially."

"Seems to me a lot of things are done unofficially in Alaska."

Delores winked at the young officer. "It didn't sit well with Heaven Ray that she was not allowed to go when she had the necessary experience."

"She's not official."

Barbara shrugged. "A technicality. None of us are military, yet Del and I work at the Fort Abercrombie Dispensary and will work at the base hospital."

"If they ever finish the construction."

"Rita here," Delores pushed the mousy-looking girl forward, "is one of Kodiak's best bush pilots and airline mechanics."

"Hard to think of a girl as a pilot or mechanic. Not very ladylike."

Rita rolled her eyes and cleared her throat, "Don't be a jerk, Ensign."

"Sorry." Mark didn't realize he said the words aloud. He had the grace to blush.

"Rita has shown your Navy pilots how to scrounge for parts and jury-rig a thing or two when they couldn't get anything," Delores paused, "officially."

"Hmm." Mark stared over their heads, hoping to see the lovely nurse emerge. A change in the conversation seemed in order. "Rumors are Heaven Ray was aggressive, even feisty."

"If a man's aggressive, he's determined and admired for it. If a woman's aggressive, she's feisty and not lady-like," Rita said, stomping her feet. "It's raining. I'll meet you inside." She crossed the street.

Delores watched her friend leave, "Just a drizzle." She folded her arms and studied the commander's son. "And how would your father have responded to aggressive and feisty—male or female?"

Mark shook his head, then grinned. "Not well, but you'd think Nurse Turner would try to dispel the rumors."

"She doesn't pay any attention to gossip." The woman's red lipstick shimmered in the sun that peeked between the storm clouds. Her mouth formed a pouty bow. "She's out of your league, Marky-boy. Best back off."

Barbara and Delores teased him about having little chance with Heaven Ray. After dating, he had remained friends with both of them. He believed himself to be honest and likable, and everyone, male or female, seemed to agree. "Girls, you're the best. Are you going to help with my "heavenly" campaign?" He wiggled his eyebrows and grinned.

Barbara said, "She's a goody-two-shoes, Mark. You'd be better off with a real woman."

"Like you?" Delores said.

"Better than you!" Barbara answered, but her tone was light.

"Now girls—you lovely dolls," Mark pleaded. "I adore you both. You know I do."

Delores looked toward the entrance of the post office. "Don't look now, but she's peeking through the glass door."

"That's a good sign, isn't it?" Mark pulled the box from under the seat. The girls giggled and reached for the chocolates. A few minutes later, Mark asked, "How long does it take to pick up the mail anyway?"

"You weren't paying attention, Mark. Heaven Ray left the building and hurried around the corner."

An elderly woman walking by with her mail paused. "You looking for Heaven? She received a letter from her father. She said the mayor would understand she needed to hurry home."

"I thought Heaven Ray's mother was a widow." Mark flashed the old woman his dashing smile.

She patted the gray hair that escaped from her headscarf and gave Mark a second look. He held out the box of chocolates. There were two left. She took them both, stuffed them into her cheeks, and talked around them, "Her father was a Navy doctor and re-gained his commission after the attack at Pearl Harbor."

"He's stationed on the Lexington," Delores added. "Apparently, aircraft carriers need doctors, too."

The following day, the embarrassed seaman recruit delivered a box of chocolates to Heaven Ray at the Fort Abercrombie Dispensary near Miller Point.

"Why are you giving me this?" Heaven Ray tapped her foot and tried to keep the irritation from her voice. *I'm sure Ensign Lawson sent this hapless young sailor to do his bidding. How crass.*

"Ensign's orders, ma'am. I'll be swabbing the decks if you refuse his gift." He forced a smile.

"I see." Heaven Ray felt sorry for the pimple-faced boy and took the box from him as the other nurses and office staff gathered around. She opened the box, and in a few seconds, it was empty. "There, I've accepted."

"Thank you, ma'am." He turned to go.

"Wait." She handed the empty chocolate box to the uncomfort-able sailor and said, "Tell Ensign Lawson the nurses were thankful for the candy."

"But, ma'am, you didn't have any."

"You can tell him that, too." *I hope you let him know I was not happy to be disturbed at work.*

Everyone laughed, and Delores said, "I don't think our Mark has ever been rebuffed."

"Do I have to, ma'am?" The seaman recruit gulped and looked

at the giggling women. Heaven Ray was nowhere to be seen.

Delores flung her arm across the flustered seaman's shoulder and escorted him out of the building. "You tell Mark that Nurse Turner is as stubborn as he is. Do you understand me, sailor?"

He grumbled under his breath and shook her arm off his shoulder. "I understand." As he walked away, he tossed the empty candy box into a nearby trash can, muttering, "She's just a nurse and not in the Navy. I don't have to obey her. I enlisted to fight, not to be a delivery boy."

Mark Lawson sent chocolates daily, sometimes with a single wildflower, whatever he found growing around the base. The seaman recruit felt like a yo-yo delivering the candy boxes, always returning with a negative report. Heaven Ray gave the chocolates to nurses, patients, even the janitor. She took the wildflowers home to her mother, who delighted in them.

Finally, the seaman recruit checked Heaven Ray's schedule and left the candy at the nurses' station when she was not on duty. On her next day off, Heaven Ray found him near his barracks. She thrust several empty candy boxes in his direction. He stood at attention and let them fall at his feet.

"You can toss me in the brig, sir. You can keelhaul me or throw me overboard. I will not take any more chocolate to that—that nurse."

"I thought everyone loved that nurse."

The young sailor lowered his eyes and gnawed on his lip. "She's polite, but—but—I think she wants you to do your own courting."

"Courting? What an old-fashioned word." The ensign rubbed

his chin. "Is that what she said? Courting?"

The unfortunate seaman shuffled his feet, swallowed, and, with a red face, mumbled, "Umm, yeah, sure—I guess." His Adam's apple bobbed, and he gulped, then threw back his shoulders and looked the ensign in the eye. "I mean, y-yes, sir."

Mark rubbed his hands together and grinned. "Dismissed!"

CHAPTER TWO

The next day, a box of chocolates gazed at Heaven Ray from the middle of her bed.

"Mom, where did this come from?"

"Ensign Mark Lawson IV, I think he said was his name. Such a lovely boy. We had a nice visit."

Heaven Ray rolled her eyes and dropped the box into the wastepaper basket next to her dressing table. "He's so shallow, a party boy."

"I think there's more to him than that. There is a restlessness underneath his charm. He's looking for something."

"He's looking for a good time, and it doesn't matter with whom. He's dated every girl on the Island." *And I'm not going to be one of them.*

"He's looking for someone worthy of love. And someone to love him, I think."

"He needs to get serious. Hitler is devouring country after country, and we've been attacked." Heaven Ray sat at her dressing table and grabbed some tissues. "The world is falling apart."

Her mother crossed the room, hugged her, and said, "I'm so thankful the Lord is keeping your father safe. God is good."

Heaven Ray shrugged out of her mother's embrace, "How can you say God is good when so many other girls have lost their fathers—are still losing them?"

"We must trust our God in the darkness, especially when evil abounds," Haven Ray spoke softly as she took the hairbrush from her daughter's hand.

"I envy you, Mom. I'm really struggling with my faith in the middle of a world gone mad." She sniffed and blew her nose.

"Take your struggles to the Lord. Give Him your feelings, even your anger and doubts. Read the Psalms; they're full of despair, doubt, and anger. They will show you the hope and strength that comes when you give all of that to the Lord. As I pray for Mark Lawson, I will pray for you. You know, I always pray for you."

Heaven Ray wiped her eyes, "Thanks, Mom."

"There. One hundred brush strokes." The older woman laid the brush on the dressing table and fished the chocolates from the wastebasket. "In the meantime, if you don't want to accept Mark's affection, at least accept the chocolates."

"One could lead to the other." *Did I say that out loud?*

"So, you're tempted?"

Heaven Ray shook her head. *I won't admit that to you, Mom, or even to myself.* "Delores and Barbara say there are no guarantees, and we should grab whatever happiness or—man that's offered."

"What does Rita have to say?"

Heaven Ray laughed, "Rita just loves her airplane," Heaven Ray sighed. The girls she had grown up with, except Rita, had become a bit wild with all the military men coming into Kodiak, especially since most local boys had enlisted or been drafted.

Haven Ray laughed again, "Maybe Rita has the right idea. I'm afraid I must disagree with the other girls' way of thinking, and I know you do, too." She hummed the old hymn—"What a Friend We Have in Jesus," I think Mark Lawson needs a friend."

Heaven Ray opened her mouth, but before she could say anything, her mother pushed a chocolate in and said, "Give him a chance. There's more to him than you think."

"It's not the right time to think about men." *Don't push me toward him. I might not be able to resist.*

As the door of the Quonset hut banged behind him, Mark said, "Elly, I need another box of candy. I'm making progress. The last one wasn't returned."

Yeoman Richardson locked the drawer and shook his head. "Nurse Turner makes it a point not to eat your candy, says it's unethical. But everyone at the Fort Abercrombie Dispensary and the local clinic loves it." The yeoman laughed out loud. "And her mother enjoys the wildflowers."

"Do you know everything that goes on around here?"

"It's my job."

"Elly, this girl is something else."

"Are you sure it's not the thrill of the chase? I can't remember any other woman rejecting you."

Mark Lawson frowned and scratched his head. "I don't know why I'm attracted to her. She's too reserved and serious, even a bit standoffish. Delores says she's overly religious. I just know I feel different when I'm around her."

"You've been hanging around Kodiak's medical facilities during all your off time. Leave her alone and stick to your duties. Besides, having the chocolate shipped here isn't easy, and you're depleting my supply. There's a war on, you know."

Mark left the Quonset hut empty-handed but vowed to approach Elly again. He needed to continue his "heavenly" campaign; chocolates were his primary weapon.

He thought about the year he had been here. Construction had slowed during the rotten winter weather. The Alaskans went hunting, trapping, and fishing. The civilians who had come North for the large paychecks huddled in their boarding houses and makeshift quarters. Most were interested in women and booze—both in short supply.

Commander Lawson tried to keep his newly arrived Seabees busy with drills and training, although the weather curtailed his efforts. Tempers flared as poker and other games of chance increased. Desperate rumors about the war blew like Kodiak's fierce wind. Accurate information on this rock in the Gulf of Alaska was hard to come by.

The short days and long nights baffled the non-Alaskans. Darkness and gloom sapped them of vigor and ambition. Like the bears on the island, many of the men just wanted to hibernate. Months later, when the earth turned on its axis, everyone breathed easier. Winter receded, and the days became longer. Young men who had never been industrious eagerly looked forward to returning to work. Construction ramped up with the long daylight hours.

Ensign Mark Lawson IV had attended every social event on the base and in nearby Kodiak, few though they were. Even during winter, he had sloshed through ice and snow to attend church socials, bingo games, and dances at the American Legion Hall. He danced with all the local girls and never found anyone that interested him beyond the moment. Now that the warmer weather arrived, he included local church picnics and fishing trips. He tried to have a good time, but each outing forced him to admit how shallow and miserable he was.

Commander Lawson swore as he looked at the paperwork scattered across his desk. He didn't need to be assigned any more responsibilities, especially a campaign Rear Admiral Charles Freeman, the man in charge of the Navy's Alaska Sector, wanted to avoid. However, the Department of Indian Affairs had delegated the responsibility to the Admiral, and he pushed it down the chain of command until it was strewn across Commander Lawson's desk.

The two civilian women sitting in his office for over an hour insisted they be included. *I'm a commander in the United States Navy, for heaven's sake, not a nursemaid.* They had obviously heard his profanity, but neither reacted.

"Pardon my French, ladies."

"You are pardoned," Miss Ruth, the elderly woman, said with a half grin, "but that's not French."

Commander Lawson looked away, cleared his throat twice, and said, "I fear for your safety that far out in the Aleutians. The Japanese have become too interested in the North."

"You do realize the Territorial Governor disagrees with a forced evacuation of these people?" Haven Ray said.

"General Buckner agrees with him, at least about the people beyond Unalaska. His report shows his concerns about taking them from their isolated islands. Their interaction with white civilization will have an adverse effect."

"Drink and disease." Miss Ruth sniffed and pushed her spectacles up, and they promptly slid to the edge of her nose. She pushed them up again.

"We have seen no plans for relocation," Haven Ray added.

Commander Lawson muttered, "General Billy Mitchell was right. He told the US Congress back in '35 that whoever holds Alaska holds the world."

"What's that, Commander?"

"Nothing, ladies." The commander, distracted by the myriad of papers on his desk, frowned. The logistics were becoming convoluted. They included proposals from the Fish and Wildlife Service, more messages from Rear Admiral Freeman, and recommendations from the Army's Alaska Native Command. Policies from the territorial government were mixed with paperwork from the Bureau of Indian Affairs. Orders from these diverse agencies and officials contradicted each other. Commander Lawson swallowed his irritation at the inefficiency of it all and forced his attention back to the two women. "I'm sorry. Who are you again?" He addressed the woman in the outdated black clothes but kept his tone polite. *Man, you look like my grandmother.*

Miss Ruth tapped the papers on the edge of the desk, "It's all there. I'm the liaison between the United States Navy, the Territory of Alaska, and the Alaska Native Brotherhood. I represent the Territorial School System, and oddly, I'm also representing the Russian Orthodox Church."

"The church?"

"I have no real religious authority with the Aleuts, so I'm bringing a priest familiar with all of the island dialects, although most Natives speak English courtesy of the United States government limiting the use of both Russian and the Native languages." Miss Ruth said.

"English is taught in Native schools throughout Alaska," Haven Ray added.

The commander pushed aside the paperwork and leaned back in his chair. He turned to Haven Ray Turner. "Mrs. Turner, I know you were a former Navy nurse and have been contracted to help wherever needed. You did a wonderful job with the station hospital evaluations. Your report was concise and thorough. But this campaign is dangerous, and I'm leery of involving civilians."

"I'm a proud veteran, and I've lived in Alaska long enough to know how difficult it will be for the villagers to leave. Culturally, they are entwined with their environment in a way we do not understand. I don't want to see them suffer any more than necessary."

The commander huffed, "These Indians—"

"They are not Indians," Miss Ruth pursed her lips, letting her displeasure show.

Commander Lawson sighed, "When the United States purchased Alaska from the Russians, the Natives were declared Indians and made wards of the federal government."

Miss Ruth shook her head, frowned, and showed her displeasure by speaking in a Native dialect. Haven Ray raised her eyebrows, patted Miss Ruth's arm, and spoke mildly, "It's still swearing, my dear, even if it's in a different language."

Miss Ruth shrugged her shoulders, "I said what I said." She turned to the commander, "Pardon my French."

Commander Lawson chuckled and said, "You are pardoned, but that did not sound like French."

Haven Ray rapped her fingers on the corner of the large metal desk. "Commander Lawson, sometimes the Natives will do things for Bozhe they won't do for anyone else,"

"Bozhe?" Commander Lawson rubbed his chin.

"It's the Russian word for God," Miss Ruth answered. "I assure you, Commander, that Mrs. Turner and I have no hesitation in doing our duty. Our paperwork is in order, and I don't see how you can refuse us. This is everyone's war."

"Hel...heck of a way to run a military campaign." He sighed and bit his lip to keep from swearing again. While there was neither consensus among the military nor comprehensive plans, these two civilian women seemed eager to embark. "Your paperwork is well organized, and I will obey my orders, such as they are."

"Bozhe goes before us," Miss Ruth said.

The commander opened the bottom drawer of his desk and saw the bottle was empty. He slammed it shut and stood, trying not to let his annoyance show. "I regret the Navy cannot guarantee your safety."

"Understood," the two women said in unison, shaking the commander's outstretched hand. "We will be ready whenever the Navy gets itself organized," Miss Ruth looked over her glasses at the untidy desk.

"Much needs to be done before this operation can be launched. I'll be in touch." He watched them leave, then bellowed for his aide. "Elly, get in here."

Yeoman Richardson stood in the doorway with a box of chocolates.

The commander scowled. "I need a drink."

Elly placed the box on the desk and shook his head. "You promised your wife, sir."

He swore again and looked for the rum-filled dark chocolates.

Ever since Mark was assigned to Kodiak, he had failed to persuade his lieutenant to submit transfer papers. There was little Mark could do to change his mind. So when Elly handed him a packet, Mark exclaimed, "My lieutenant came through!"

"Do you really think he would send your request up the chain while your father is in command?" Elly grinned.

Mark shook his head and wondered what Elly was up to. After pulling the papers from the manila envelope and glancing through them, Mark tossed them onto the desk. "Explain this to me, Yeoman."

"Seems rather self-explanatory. You can read."

"Using the Navy to move a bunch of Aleut families off-island and letting civilian women and a priest help? You've got to be kidding!"

Elly unlocked a battered wooden cupboard under the window and pulled out a familiar-looking box of confections. "A tentative plan is in place, but your father doesn't like it. It took an enormous amount of chocolate to calm him."

"You've been holding out on me, Elly. I thought you were out of candy. In fact, I confiscated your keys a few days ago and searched your filing cabinet." Mark raised his eyebrows and stared at the battered metal cabinet where the candy used to dwell.

Elly laughed, "I have more keys and hiding places than you know, and I move my stash around to keep it safe. Never mind the candy. This mission is as close to a battle as you will get."

"Why is it a Navy problem? Why doesn't the territory take care of it? Why don't the people just leave if they feel unsafe?

"All of that is above your pay grade, my boy."

"Did you write my name on these orders?"

"You think I volunteered you? Talk to your lieutenant. I think he's irritated with you."

"C'mon, Elly. I know you. Besides, I've never complained, just asked for a transfer a time or two."

Yeoman Richardson snorted, "A time or two?"

Ensign Lawson narrowed his eyes and sat on the edge of the yeoman's desk. "I think you can rewrite these orders and get me out of this. I'm no taxi driver or babysitter. Transporting a group of primitive people is not my idea of a naval campaign."

"Afraid?"

"Don't question my courage. You know I want to be on a battleship or cruiser. I'd even take a destroyer." Mark spoke through gritted teeth. Elly was as close to him as his own grandfather, but there were lines he shouldn't cross.

"It's nearly fourteen hundred miles of treacherous seas and vile weather to these islands. The villagers may not cooperate. They might have to be forcibly removed."

Mark Lawson scowled, "It's not a combat zone, and they are not the enemy."

"It's not a combat zone—yet. Do your duty."

"Come on, Elly. Don't make me call my mother," Mark grinned but knew Elly would take his words at face value.

Yeoman Richardson stared at the young man, then sighed and reached for the appropriate forms to remove Mark's name. "I don't want to see you in this office for a long time. And don't say anything to your lieutenant. I'll have to do some creative paperwork to circumvent the chain of command."

"Thanks, Elly."

"Get out!"

True to his word, Mark stayed away from the office until the rumors flew across Kodiak like the island's bald eagles.

"Scuttlebutt says the Japanese bombed Dutch Harbor. Is it true? Have we launched a counterattack? I can't believe I'm stuck on this rock. I'm never going to see any action." Ensign Lawson's staccato voice bellowed before he was three steps into the office. "What's being done about it?"

Yeoman Richardson motioned for Mark to be quiet while he finished his phone call. He riffled through the papers scattered across his desk. "Yes, sir..." He picked up a single sheet, "Here it is... we lost 43 men, 50 or so wounded, 14 aircraft destroyed, the hospital was hit...I don't know...Yes, sir. Right away, sir." Elly replaced the handset, ran his hand over his balding head, searched through the messy desk, and said, "I don't have time for you."

"Get me on a ship!" Mark's heart rate accelerated, and his palms felt clammy.

Yeoman Richardson turned and stared at the map of Alaska behind him. His face was ashen, showing his age, his tone sober. "No ships are moving in that direction, and the situation is worse than you think. After they bombed Dutch Harbor, the Japanese invaded Attu and Kiska. In fact, they are dug in and occupying them. But you didn't hear it from me. In fact, the Navy is trying to keep a lid on it."

"Attu and Kiska?"

"Islands at the end of the chain. Near Dutch Harbor. Close by Alaskan standards anyway, Attu is over eight hundred miles west of Dutch and less than six hundred and fifty miles from Japan."

"Whoa." Mark scratched his head and fell into the nearest chair. He stretched his arm toward the chocolate and then pulled back. It wasn't possible. The enemy had occupied American soil—barren islands in the middle of nowhere, but still.

Yeoman Richardson pointed to the large map. "Look at the map, Mark. If the Japanese build an air station on these islands, they can bomb the Boeing plant in Seattle and the NavyYard at Bremerton. It's about an eight-hour bomb run. For Japan, Alaska is the back door to America."

"We had so many classes at the Academy on various strategic scenarios, but Alaska seemed so remote I didn't realize how strategic it really was," Mark gulped, and rage fueled his voice. "We need to do something!" It was hard to imagine those isolated rocky islands at the edge of the Alaska Archipelago were part of his country. And it was equally challenging to think of those primitive people as American citizens.

Mark barely gave the map a glance. "The Academy trained me for war, and I want to be a part of it. Now!" *The commander won't be proud of me until I've been battle-tested.*

Yeoman Richardson snapped. "We are in no position to counterattack. We don't have the men, the armor, or the tactical support. We don't even have enough cold-weather gear for the men on this base or at Dutch Harbor. Supply has been a nightmare. It will be months, possibly a year before we can assemble enough supplies, ordinance, and men to mount an offensive."

Mark clenched his fists and frowned as Elly continued, "We

assume the people on Attu and Kiska were either killed or taken prisoner. That evacuation mission you wanted no part of will happen sooner rather than later. We don't know how many islands the Japanese will invade."

Mark stood before the map and stared at the tiny islands, home to American citizens in danger. An isolated people he knew nothing about, but still his countrymen.

Elly sat with his feet on his desk, leaned back, and laced his fingers behind his head. "Too bad, my boy, you had your chance."

"Why are you looking so smug, Elly?"

"Did I forget to mention that a nurse you claim is too serious and reserved is leading a triage team and performing medical checks as each Aleut is processed? She'll work closely with whoever is part of this campaign."

"Are you telling me it's…?"

"I can't say. Besides, you're not a babysitter or taxi driver, remember?"

"Come on, Elly. I didn't mean that."

"I had to do a lot of fancy paperwork to deny your lieutenant's request," Richardson grumbled, picked up his chocolates, and locked them away. "I'd have to do even more to put you back." He shook his head and frowned.

"This would be good for me, Elly. I need to do something. I need to be at sea." *It wasn't combat, but it would put him close to Heaven Ray Turner.*

"Ha!" Yeoman Richardson put his ear to the inner office door, then returned to his desk. His voice was as low as he could make it. "Your lieutenant will hate me if I force him to rearrange his paperwork again. I can make this happen, but it will cost you."

"Anything, Elly."

"Leave my chocolates alone for the duration of the war."

"Done."

"As soon as your orders are cut, see if the quartermaster can outfit you with cold-weather gear. Make sure it's waterproof." Elly shuffled through several papers on his desk, then looked up. "Are you still here?"

Later that week, Mark picked up his new orders and read them on his way across the base. He let the door slam behind him, and the Quartermaster growled around the unlit cigar clamped between his teeth, "Whatever you want, we're out." He took the list from the ensign and growled, "You'd be better off going into town and buying from the locals. I only have three items on this list."

Mark took what was offered and would make do. He refused to go local; he wasn't a hunter, a fisherman, and definitely not a tourist. He was a fourth-generation Navy man, and he would look like it.

"Sir, may I recommend you put Ensign Lawson in charge of this operation?" Yeoman Richardson stood in the doorway to the commander's office.

"Mark? Are you kidding?"

"Your son needs some responsibility, and while he's chafing for a combat mission, this is the next best thing. It will get him away from the base and on a ship. Give him some responsibility."

"He'll botch it. The boy is soft. I wouldn't authorize him to feed my dog."

"You don't have a dog." The yeoman leaned over the desk. "I seem to remember your father, Admiral Mark Lawson, Jr., saying the same thing about a certain young officer."

"My father was a salty old sailor who didn't cut me any slack." He leaned back in his chair and pictured himself as a young officer. He shook his head and frowned. "But putting Mark in charge?"

"Second in command only. Mark needs a chance to prove himself."

"The Lawsons are Navy all the way, and expectations are high. But I don't think Mark is as committed to the Service as I'd like him to be. He's more like his mother than the Lawsons."

"I agree Mark is like your wife, sir. If I may be so bold, she is gentle and kind but has courage and grit when needed."

"Sometimes I forget that you've been a part of our lives forever." The commander rubbed his jaw, "Second in command?"

Elly looked him in the eye and spoke more harshly than he intended, "He needs to get away from you."

"Careful, Yeoman." Caramel from one of the chocolates lodged in the commander's throat, and he choked, "Isn't it time for you to retire?"

"No danger of that until the war's over. Besides, Natalie would have my hide if I left you alone in this Alaskan wilderness."

The commander chuckled, "She would indeed."

"Sir, remember how you chafed under your father and grandfather's reputations. Imagine how Mark feels with three generations before him."

"He needs to toughen up."

"Don't mistake his tender heart for weakness. He made it through the Academy with good grades. You should be proud."

"I'm sure the Lawson name helped." He searched for another chocolate.

"You know better than that." Elly ignored the commander's scowl. "Besides, I've heard stories about that Miss Ruth person. She and Mrs. Turner know the villagers and will no doubt be helpful. I believe they are a force to be reckoned with."

"Cut the orders. But if he fails, and I'm sure he will, it'll be on your head."

Yeoman Richardson smiled as he closed the door. The orders had already been processed and were in Mark's hands.

CHAPTER THREE

"How was your shift, Heaven. You look tired." Delores breezed into the Army's clinic at Fort Abercrombie.

"It's been quiet for the past hour, Del. The rest of the day was wild."

"Ensign Lawson gave me a ride. I told him to wait for you."

"Why did you do that?" Heavan Ray snapped. *I don't want to see him again. He's entirely too self-confident.*

"Mark's a nice guy. You're a nice gal. It's meant to be." Del adjusted her nurse's cap and refreshed her bright red lipstick. She slipped her mirrored compact into her purse. "Seriously, Mark could be just what you need."

"Seriously, Delores!" Heaven Ray mimicked her friend, "I don't need a man in my life." Heaven Ray quickly hugged her to take the sting out of the words.

The town of Kodiak was a short four-and-a-half miles from Fort Abercrombie. Heaven Ray looked through the clinic's window to the temperature gauge—fifty-six degrees. She slipped out the back door and around several buildings to keep out of Mark's sight, then waved to the military guard as she left the Fort and walked along the edge of the gravel road. He returned a sharp salute and gave a loud wolf whistle when she was a few paces away. Heaven Ray grinned but did not turn around.

It had been a while since she had enjoyed the beauty of Kodiak

Island. The forested cliffs and craggy bluffs overlooking the ocean at Miller Point never ceased to amaze her. The island had many sheltered bays and coves, perfect anchorages for its fishermen. The blue-green spruce forests had enchanted her since her yearly treks with her father to choose the holiday tree. The piney scent of blue spruce always smelled like Christmas. Those were wonderful years, and she stood for a moment, filling her lungs with the sweet scent of her memories. Even though it was now the middle of summer, she belted the chorus to "Jingle Bells" and danced down the side of the road. She felt about eight years old; the present world conflicts fell away until a military vehicle roared toward her, spewing dust and gravel behind it. The Jeep full of GIs whistled, waved, and laughed. One yelled, "Merry Christmas."

As she neared the small town of Kodiak, she wondered if Mark was still waiting outside the clinic. She felt a bit guilty but quickly pushed the emotion away. *I need to think about what I can do to help the war effort, not moon over some handsome officer in the United States Navy.*

The gravy congealed on her mashed potatoes, and the venison roast grew cold. Heaven Ray wasn't hungry anyway. She took a sip of water and sighed. Her father always encouraged her to bite the bullet and do what must be done sooner rather than later. She regretted she had delayed this conversation with her mother. "I need to talk to you, Mom, but I'm unsure how to begin."

Haven Ray rose from the table, poured hot water into the ceramic teapot, and added loose Darjeeling. She took two china cups and saucers from the sideboard and placed them on the table. After pouring the tea through the small bamboo strainer, she inhaled its fragrance and told her daughter to begin wherever she felt most comfortable.

"Before he left, Dad and I had several long talks. He knows how I long to follow his example. The Navy needs nurses, and he said he was proud of my desire to serve my country." She reached for her mother's hand. "Can you be proud?"

"I am proud of you." Haven Ray took several sips of tea, giving herself time to think. "You're an excellent nurse, and I appreciate how you work with me in the Native villages. I respect the strong woman you have become."

"I have the skills to do more."

"Your work at the Fort Abercrombie Dispensary and the town clinic is important," her mother said, "And I believe the Navy hospital is almost ready to open."

Heaven Ray shrugged, "Today I set a broken leg, bandaged a gash on a forehead, and stitched several lacerations. Mostly accidents. The sailors are bored and irritated by the endless drills. Most want to be where the action is. It makes them careless. The construction workers, whether military or civilian, are in such a hurry to finish all their projects that they don't always take the necessary safety precautions." Heaven Ray stirred half a teaspoon of fireweed honey into her tea. "I'm a trained surgical nurse and know I can do more."

"You're needed here just as much as anywhere else."

"No, Mom! Wounded sailors who require life-saving surgery have a greater need. Can you be proud that I applied for a commission in the Navy Nurse Corps?"

The color fell out of Haven Ray's face. She stared out the window and gnawed on her lower lip. Choosing her words carefully, she said, "I pray daily for the Lexington and all the men on it. I am confident the Lord will keep your father out of harm's way. It would stretch my faith to have you in a war zone as well." She turned to face her daughter, "Silly, I know. God watches over us wherever we are. Your father is doing what he must to protect the rest of us. And now you?" She reached for her daughter's hand.

"I pray for Dad every day."

Haven Ray picked up the dainty china cup, then set it gently on the saucer without drinking. "Let's pray now."

The two women bowed their heads and gave the man they loved into the Father's hands. They prayed for all the military personnel they knew and those they didn't. They prayed fervently that good would overcome evil, light overtake darkness, and peace overcome violence. As they said amen, a deep calmness settled over them, and they were reluctant to break the silence.

Heaven Ray gave her mother a moment and said, "Admit it, Mom, you're proud of me. After all, you were in the Navy. I'm just following your example."

"It was peacetime then." Haven Ray sighed and clung to the feeling the prayer had given her. "When do you leave?"

"If my commission is accepted, I imagine I will have to report to the San Diego base as soon as possible. I'm unsure where I'll be assigned."

"Officer's training for nurses was always in Newport, Rhode Island. Do they have a training center in San Diego now?"

Heaven Ray shook her head. "I don't know, but I'm sure I can forgo those classes."

Haven Ray didn't say anything to dissuade her daughter, although it seemed implausible that anyone could skip officer's training. "Perhaps you will be deployed here. I was hoping you could help with the Native evacuation."

"I've requested a hospital ship in the Pacific."

"A hospital at Pearl Harbor or somewhere in Australia would be much safer," Haven Ray said as she cleared the table.

Heaven Ray changed the topic of conversation. "Mom, I'm worried about this so-called evacuation. You know the Aleuts don't recognize the separation between self and place. How will they fare once removed from their islands?"

"I've talked with Governor Gruening."

"When? How?"

Haven Ray sighed, "Sometimes it's extremely inconvenient not to have telephone service here. We talked over the mayor's ham radio. The governor wanted someone from the Office of Indian Affairs to meet with the elders and discuss the matter fully so the villagers would understand exactly what was happening."

"That's a good idea."

"It's not going to happen." Haven Ray looked deep into her daughter's eyes. "I didn't want to tell you, but the Japanese have bombed Dutch Harbor and invaded Attu and Kiska. The evacuation of nearby islands must happen as soon as possible."

Heaven Ray shuddered, "I wouldn't let myself listen to those rumors. They sounded so impossible. We must get the people to safety."

"According to what I've heard, too many military and governmental agencies are involved, and no one will take responsibility. Nobody appears to be in charge. I'm afraid it's the Natives who will suffer."

"I hope I'll be here to help." Her shoulders fell, "Have you heard from Ensign Lawson?" *Why did I ask about him?*

"Funny you should ask. Did you know Mark is part of the evacuation team? Yeoman Richardson sent a message for me to be packed and ready to go at a moment's notice. They could send a Jeep for me any day. In the meantime, since Miss Ruth is in town, let's have a tea party-prayer meeting like we did when you were a little girl."

CHAPTER FOUR

Yeoman Richardson sat at his desk and wondered if he had done the right thing, assigning Mark to the evacuation campaign. His concern for the young ensign grew by the day. Yesterday, Mark was in the commander's office. Elly kept his eyes and ears close to the inner office door as usual. Although their voices were so loud, he could have heard them across the Gulf.

"What do you mean there are no ships available? I saw half a dozen in the harbor on my way here."

The commander bellowed for Elly to bring more coffee, then turned to his son, "Let me explain what I'm sure you already know. Ports on the West Coast are on a war footing. Ships sail north, crossing the Gulf of Alaska, transporting men and supplies to Army and Navy bases in various stages of operation in Sitka, Seward, Whittier, Kodiak, Dutch Harbor, and beyond. The Alaska Steamship Company transports civilians to high-paying jobs constructing those bases. Tensions are high, most bases are unfinished, and the Japanese are on American soil."

"I know all that, sir."

Commander Lawson gave his son a look that would wither a career Navy man more experienced than Mark. "Sorry, sir."

"All that means is no Navy ships are available for evacuation, Son."

Ensign Mark Lawson IV took a moment to quietly look at the

commander. It was unusual for the man to call him son. "What's bothering you, sir?"

"I wish you hadn't volunteered for this campaign. It won't do your career any good."

"You mean, you don't think I can handle it." Mark berated himself for sounding hurt and unsure.

The commander rubbed his hand over his eyes, bloodshot from lack of sleep. "I mean, there is no agency in charge. I don't even know exactly where these people will be settled, but I believe it will be somewhere in Southeast Alaska. I have memos, messages, and telegrams from several government agencies, including the Army and Navy. Most are convoluted and contradictory, and I don't have the authority to create a coordinated plan. I'm afraid this ill-fated mission will fail. I wanted to spare you that."

Mark ignored his father's negativity. "So, there are no ships available. But you always have a solution, sir."

"The Army is transporting the Natives from the Pribilof Islands as far as Unalaska, and then the Navy is responsible for taking over."

"Can't we use their ship?"

"I'm told it's assigned another mission once they unload. The Alaska Steamship Company has a ship here in Kodiak. It's being fueled and prepared right now. You'll leave in the morning. It's the best I can do." He pulled a handkerchief from his pocket and wiped the sweat from his forehead.

"That's civilian."

"The government has taken control of almost all US registered ships. So, the Alaska Steamship Company has become an agent for the War Administration."

Ensign Mark Lawson frowned and then shrugged. It wouldn't

look like a Navy ship, but for all intents and purposes, it was. "Scuttlebutt says we have no plans for an offensive on Attu and Kiska. When can we expect that to take place?" Mark asked the distraught commander.

"Few people realize how far away Alaska and the Aleutians are. The logistics are mind-boggling. Transporting men, weapons, gear, food, ordinance, and all the supplies needed will take months, provided we can get them. Almost everything is allotted to Europe. What we can get will be delivered to an, as yet, undetermined staging area, and then we wait."

"Wait? What for?"

"The weather! The blasted weather! I've been told those islands are the foggiest, rainiest, and windiest in the Western hemisphere, with year-round, violent, blistering storms with waves sometimes fifty feet high. The commander at Dutch Harbor has authorized several bombing sorties over Attu and Kiska, most of which have been turned back because of the weather. The shoreline is too rocky for landing troops, but land them we will."

"We prepared hypothetical plans for different invasion scenarios at the Academy, but never for the Aleutians." Mark raised his eyes to his father. "I never considered the implications, the reality..."

"Of knowing your decisions could send men to their deaths?"

"Yes, sir." There was a growing respect for his father in Mark's eyes.

"I don't have the final say, but I've been asked to give my recommendations. It will be a difficult battle at the end of the Chain, with high casualties."

"Is the weather expected to clear?"

"The weather is as vile and stubborn as the enemy. The clouds hang low, and the fog blankets everything. As I said, a few sorties have already been launched from Dutch Harbor. Even if the skies were clear and the wind nonexistent, bombs would do little damage. It's not like the war in Germany, bombing munition factories and infrastructure like bridges and rail lines. The Aleutians lack infrastructure, and the Japanese are dug in on those barren islands."

Mark sat a little straighter. "I'm ready for the battle, sir, whenever it commences, and I will succeed in this evacuation mission."

"Dismissed, Ensign." Commander Lawson bent his head over his paperwork but looked up when the door closed behind his youngest son. Mark said all the right things about wanting to fight, but Commander Lawson knew his son's true desire was to please him. The other boys had obeyed orders without question. Mark needed to understand the whys and wherefores. It had always been difficult for his youngest son to put his thoughts and opinions aside and carry on. In a way, the commander respected that, but he wouldn't want a fleet of sailors who reacted like that. Commander Lawson saluted the closed door and whispered a traditional Navy blessing, "Fair winds and following seas, my son."

As Mark, presently unmindful of the sights and sounds of construction, wandered through the base, he thought about how, in the late 1930s, the intelligence reports about Japanese interest in the North caused many in Washington to scramble to prepare for war. Construction began on a plethora of military installations in the territory of Alaska and was in various stages of completion when the Japanese attacked Pearl Harbor.

He wandered into the dispensary, but Nurse Barbara said

Heaven Ray was working at the Fort Abercrombie Clinic. He waved goodbye and ran toward the commander's Quonset hut, yelling, "Elly, I need the key to the commander's Jeep."

"What are you doing here, Mark?" Delores asked as she came out of the clinic.

"I thought I'd give you a ride home, Heaven Ray, too." He craned his neck and peered into the clinic as several bandaged Seabees emerged and climbed into a waiting truck.

Delores laughed and climbed into the Jeep. "You are so thoughtful, but Heaven volunteered to stay late."

"All that girl does is work," Mark complained as he glanced again at the building.

"With twenty hours of daylight, more civilians have been hired, unskilled and untrained in construction, so more mishaps and accidents. It keeps us busy."

"Just put a hammer or saw in their hands and let them go." Mark had difficulty listening to Delores. His only thoughts were of Heaven Ray.

"There's a lot more to construction than that, as we have found out." Delores shivered, "I can't begin to tell you how many men I've stitched up today. I should have been a seamstress."

Mark put the Jeep into gear, "Where to?" As he drove away, he glanced into the rearview mirror, picturing Heaven Ray in her cute nurse's uniform.

"There's a dance at the American Legion Hall. Let's go there."

"Why not? This northern sunlight gives me so much energy that I have difficulty sleeping."

The wooden building stood in the middle of Center Street. Its peeling paint and the American Legion motto, VETERANS

STRENGTHENING AMERICA, were splashed across the entry. The recorded sounds of Benny Goodman's band roared out of the open windows. As they entered, Mark and Delores were assaulted by the odor of egg salad sandwiches, strong coffee, stale cigarettes, cheap perfume, and unwashed men straight from their jobs. She wrinkled her nose, almost gagged, and said, "Let's dance. Maybe then we won't notice the smell."

Mark followed her onto the crowded floor and frowned his way through a foxtrot and jitterbug. The waltz had him even more stiff and distracted. Delores stopped in the middle of the dance floor before the music ended, "What's wrong, Mark?"

He shrugged. She grabbed his wrist and pulled him outside. "How much gas does that thing have?" she pointed to the Jeep.

"I filled the tank before leaving the base."

"Must be nice not having to worry about rationing."

Mark ignored her sarcastic tone. "Where to?"

"Somewhere near the water, you and I are going to have a heart-to-heart talk. Get that look off your face, sailor. I promise it will be painless."

Mark parked the Jeep on a bluff overlooking St. Paul Harbor. Several fishing boats bobbed in the choppy sea, others headed to the marina. Delores tied a scarf over her hair as the breeze became stronger. "Tell me what's going on?"

Mark gazed at the horizon and didn't answer. How could he put into words all the emotions swirling through him? How could he explain that a world in chaos and crisis had thrown him off balance? He questioned the meaning of it all. "I can't live for the moment anymore." His hands felt clammy, and his face hot.

Delores leaned toward him and looked deep into his eyes.

"Grab all the fun you can because the world may end tomorrow, isn't it for you?"

His bleak face told her what he could not voice.

"It's Heaven. She's changed you, and she doesn't even know it."

Mark raised woeful eyes to the girl beside him, "Every time I try to return to my old way of thinking, I see her face."

"Heaven Ray seems to have a strange effect on people. They either admire her or resent her. Which camp do you fall into, Mark?" She tucked an errant wisp of hair back into her scarf. "As if I didn't know."

Mark grimaced, "I can't get close to her, and that irritates me, but I admire her for having high standards. I guess I alternate between camps."

"Have you told her?"

Mark's knuckles tensed as he gripped the steering wheel of the parked vehicle. "Of course not. She won't see me anyway, not to go out."

"I'm not talking about dating her. I'm talking about sharing your feelings, just like you did with me just now."

Mark laughed and started the Jeep. "I didn't share a thing. You pulled those thoughts out of me against my will. Let's go for dinner."

Delores leaned toward him. "Come to my house. My mom is the best cook in Kodiak." She winked and added, "I am going to devise a plan for you and Heaven Ray to have a meeting of the mind, if not the heart."

"Sure, sure."

"Trust me. I can be extremely devious when the situation calls for it."

He took her hand for a brief moment and choked. "Thanks,

Delores. You're quite a gal."
    "That's what they all say."

CHAPTER FIVE

Heaven Ray's paperwork arrived stating she was to report to the Officer Development Training Program in Newport, Rhode Island, for five weeks of classes and then to 32nd Street Naval Station in San Diego to receive a permanent assignment.

"Five weeks! We'll see about that." Heaven Ray crumpled the papers and headed to Kodiak's naval base.

"So, Yeoman Richardson, because of my work here for the Navy and my surgical expertise, it's unnecessary for me to spend more than a month on further training, not to mention the week-long voyage to Seattle and then several days on a train trip across the country and then back to San Diego. It's a waste of time criss-crossing the country."

"I can understand how you feel, but the Navy does have its standard operating procedures." Yeoman Richardson frowned, "I don't see how I can help you."

"There is always a way," Heaven Ray began.

"And then there is the authorized way, the Navy way," the yeoman finished.

They both laughed, although Heaven Ray's chuckle was forced. "In Alaska, we find the best way to get things done and do it, authorized or not."

"Your orders are to make your way to Newport, Rhode Island, as soon as possible, correct?"

Heaven Ray nodded and wondered what the yeoman was up to as he went into the inner office without a word. She sat in the uncomfortable wooden chair for the next hour and forty minutes. She pulled a small New Testament out of her oversized purse. Although she read and prayed, she couldn't concentrate. She pointed to the commander's door as several sailors came looking for Yeoman Richardson. She pretended not to notice when they snatched a piece of candy from the ever-present box on the corner of his desk. Some left papers for him, and others said they would return later. The phone rang often; she ignored the first few calls, answered the shrill ring of the fifth, and took a message. *How different life will be when telephone service extends beyond the military bases. I wonder when that will happen.*

Yeoman Richardson returned to his desk, smiling like a Cheshire cat. He nodded toward the door. "You can go in now."

As Heaven Ray stood, the yeoman's grin grew more expansive, and he said, "Nurse Turner— you can thank me later." He laughed at her puzzled look and returned to his duties.

Heaven Ray sat with her hands folded in her lap and returned the commander's intense gaze. He crumpled an empty package of cigarettes and threw it in the trash. He leaned back in his chair, tapped a pencil on the end of his desk, and continued to regard the young lady sitting across from him. Heaven Ray wondered if the military man knew he was tapping SOS. Finally, he laughed.

"Excuse me?" Heaven Ray said.

He tossed the pencil onto a pile of papers. Unnoticed, it rolled and fell off the edge of his desk. "I remember the first time you came into my office with all the reasons you should be part of the station hospital inspections."

"And you agreed with those reasons."

"You came in two other times with outlandish requests."

"As I recall, they were perfectly legitimate things the Navy needed to do, and you found a way to accomplish them."

The commander shook his head and looked for his pencil. "This is above my pay grade, way above."

She gazed at him without comment.

He ruffled through the papers on his desk, found a blank one, picked up the fallen pencil, and said, "Okay, tell me everything you said to Elly."

"Eighteen months ago, my father organized a civil defense for Kodiak. His unit included fishermen, Native villagers, and townspeople. He used military procedures to train us. Almost everyone was already proficient with a rifle, but he instructed us in small arms and hand-to-hand combat, even the females. I was his second in command. I have his old Naval Officers Training Manual practically memorized and am sure I would excel in any test, written or oral."

"That's quite an accomplishment—forward, out-of-the-box thinking."

"After the attack at Pearl, he resumed his commission and left me in charge of the unit."

Commander Lawson nodded, "And I understand that you and your mother have instructed many Natives in basic first aid."

"No, sir."

His eyebrows rose. Heaven Ray raised her chin and said, "We worked with Native elders and gave them advanced medical training. We tried to incorporate their herbs and medicines since sometimes that's all they would have available. We learned from them as well."

"Hmmm. Once again, you seem to have everything covered. We just have to find a way to make it official."

"I have every confidence in you, Commander." Heaven Ray said calmly.

Again, the man's eyebrows traveled toward his receding hairline.

"Much like the men of Alaska, I think you assess each situation and find a way to get things done. Forward, out-of-the-box thinking. You would make a great Alaskan. I can give no higher praise," Heaven Ray's tone was serious, but there was a twinkle in her eye.

The flustered but pleased commander folded the paper and stuffed it into an envelope. "A letter to my wife."

"You wrote your wife a letter while we were talking?" Now, it was Heaven Ray's eyebrows that lifted.

He licked the envelope and stamped it. "It's a written record of everything you just told me."

"I don't understand."

"Sometimes, Miss Turner, it's not what you know; it's who you know. In your case, it's both. When I was stationed at Newport, Rhode Island, my wife served on a committee at her church with a woman who happened to be the Navy's Superintendent of Nurses. They're good friends. She might agree you can bypass the officer's training because there is a considerable shortage of nurses in the South Pacific. That is if you can pass the examinations."

"You've already spoken with them?"

"Rank has its privileges. Placing long-distance calls immediately is one of them. This letter is merely a confirmation of your qualifications and experience. I am leaving it to my wife to contact the Superintendent."

Heaven Ray stood and shook the commander's hand. "Thank you, sir. When do you expect an answer?"

"I will let you know. You must pass the examinations before you are deployed. I hope the test booklets can be mailed to San Diego, where you will be proctored by the naval hospital's head nurse. There is a troop transport heading south soon. We'll put you on it."

"Thank you."

"Of course, if the answer is no, you will still have to take that train trip across the States."

Heaven Ray nodded, "And if I could ask a favor? Please keep this quiet. There is a certain ensign," Heaven Ray looked away from the commander's eyes, "Let's just say I'd rather slip away from Kodiak without any fuss." *I don't want to look into Mark's bright blue eyes and say goodbye. Oh, why am I thinking like this?*

"Commendable." He stroked his chin as he watched her leave. There was something about that girl. "Elly!" he yelled.

"Yes, sir."

"See if you can get Nurse Turner on that troop transport heading south, and Elly, keep it quiet. She doesn't want Mark to know about her departure."

"Yes, sir." Elly agreed. It seemed the commander was focused on other things and had put the evacuation out of his mind. Mark was no longer on Kodiak. His ship was well out to sea, and he must be aware Nurse Heaven Ray Turner was not a part of the Aleut evacuation. Yeoman Richardson hoped the ensign's anger would be tempered by the time the mission was complete.

CHAPTER SIX

Ensign Lawson was informed that the SS Columbia had docked and was ready for him and his evacuation crew. He packed his duffle bag and ordered a seaman recruit to drive him to the pier. Supplies and freight bound for ports between Kodiak and Dutch Harbor had been loaded, and the ship's horn blasted twice. He found his assigned room, stowed his gear, and went in search of Heaven Ray Turner.

With another blast of the horn, the gangplank rose, and the ship vibrated as it backed out of its berth and began its long journey to the Aleutians. The low-hanging clouds let loose, and Mark hoped it was only rain and not one of the Gulf's furious storms. He returned to his cabin, cursing the Quartermaster for his lack of supplies and himself for not shopping at the local general store. He put on his pea coat and watch cap and went topside again. He found the priest in the salon reading a book, but no sign of the women. Another turn around the deck was fruitless, so Mark made his way to the navigation bridge.

"I'm looking for Captain Nelson."

Short, stout, and gray, Captain James scowled, moved the gnawed cigar to the other side of his mouth, and growled, "I received a radio message just before we embarked. Apparently, he can't waste time on this civilian ship and will fly to Dutch Harbor. He should be there by the time we arrive."

Mark stifled his anger. He was supposed to work out some of the mission's logistics with Captain Nelson during the voyage. He turned to go.

"Wait, this is for you."

According to the paper thrust into his hand, Mark discovered Captain Nelson had ordered him to create an organizational chart for triaging the Natives, destroying their villages, and assigning their quarters on board the Columbia. He was also required to list their needs from the Aleutians to Southeast Alaska. He crumpled the paper and muttered, "And just what will you be doing, Captain Nelson?"

"What's that?" The steamship's captain asked.

"Er, thank you for the use of your ship, sir."

"It's everybody's war. We're happy to do our part."

As Mark left the pilothouse, he uncrumpled the communication. After rereading it, he threw back his shoulders and stood a little straighter. This was an excellent opportunity to show his father what he could do.

He checked his watch; it was nearly time for the evening meal. He would sit with Nurse Turner, and if he were lucky, it would stop raining, and she would agree to a stroll around the deck. He foresaw many meals and conversations with the lovely Alaskan nurse.

The rain had dwindled to a soft drizzle. The evening sun dropped below the cloud cover and streamed over the water. Its amber light infused him with an optimistic energy. Ensign Lawson stood in the stern and stared at the patterns of the ship's wake. Its ivory foam churned a trail behind them, and the slate-blue water contrasted with the brilliant cerulean sky. It was hard to imagine that just a few weeks ago and over twenty-three hundred miles south, other sailors had no time to stare at their ships' wakes. They fought for their lives at Midway, a tiny dot in the middle of the Pacific—a place no one had ever heard of.

Mark shook off his musings, not sure what he felt. Anger that he hadn't been part of the battle? Relief that he remained far away from danger? Grief over the death of his eldest brother? Worried that he didn't know where Eugene's ship was currently engaged? He pushed his thoughts away and rechecked his watch. If he hurried, he had just enough time for a quick shower and shave.

He stepped out of the shower and grabbed the bottle of Old Spice aftershave his mother had included in her latest package. He was anxious to see Nurse Turner's reaction to it. From the expressions of the stewards he passed in the hallways, he had been too generous with his mother's gift. He sniffed, but all he could smell was the aroma of roast beef wafting from the galley. He scanned the dining room. Mrs.Turner, a priest, and an older woman sat at Captain James' table, but there was no sign of Heaven Ray. Perhaps she was seasick or just late. As he approached a nearby table, Mrs. Turner indicated the empty chair beside her. "Ensign Lawson, please sit with us."

He smiled, "Thank you, ma'am, but I'm sure you'd rather have your daughter next to you."

"Since that's not possible, perhaps you will take pity on me."

"Is she ill, seasick?"

Haven Ray smiled, and her eyes had a speculative glint, "Heaven Ray is on her way to San Diego."

"I don't understand."

I'm not sure where she'll be stationed after that," Haven Ray's smile was tinged with concern.

Miss Ruth stood, took the ensign's arm, and led him to the empty chair, "I gather you didn't know Heaven recently received a commission in the Navy? I'm Miss Ruth, by the way."

"M-Mark. Call me Mark," he mumbled with unfocused eyes and a distracted tone.

Haven Ray put her hand over Mark's. "I'm hoping she'll be assigned here in the north or a hospital at Pearl Harbor, but she intends to volunteer for a hospital ship."

"She can't do that," Mark exclaimed, "It's too dangerous!"

"Ensign Lawson—Mark," Miss Ruth began, "We are all called to do our duty no matter how threatening."

"Except me. I may never do anything significant."

"You are exactly where Bozhe wants you to be. Now, my boy, eat your dinner."

"Don't mind her," Haven Ray said, "She's been talking to me like that since I was a little child."

Mark smiled, and although his appetite had fled, he picked up his fork. He sat through dinner in a daze, without tasting what he ate or knowing if he ate. By the time dessert arrived, he had forced himself to participate in the dinner conversation.

"Who is Bozhe?" Mark asked the old woman in the outdated black clothes. They had not actually been introduced, but he assumed she was part of the evacuation team.

Miss Ruth gave a detailed answer, but Mark's mind was in the middle of the Pacific, imagining Heaven Ray in all sorts of difficult situations. It galled him that he was on his way to the Aleutians. He should have been near Heaven to protect her.

Back in his cabin, he struggled to sort out his mixed emotions: frustrated that Elly misled him about Heaven Ray and disappointed he meant so little to her that she didn't say goodbye. He threw his uniform on the floor and pulled out the pajamas his mother insisted he wear; they soon joined his uniform. He'd sleep in his skivvies like a good sailor.

After a few minutes of tossing and turning, naval discipline took over. He hung his uniform, brushed out the wrinkles, and folded the pajamas. He lay on the bunk and thought about life late into the clear Alaskan night. The endless hours of daylight both energized and unnerved him. It was difficult to fall asleep. Finally, Mark dressed and walked the deck. His restless thoughts accompanied him topside.

It pained him that he had never measured up to his father's expectations, not the way his two older brothers had. Even in death, Brad had made their father proud, and Eugene, somewhere in the South Pacific, caused the old man to stick out his chest and brag about his middle son. *Dad, why are you proud of them and not me? How can I measure up?*

CHAPTER SEVEN

"How much further, captain?" Mark visited the bridge often and would have enjoyed the seafaring stories of Captain James if he had not been so irritated that his girl was on her way to who—knows—where in the South Pacific. *When did he begin to think of Heaven Ray as his girl?* Mark shook his head and refocused on the wily old man of the sea.

"Another three days, but the closer we get to the Chain, the more likely we will be delayed by its adverse weather."

"The Chain?"

"The Aleutian Islands drag across the sea like a chain. Visibility can drop from twenty miles to nothing in minutes, and the fog can blanket us like a shroud before we're even aware. The winds from the Arctic are sometimes as fierce as an Atlantic hurricane or a Pacific typhoon."

"You old sea dog, are you sure you're not trying to put the fear of God into me?" Mark laughed.

"I may not be Navy, but I've sailed the Gulf of Alaska for over thirty years, and I hate this route. Other oceans and seas will give you a period of calm after a storm. Not here. Most of the time, it's one front immediately after another." He tossed his still-smoldering cigar into his empty coffee cup and shouted, "Ahead full."

"Ahead full. Aye-aye, cap." The first mate pulled the engine order telegraph and annunciator lever.

Captain James continued educating Mark. "The weather in the Chain is unpredictable and dangerous. The storms it sends across the Gulf are treacherous." The rheumy eyes of the experienced seaman showed his respect for the fierce Alaska weather. "Don't you think any different, son. It could get you killed."

"I'd like to stay on the bridge as much as possible and learn from you, Captain James." *Anything to keep my mind off Heaven Ray and her journey into harm's way.*

The next day, a heavy snowstorm with glacial winds of fifty knots assaulted the ship. The turbulent sea produced swells of over forty-five feet. The temperature plummeted, and visibility was nonexistent.

"Help me hold the wheel," Captain James yelled to Mark, "We're taking green water over the bow."

The ship plowed into the waves of the rough seas. Together, Mark and the captain held the wheel steady. Mark's arms felt like they were being torn from his shoulders, and his legs burned with tension. The cords in his neck bulged, and he knew the wheel could be pulled from his hands with an upward jerk of the ship. *Hang on! Hang on! Lives will be lost if you let go!* His breathing became labored within twenty minutes, and sweat ran down his face. Captain James yelled for the first mate to take over.

Mark gripped the wheel tighter, "I can do it." He felt a blush of inferiority heat his cheeks.

"You will obey orders. There's a thermos of coffee around here somewhere."

"On the floor, sir. It rolled into the corner," the first mate said.

The captain nodded and looked at Mark with a steely glare. "You'll drink it and sit down for ten minutes. Then you'll pull the bottle out of my locker and spell me."

"Yes, sir."

The storm lasted three days, and the ship made little headway. The wind blew the clouds away, and the sun's summer light infused him with a wide-awake energy he enjoyed but did not understand. Mark couldn't track the intense, slow-moving hours. The sun did not set until almost midnight; dawn came six and a half hours later. He rarely glanced at his watch anymore. The days were long, and the nights were short.

Another less fierce weather disturbance was coming, but Captain James felt his crew could handle it. "Ensign Lawson," Captain James held out his hand as Mark left the pilot house, "If you ever decide the Navy's not for you, there's a place for you aboard my ship."

"Thank you, sir." Exhausted but yet not sleepy, Mark's spirit soared at the captain's words. He saluted the man and stumbled to his cabin. He fell onto the bunk and, to his surprise, awoke nine hours later. He berated himself as he washed the tiredness from his eyes. Navy men were trained to go without sleep. He was better than this. *It must be the lack of meaningful activity on Kodiak that's made me soft.* After grabbing something to eat, he returned to the pilot house, and the captain handed him a pair of binoculars. He was told Dutch Harbor was on the horizon, although obscured by low clouds.

"Looks like fog to me," Mark said.

"The clouds are low, and the fog is dense. They mesh together and hang like a heavy curtain—devil of a thing." The captain once again cursed the weather along the Chain. "When you discern a thin, dark line on the horizon, that's Dutch."

Eventually, Mark and his evacuation team, including Mrs. Turner, Miss Ruth, and the priest, who seemed to have no name and didn't speak, huddled on the dock, barely able to see who was standing beside them. With some difficulty, they made their way through the fog to headquarters to learn where they would be billeted and when the evacuations could begin.

"We should ask if the transport from the Pribilofs has docked and where those evacuees are being held." Mark pulled his orders from his vest pocket. "I'm not sure Captain Nelson's plane has arrived. If not, we will do what we can."

A nearby seaman overheard him. "Island's been socked in for the last five days. No planes can land or take off." He laughed at the scowl on Mark's face. "You will learn that the weather is as vile an enemy as the Japanese. Here in Dutch, low clouds, high winds, and thick fog can delay or cancel many of our duties. Never seen anything like it. Not much gets done."

Mark swore and then apologized to the two women.

The seaman laughed, "You better get used to such language, ladies. That's all you'll hear in Dutch."

They ignored him. He turned and addressed Mark. "Ensign, rumor is, over five hundred Natives were taken from the Pribilofs last week and are quartered in a couple of Quonset huts just off base near Unalaska."

"That will be our first stop," Miss Ruth said, "We need to check on them."

CHAPTER EIGHT

Even when the fog cleared, there was no sign of Captain Nelson. Mark determined they would carry on without him. The frigid, wet wind did not abate, and Mark looked longingly at the foul weather gear the two women wore. Miss Ruth winked and patted his arm. "Is there anything you'd like to say? Anything you wished you had?"

Was he that easy to read? He felt his face flush and cleared his throat. "No, ma'am. I'm fine." He turned up his pea coat collar and pulled his watch cap over his ears.

"We heard you refused to look like a local." Miss Ruth laughed at the look on Mark's face, "Kodiak's a small town. Everybody knows everything. You look as wet and frozen as an ice cube in the Arctic."

"Don't tease the boy, Miss Ruth." Haven Ray showed Mark the bundle she carried. "These will keep the cold rain and wet wind from penetrating your clothes."

Miss Ruth laughed, "Me, tease? I just want him to admit that we're drier in our sou'westers and mukluks than he is in that ill-advised uniform."

"You know how hard it is for men to admit they're wrong. Look, his eyelashes are dripping, and his nose is as red as—what was that story that came with the Montgomery Ward Catalog last Christmas? Rudolph? That's it. He looks like Rudolph the Red-nosed Reindeer."

Did they have to talk about me as if I'm not here? And who's Rudolph? Mark stamped his feet and clapped his hands, trying to generate some body heat. He must admit they looked warmer than he felt. Drier, too.

"We've got eight villages to evacuate within the next few weeks, and Captain James says the weather will get worse." Haven Ray winked. "It might be easier for the villagers if you didn't come in uniform."

Miss Ruth pointed to the nearest barracks. "Go and change. Don't worry. You won't lose any of the authority your uniform grants you. And your dignity will remain intact."

Haven Ray handed him the bundle. "You're about the same size as my husband, who prefers Native raingear. It's hard to come by these days. Sadly, the old ways are disappearing. The mukluks might be a little large," she pulled the fur boots from the bag and showed him, "but I packed extra socks."

The constant icy winds chafed his face, but Mark was protected by the borrowed clothes. He wore a hooded kamleika—a light waterproof coat made of otter intestine—over his navy peacoat. The sealskin mitts and boots were a practical defense from the elements. The Native clothes were definitely a barrier against the weather. He looked at himself, grinned, and let the awkwardness drain away. "I can't believe how much drier and warmer I am."

"The Natives have adapted to their environment. We could learn much from them," Miss Ruth said.

"Thank you, Mrs. Turner."

"Call me Haven Ray."

The Columbia blew its whistle, backed out of its berth at Dutch Harbor, and headed to the first island to be evacuated. Several crewmen groused about the need to ferry the Aleuts from their villages to the ship in small boats. Captain James soon put a stop to that. "If I need you to be taxi drivers, that's what you'll be," he yelled.

"You'd make a good naval officer," Mark said.

"I run a tight ship, my boy. See that you run a tight mission. I'd like to get this over with as soon as possible. It doesn't sit well with me." He pulled his half-chewed cigar from his mouth and threw it over the ship's rail. Mark bit his lip to keep from agreeing with this civilian seaman.

Their first stop was the village of Nikolski on a nearby island. Ensign Lawson was surprised and felt ill at ease in traditional clothing because the Aleuts wore Western styles. He received several odd looks which were difficult to ignore. He supposed that if he had thought about the people in this isolated part of Alaska, it would have been the stereotype of an Eskimo in furs sitting in front of an igloo gnawing on whale blubber. True, the people in Nikolski lived a subsistence lifestyle, seeking food from the sea, but they lived in houses with electricity and plumbing. He coughed to cover his embarrassment and stammered his orders to the village elders. Most stared and remained unmoving, and he barked at them to get moving.

An old man, bent almost double, approached Mark. "I do not wish to leave my home."

"I'm sorry, but you are not safe here."

"I do not wish to leave my home."

"We'll transport you across the Gulf to a more civilized area."

The old man turned his face to the sky, "We are the people of these islands. We live close to the things we love, the sea, the sky, and each other. We do not want your civilization."

"I have my orders." Mark clenched his jaw and forced himself to sound stern even though he pitied the elderly man.

The faint droning of Japanese bombers and several dark specks near the horizon alarmed the old man. "Are they coming here?"

The sound of the bombs whistling through the air and exploding on a far away island unnerved the elder. Mark patted his shoulder and said, "Not today, but that is why you must leave."

The old man nodded and shuffled back to the others, but Mark saw the despair in his eyes. Mark swallowed his own misery and barked out orders once more. He repeated them in a loud voice. One little boy started to cry. Mark turned away.

"Here." Miss Ruth handed him a bag of lemon drops and lollipops. "Give these to the children. It will make them feel better—a little distraction."

"Really, Miss Ruth, I hardly think..." Mark refused the bag.

"It will make you feel better, too." Miss Ruth held it high above her head. "Come, children. Mr. Mark has a treat for you." She shoved the candy into his unwilling hands as a dozen young children swarmed around him. Hanging onto his knees and pulling at his arms. Their dark eyes twinkled as they tasted the candy.

They clung to him, jabbered, and giggled, "Mr. Mark. Mr. Mark." They pulled him down to their level and scampered into his lap. "Mr. Mark. You nice. Good man." The words were a jumbled mixture of Aleut, Russian, and English, but their delight transcended language.

Ensign Lawson struggled to hang on to all the discipline and dignity of the United States Navy. But it fell away as these children tumbled into his heart. *I needed this diversion more than the children.* All too soon, their mothers called for them. Mark's eyes followed as they led their children away. They were like mothers everywhere, eyes full of love for their children and fear for the future. Playtime over, Mark brushed himself off, shook his shoulders, and stuffed a handful of lemon drops into his mouth.

He saw his men had taken a break and were standing in groups of two or three, joking and ignoring their orders, or perhaps he hadn't been explicit enough. He stiffened his resolve to fulfill his duty with proper naval discipline and order. "Get moving, men. You have a job to do."

Each villager was ordered to bring one knapsack or suitcase plus a blanket. Watching these grim-faced people trudge from their homes, he wondered if they chose to pack clothes, fishing gear, household goods, baskets, family treasures, or dried salmon?

Haven Ray Turner led the people to a makeshift triage area, giving them a cursory medical check. Outside the church, Mark saw several villagers huddled around the priest. Although their village had no full-time priest and this cleric was a stranger, they looked to him for counsel. They fell to their knees as he prayed over them. Mark hoped it made them feel better. Anything to make his job easier and the people more manageable. At the edge of the village, Mark saw a couple arguing. The woman pulled on the man's arm, crying and shouting. He repeatedly shook his head no. Ensign Lawson ordered one of his men to check it out.

"Sir, the man has taken apart his boat motor and stuffed it into his suitcase. His wife is angry because there's no room for anything else."

Mark shook his head. What good was a motor without a boat?

"Sir...sir, what should I do?"

"Nothing, it's his choice."

The couple continued toward the beach with raised, angry voices. The small boats from the steamship were crewed and ready to ferry the villagers to the ship.

One woman waddled past Mark, looking much broader than she had an hour ago. Miss Ruth tugged Mark's arm, pointed, and said, "That's one clever mama. Look at how roly-poly her children are. I think they are wearing all the clothes they own, which allows them to fill their suitcase with other necessities."

"These poor people don't know where they are going or what they will need. It's horrible." Haven Ray called as she hurried across the open space. She asked Miss Ruth for more candy, then headed toward the crowd on the beach. More lollipops and lemon drops made the children smile. Nothing eased the sad tension in the adults.

Mark fisted his hands and shoved them into his pockets. His mood was as overcast as the sky. His eyes were as misty as the fog surrounding him, threatening to betray his emotions. He couldn't see the gulls and seabirds overhead nor hear their squawking. Two shrill blasts from the steamship signaled Captain James' impatience. Mark shook away his melancholy and nodded to the evacuation team. At his command, the sailors rushed to place a can of gasoline in the middle of each dwelling and set them ablaze. Whatever the people had not brought out of their homes was destroyed. Every structure in the village was burned to the ground, including the school, storage sheds, and food caches. The church, with its precious icons, was also burned. A culture destroyed.

A wail rose like smoke from the villagers as they saw their houses blazing. They obviously had no idea the government had intended to destroy their homes. Should the Japanese invade this island, they would find nothing of value.

A little boy ran toward one of the flaming houses, and Mark scrambled after him. The heat stung his face and scorched his eyebrows as he carried the struggling boy away. "What was in the house, little buddy. What did you go back for?"

A terrified mother tore the boy from Mark's arms. His stomach clenched, and he swallowed the bile that rose to his throat as he watched her weep for her lost home. Then she turned and thanked him for saving her son. He could only nod as she hurried back to the beach. Ensign Mark Lawson, a fourth-generation naval officer, thrust the shame of carrying out his orders deep into his soul, glad he wasn't responsible for determining if this campaign was right or wrong. He stared at the inferno and wondered if those in authority knew it wasn't just houses they were destroying. Lives were disrupted, and a culture wounded, perhaps fatally. Mark hadn't realized any of this until he looked into the frantic face of the little boy and the mother's anguished eyes. *It's not my fault. I'm just following orders. Besides, it's for their own safety.*

The old man looked at Mark as he stepped into the small boat, "You have taken my life."

Over the next few weeks, Mark's temper frayed, and his mood worsened, as did the weather. He avoided eye contact with the villagers and tried not to think of them as persons. He concentrated on the mission. Fortunately, he did not have to set any other island homes ablaze. His orders stated that the US Military conscripted the houses and outbuildings on the remaining islands for their own use.

Captain James stood at the rail and watched the activity on shore through his binoculars. He became as irritable as the ensign.

It was a harrowing time for everyone.

Just two more villages, then the voyage across the Gulf, which should take eight days, weather permitting, and I can forget about this messy business and these God-forsaken villagers.

The next village had around three hundred inhabitants, containing both whites and Natives. No one had received orders to evacuate. Mark called for the entire population to assemble and read his orders. Everyone was in shock. Mark gave them two hours to gather their belongings.

"We are to evacuate the Natives and leave the whites."

"That makes no sense," Haven Ray said.

"How can it be dangerous for the Natives to stay here and safe for the whites?" Miss Ruth asked.

Mark looked at his paperwork. "It says because the Natives are wards of the federal government, they can be forcibly removed. The white citizens are free to go or stay as they choose but must arrange their own transportation."

"That is the stupidest thing I've ever heard, and it's unjust." Haven Ray bit her lip to keep from saying more.

"What about mixed families? There are several where the husbands are white, the wives are Natives, and the children are both."

"We will take the wives and children and leave the husbands. I cannot alter these orders. There is nothing I can do."

Tension was high, and Mark threatened to use force to carry out his orders. A fistfight broke out when one of his sailors pulled a woman from her husband's arms and pushed her toward the boat. Mark swore and stepped between them. The husband didn't pull his punches, and Mark took one on the jaw. Ensign Lawson stepped back, rubbed his jaw, and apologized for the actions of his men.

Once all the Natives were aboard, Captain James blew the whistle, and the ship's engines rumbled. Miss Ruth and Haven Ray joined the wives and children at the ship's rail. Weeping and crying, they waved frantically to their husbands. The men cursed and yelled, begging to know where their families were being taken.

"I can't tell them our destination," Mark moaned, "Somewhere in the Southeast. Thank God, there is only one more island to evacuate."

"Where is it?"

"I'll be told when we stop back at Dutch Harbor to pick up the villagers from the Pribilofs, then just one more village to go. I hope Captain Nelson has arrived. He's in charge of this fiasco."

Miss Ruth cleaned her spectacles and smiled at Mark. "You have done an admirable job under the circumstances, Ensign Lawson."

Mark disagreed but gave her a brief nod.

After the morning meal at Dutch Harbor's Officer's Mess, Haven Ray's anxious voice asked, "Mark? Miss Ruth and I have a request."

"Is anything wrong? Your daughter is okay?"

"We must delay evacuating the last village and sail to Pleasure Island."

"Pleasure Island? Where's that?"

Miss Ruth reached for the salt shaker in the middle of the breakfast table. "Surely, you've heard the rumors? I can tell you they are true, and we must do something."

"Rumors?" Mark shook his head, "Our mission is almost complete. Captain James is anxious to return to his civilian schedule. We don't have time for anything else."

"We must make time."

"The Natives are not happy crammed into the cargo hold. It's cold, dark, and damp. I want to sail as soon as possible." He drained his coffee and motioned for the steward. He knew he wouldn't like whatever these two women had planned.

Haven Ray dabbed her eyes as Miss Ruth said, "The priest has talked to several elders, and they have confirmed the rumors. The youngest is twelve."

Mark instantly assumed the worst, and he was correct. "It's an unfortunate situation, but I hardly think it's the Navy's responsibility, Miss Ruth." Mark tried to sound harsh, but the image of the village children kept his voice soft, and he felt something stir in him for this trapped twelve-year-old girl.

"I wonder what I would have done if Heaven Ray had been caught up in such an evil circumstance. These poor wretches are someone's daughters," Haven Ray sighed.

Ensign Lawson thanked the steward as he refilled everyone's coffee. He stared into the dark liquid while his mind planned a rescue he knew he shouldn't get involved in. "I will speak to the commander of Dutch Harbor and see what can be done."

"I hardly think he will be accommodating. Obviously, he has turned a blind eye to the situation. The man has apparently allowed these particular vile activities to flourish," Miss Ruth's flashing eyes and harsh tone left no doubt of her anger.

"Nevertheless, I will need his permission, and hopefully, he will assign armed men to accompany me."

"Accompany us." Miss Ruth interrupted.

Mark threw his napkin on the table. "No. I cannot allow it!"

"We're going. I imagine the sight of armed men will cause them some anxiety. It will be helpful to have us along," Haven Ray insisted.

"Things could get ugly," he warned.

"They're already ugly," Haven Ray shuddered.

Mark tried for several days to make an appointment with the commander. He was seldom in his office. Mark finally found him at the base's airport, questioning a bomber pilot who had just returned from his sortie.

"Sorry, sir," The frustrated pilot said, "The fog took visibility down to nothing, and we had to turn back. We almost lost one of the planes due to the high wind."

"Have your men eat and rest, but be on alert. We will try again as soon as the weather breaks."

"Sir?" Mark introduced himself.

"You're the ensign who left messages about Pleasure Island? Leave it alone. It keeps the men, both naval and civilian, from going off. It's like a valve on a pressure cooker. This is a harsh environment, with very little to entertain the men. Things could get dicey if they don't have a little distraction, making my job more difficult."

"Surely, you can do something."

"This rock in the middle of nowhere has little to offer. There are only two things the men want. Booze, which is easy to get, and women, which are not."

"The women on Pleasure Island are trapped in a vile life."

"I assume it's their choice."

"Even the twelve-year-old?" Mark growled. "She has a choice?"

The commander of Dutch Harbor paled, then shrugged and said, "I didn't know there was a child on the island. Still, some of these Native girls marry at that age."

"With all due respect, sir, I am going to Pleasure Island with or without an armed escort."

"Look, Ensign, there is a war right here in the Aleutians, and between the incessant fog, wind, and rain, I'm having a devil of a time coordinating bombing sorties over Attu and Kiska. I don't have time for this."

"All I need you to do is give me a boat and assign six men to my command."

The irritated commander threw his cigarette on the tarmac and swore. He pulled a scrap of paper from his pocket, hastily scrawled instructions, and shoved it toward Mark. "Give this to my yeoman, and don't bother me again."

Miss Ruth and Mrs. Turner praised Mark for his success. He blushed and didn't offer any details. *Let them think I talked the commander into it. They don't need to know he just wanted to get rid of me.*

Early that evening, the fog cleared, and the wind died. The reluctant sailors who had assembled on the dock raised their eyes and cheered as the rumble of the American bombers roared overhead. They grumbled and muttered to themselves as Mark ordered them into the boat. Miss Ruth and Haven Ray sat in the bow and faced them. Miss Ruth lifted her voice over the sound of the engine and lectured the men on the evils of drunkenness and fornication as the boat crossed the narrow channel to Pleasure Island. Haven Ray Turner stared intently at each sailor. Many lowered their eyes. One returned her intense gaze and then spat tobacco juice over the side. She prayed fervently for him, then turned her face toward the youngest sailor, who blushed and stammered, "I only went there once, ma'am. Honest."

CHAPTER NINE

Pleasure Island looked anything but pleasurable. An unpainted, ramshackle two-story building sat on the edge of a slight rise not far from the beach. Ragged lace curtains hung askew in the dirty windows. Mark saw a subtle movement and lifted his eyes. A young girl's sad face peered from the upstairs window. When their eyes met, she quickly turned and was lost from his sight. He swallowed and addressed the men. "I don't want any trouble. I don't care how many times you have visited this establishment in the past. We are here to shut it down."

"It ain't right."

Mark towered over the man, "Excuse me, sailor. Did I hear you say something?"

"No, sir." The man swallowed his wad of chewing tobacco.

"Let's keep it that way."

The madam welcomed Mark. It wasn't often an officer came to see her girls. Her smiles turned to curses when she was informed of the Navy's intention to close her establishment. "You can't do this. I'm an American, and I have rights."

Mark looked her in the eye. "Actually, the United States government outlawed prostitution years ago."

She put her hands on her hips and talked around the cigarette dangling from her red lips. "We ain't a state, so what do you say about that?"

"The federal law still applies, and these women are free to go."

"None of my girls will leave me. I take care of them—give them a good life. The money they make helps their families, them that gots families."

"I'm not arguing with you, ma'am. If I have to, I'll burn this place down."

"Take the girls, but leave me my house. I ain't got nowhere else to go."

"Don't let them take us. We'll starve." A hard-faced woman said. She appeared to be the oldest and looked tired and worn. Her rouge had settled into the crevices on her wrinkled face, and Mark thought that any man who had paid for her services must be desperate indeed.

"I ain't goin' nowhere." A pretty woman who appeared in her mid-twenties said, "Never had it so good. Here, nobody beats me, not like in 'Frisco." She flicked the ash from her cigarette toward an ashtray but missed, then pulled a flask from the folds of her pretty pink kimono.

"Maybe life will be better somewhere else," a young, delicate Creole, hardly more than a girl, whispered.

"You don't have a choice, ladies. You have one hour to pack your things. Cooperate, or we will force your cooperation."

"Best you go so they don't burn my place."

The women slowly left. The oldest patted the madam's shoulder and whispered loud enough for the rescuers to hear, "Don't worry, we'll be back."

The skinny but pretty twelve-year-old crept close to Miss Ruth. "I'd like to leave, but I got nowhere to go." She bit her lip to stop its trembling.

"What's your name, my dear?"

"She's mine! You can't take her!" the madam shrieked, pulling the girl toward her. "Tell them, Angel. Tell them I'm your mama."

Angel stomped on the madam's foot and jerked out of her grasp. She was slapped across the face.

"Don't touch her!" Haven Ray cried. The girl hid behind Haven Ray, her voice a soft, timid whisper, "My mama died birthin' me. That's what they told me."

One of the women turned in the doorway and nodded. "That's right. Her poor mother was too innocent when she came here. She didn't know how to take care of herself."

"Stupid girl. Got herself pregnant right away. Didn't know it until it was too late," the madam growled, "She wouldn't let me help her get rid of it."

The oldest woman returned with her small suitcase. She set it on the floor and stood before Miss Ruth. "Best you take her. She just turned twelve, and some of the men have been eyeing her. Her innocence is going to be auctioned to the highest bidder."

Haven Ray Turner gasped and pulled Angel into a fierce hug. "She's coming with us."

"I need her," the madam whined. "You know I love you, Angel-baby. Stay with me."

Haven Ray glared at the Madam. You'll not take her innocence."

"Haven Ray, take the girl outside," Miss Ruth said and then turned to the owner of the brothel. "You will not perpetrate your evil on this young girl or use her to make money."

Mark rubbed his forehead. "What are we going to do with her? This is getting complicated. What will we do with any of them?"

"We'll take Angel with us to Kodiak and figure it out from

there," Miss Ruth said, "We'll take the others to Unalaska and interview them. Hopefully, they have other job skills. We will help them in any way we can. I'm sure Captain James can make room for those who want to go elsewhere."

Mark nodded but thought the women lacked other skills or resources. It seemed Pleasure Island could only be a last resort for any female.

As the women were installed in the open boat and taken from Pleasure Island, they refused to be interviewed and said they would be fine in Unalaska. They also refused passage to Anchorage, Kodiak, or the Southeast. Ensign Mark Lawson, relieved of arranging transport for these women, found himself wondering if they would return to their former line of work. He said as much to Miss Ruth and Mrs. Turner at dinner that evening.

"We have counseled each one and paid for a few nights lodging in Unal. We've offered to help them find honorable jobs." Haven Ray wiped her eyes.

Miss Ruth lifted sad eyes to Mark's. "I suspect you are right. But one little lamb, our Angel, will be safe."

"All that trouble for one?"

Miss Ruth smiled, "Yes, Mark. Jesus left the ninety-nine sheep to find one lost little lamb."

Angel sat between Haven Ray and Miss Ruth. She kept her head down and squirmed in her seat, refusing to speak. He noticed she had no concept of table manners. She wore a shirt he had seen on Haven Ray a few days ago. On the slim, malnourished child, it was as long as a dress. He presumed she had spent a long time in the shower. She looked well scrubbed, her hair clean and plaited in two long braids that hung below her shoulders.

"Timid little thing," he whispered.

Haven Ray frowned at him and put her arm around the girl, "Perfectly understandable."

"There's nothing wrong with her hearing, Mark. Angel spent her life in that house, only going as far as the beach. Everything is new and perhaps frightening."

"Sorry, Miss Ruth." Mark felt his face redden at his insensitivity. He gulped his coffee and addressed the girl, "I apologize, Miss Angel. Thank you for joining us for dinner. We will have ice cream for dessert. I'm sure you will like it."

The little girl lifted her head and risked giving this imposing man in uniform a quick glance. He winked, and she lowered her head again and shivered.

Miss Ruth leaned over and whispered in Angel's ear, "He is the man who rescued you, dear one. You can trust him."

Angel shrugged her shoulders and slowly reached for her biscuit. Mark was surprised at the disappointment that punched him in the stomach. Miss Ruth said, "It will take time, but our little Angel will be okay."

CHAPTER TEN

The sun rose high above Dutch Harbor, and the hillsides on the outskirts of the base exploded with wildflowers and berry bushes. Ensign Lawson didn't realize how much he had missed the sun. The bald eagles overhead captured his attention, and he let his gaze follow them. They soared above foxes so well-fed they looked like chubby dogs. Mark laughed out loud, and the foxes ran into the brush. He turned and saw several otters floating on their backs, and a lone harbor seal barked as he caught fresh fish for lunch. Mark lifted his face to the heavens and breathed in the delicious fresh air. Then his gaze fell on the Alaska steamship, and his good cheer evaporated.

The Natives he evacuated had been sequestered on the ship while he made the detour to Pleasure Island. He had hoped to sail upon his return, but a thick fog had halted all travel in and out of Dutch Harbor for the last three days. It had lifted this morning, and Captain James was preparing the ship to sail. Mark took the opportunity to stretch his legs.

He knew that Captain James, while sympathetic to Mark's mission, had other concerns. Mark was informed the white civilians of Unalaska who were leaving had purchased tickets and reserved every available stateroom. There was a lot of freight in the hold, so the Natives were stashed between packing crates. It was dark, damp, and not well-ventilated. While they were in port, the captain had allowed the villagers to camp on deck, which irritated his crew. Once underway, the Natives would be confined to the hold.

Ensign Lawson chomped on the last lemon drops Miss Ruth had given him. The sour candy left a bitter taste in his mouth. He ran to the dock, determined to evacuate the last village and sail for the Southeast before the weather turned again.

"No, it's impossible. You must bring him back." Mark looked over his shoulder at the ship anchored in the dark water. As soon as these Aleuts were aboard, they could set sail. He towered over the short village elder, intending to impose the will of the United States Navy on the man.

The man refused to be cowed. "When the government man came to our island and told us we would be forced to leave, we were not happy. He said the Japanese would come and kill us, so we go."

Mark ran his hand through his hair. "But the boy?"

"Once you have killed your first seal, you are a man, and your life is what you choose."

"It's not his decision to make. I have orders to evacuate everyone. Call the men of the village. We will conduct a search."

The elder raised his eyes. "The sky is angry; bad weather comes."

"We must find him."

"You will not."

"What about his parents? They cannot possibly agree."

"His mother weeps but is proud. His father is dead. The boy is like his grandfather's father—a hunter. Fearless."

Mark sighed in frustration, his shoulders slumped, and he wished Miss Ruth and Haven Ray were here instead of triaging the villagers. He turned to the priest. "Can you reason with him?"

Mark paced as the two men talked. After a short time, the

priest shrugged and motioned for Mark to come. "There is nothing to be done."

"How will the boy live? What if the Japanese invaded? He cannot fight the entire Japanese military." Mark glared at the elder, who returned his gaze unfazed.

The village elder spoke in a soft voice. "On the island's other side are many hidden and secret caves. The boy has taken all the food we have gathered this summer and stashed it. He has hidden extra clothes, tools, and supplies, plus a kayak."

"A few baskets of dried fish will not sustain him for long, and he cannot escape in a kayak." Mark hardened his voice as his frustration mounted. He gazed across the treeless island to the far hills, trying to see where this young, lone Aleut could have hidden.

"He has many baskets of dried fish and seal, as well as whale blubber. He has taken several large containers of seal oil and eggs from puffins, murres, and the long-tailed duck. Packs of dried greens and berries have also been collected. The boy has traveled to several nearby islands in his little kayak, but he will remain hidden and survive as our people have always survived. If I were younger, I would remain."

"It has been decided," the priest said, "None of the villagers know where the boy is, and they will not help you search. If you look toward the sea, you will see a dense fog rolling in. We must go."

Mark felt like storming into the hills alone and dragging the boy back. His lack of knowledge of the island, the boy's apparent ability to hide, and the persistent, thick fog prevented him. Defeated, he pulled the papers from his inner jacket pocket and muttered, "My tally sheet will be one short. Unacceptable."

The elder looked at the overcast sky. The black clouds dropped closer to the earth, and the haze thickened. "Best we go while we can see."

Mark's crew escorted the elder and his people to the ship as the fog enveloped them. Mark followed, guided by the women's quiet voices and the men's bitter words. The weather had swallowed them, and he had trouble seeing his feet as he took careful steps after them.

"The boy is in Bozhe's hands," the priest's voice came out of the gray mist, trying to comfort Mark, "He has learned the old ways from his grandfather. Do not concern yourself."

Captain James yelled to his crew, "Get them settled below. I want to be ready to sail when the fog lifts; we should be so lucky."

"They are hungry, Skipper. What shall I give them?" a seaman asked.

"The Navy sent several pallets of C-rations for the Indians, sir," the first mate said.

"They want to be called Aleuts," the captain said, disgusted at his crewman and annoyed he had to carry these Aleuts across the Gulf in the dungeon-like hold of his ship.

"I don't think they'll eat it." The seaman ignored the captain's reprimand and was back an hour later, "I was right. They won't eat it. I tried everything except crammin' it down their throats."

Captain James scratched his head, tossed his unlit cigar across the room, and barked at Mark, "These people are your responsibility. Fix it!"

Mark found Haven Ray and Miss Ruth in the galley arguing with the cook. "What's the problem?"

"We have several bags of clams and mussels which need to be cooked."

"This is my galley, and I'm in charge, and I ain't cooking for no savages."

"He's right, ladies." Mark motioned for the two women to leave.

"Thank you. Interfering old busybodies!" He slammed a frying pan on the stove.

"You're the cook," Mark growled as he hefted the 50 lb. bags of shellfish onto the counter, "Now, cook!"

"But..."

"And don't try anything foolish. I'm going to taste test every dish and they better taste good. Got it?"

"Yes, sir!" The cook saluted, forgetting he still gripped a large metal spoon.

Miss Ruth and Haven Ray had been peeking through the half-open doorway and chuckled when the cook smacked himself in the eye.

"Good job, Mark," both ladies congratulated him. He discovered they had brought dried salmon, preserved seabird eggs, dried berries, and other food natural to the Native's diet. There was enough for the voyage.

"I just assumed they would eat the C-rations. They aren't too flavorful, but the Marines manage to choke them down," Mark said.

"I heard they call them C-rats," Miss Ruth laughed.

Haven Ray patted Mark's arm. "We thought the trip would be less harrowing if they had familiar foods. We raided their homes once they left and brought as much food as possible."

Captain James didn't want to know what was happening below deck. He pushed his ship to the limit, anxious for the voyage to end even though it had just begun. "I'll not take human cargo again. I don't care how many times the Navy orders me. I won't do it."

Mark took off his peacoat and flung it into the corner. He took a turn at the wheel. "I wish I had that option. This feels wrong, but what can I do? We couldn't leave them behind, not with the threat from Japan."

"I get it, but there's a lot of things happening in this war, son, and people are going to say they were just following orders." The captain's steely gaze focused on Mark.

Mark's face reddened, and he bit his tongue to keep himself from responding to the man's accusatory tone. With averted eyes, he pictured the previous generations of his family. All Navy men. Had any of them ever violated their principles? Obeyed orders they thought were morally wrong, although legal, even necessary? He had a class at the Academy on ethics and morality, all theoretical. It was different when one was caught in the vortex.

CHAPTER ELEVEN

The Gulf of Alaska was notorious for storms, and it lived up to its reputation as Captain James struggled to keep his ship from capsizing due to the high waves and strong winds. He had received reports that seasickness was prevalent among the people suffering in the hold. He couldn't spare a thought for them as he saw a wall of green water spill over the bow.

The buckets used for human waste overflowed, and the Natives spewed vomit everywhere. The odor sickened many, especially the elders and the children. The disorientation caused by each pitch and roll of the ship inflicted the people with nausea, fear, and pain. The steel of the ship's hull felt as cold as the water it held back. There was no heat in this dungeon. There were no cots or bunks. The people huddled together on the cold metal floor. Some of the agile, adventurous children scampered atop the cargo, those who did not moan and puke. They assured their mothers they would hang on and the ship's rocking would not dislodge them.

Mark made his way to the wheelhouse, hanging on to every rail and stable handhold. "Can't we do something for the Natives?"

"It's all I can do to keep this ship afloat. It's one of the worst storms I've ever experienced. I've given orders for everyone to stay in their cabins."

"But, surely..."

"There is nothing to be done, no place for the Natives to go.

I only hope I can land them in the Southeast alive. I pray all of us survive this storm. You get me?"

"What can I do?"

"Stop talking and check with my first mate."

The storm abated two and a half days later, and Mark inspected the hold. The stench was unbearable, but he forced himself to proceed. He sent the Natives to the deck a few dozen at a time and pushed his evacuation team to clean up the overflowing refuse buckets. Miss Ruth and Haven Ray took bundles of filthy, vomit-stained clothing to the ship's laundry and insisted they be cleaned before any of the paying passengers' slightly soiled clothes.

Haven Ray and Miss Ruth invited the women, a few at a time, to their staterooms, introducing them to the lavatory's tiny shower. The mothers were delighted to bathe themselves and their children. Angel watched the interaction between the women and their children. She had never seen little ones before and was enthralled.

"Captain!" Ensign Lawson burst into the pilot house again. "There's been a death aboard!"

Captain James turned the wheel over to his first mate and led Mark to his cabin. "Calm down, man."

"When the last of the Natives came on deck for air and exercise. They brought the oldest man from Biorka—dead!"

"The cause?"

Mark removed his cap and rubbed his hand through his dark hair. "I don't know. The conditions in the hold are dismal. I imagine his heart gave out."

"Hmmm." Captain James tugged at his mustache. "We must bury him at sea. The priest can officiate. It would not do to speak of this."

"But…"

"You know the Navy wants the least amount of publicity about this mission. If you offload a body, things will not go well for any of us. I'll have my men wrap the body in canvas and weight it with chains. You get the priest."

"But, sir…"

"Tell the priest to say a quick prayer. We'll do it when the passengers, the white passengers, are at dinner. No sense upsetting them."

"But, Captain…"

"Go."

As Mark bellowed the captain's orders to the Natives, he refused to look them in the eye. *So this is what it is like to be in command. It's not for me. Could this mission get any worse?* Ensign Mark Lawson's clenched jaw and tight muscles told him he didn't think so. He stood aloof and alone at the ship's rail as his orders were carried out. He couldn't force himself to join the mourners, although he was glad to see Mrs. Turner and Miss Ruth offering what comfort they could.

The choppy waves were an angry gray-green topped with foaming whitecaps. Dark clouds filled the sky, cutting off the sun. The stormy air whipped around him, and he pulled his coat tighter. The chill reached his heart. He felt as angry as the waves, as devoid of sunlight as the sky.

Captain James had ordered his crew to prepare for the funeral while everyone was at dinner. The clandestine service was to occur with no one except the man's wife and family, which seemed to include all of the island's inhabitants. They stood around the canvas-wrapped body. The only sound was the whispered prayers of the priest and Haven Ray Turner's sniffing. The canvas-shrouded body lay stiff on a cedar plank. A seaman balanced the board on the ship's rail and tipped it during the priest's final prayer. Everyone was hustled back to the ship's hold as the body splashed into the sea. The short service ended, and Mark pushed himself away from the rail.

With heavy hearts, Mark and the two women made their way to the ship's salon and sat apart from its other occupants.

"I don't understand how this happened. We should have left them in their own villages," Haven Ray cried.

"As awful as this relocation is, I imagine that the Natives on Attu and Kiska would rather have been evacuated than executed by the enemy or held as Japanese prisoners of war," Miss Ruth said and motioned for the steward to bring a pot of tea. However, she was sure the ensign would prefer something more potent. "I wish those on Attu and Kiska could have been removed before the Japanese invaded. Our government had the best intentions, but that does not excuse their lack of planning."

"At least they won't be prisoners like the Japanese Americans who were forced into camps in the lower forty-eight. It breaks my heart." Haven Ray wrung her hands, sniffed, and stood. "I'm going to turn in."

Mark sighed and shook his head when the steward set a tray on the table and placed a teacup before him. Miss Ruth poured the fragrant Earl Gray tea. "Drink your tea, Mark. It will make you feel better."

"This has been a disaster from the beginning. Nothing will make me feel better. This was an unnecessary death. The whole mission was ill-advised."

Miss Ruth let two lemon drops slip from her fingers into the tea and handed him a cup. He gulped the too-hot liquid and choked.

"I'm not even sure of our destination. Neither is Captain James. He's waiting for orders. And I'm still waiting for Captain Nelson to show up. It's all a muddle."

"Yes, it is, but the governor has assured me there will be no barbed wire or armed guards around their settlements like there are for Japanese Americans. If the Aleuts choose to leave, they can."

"I've been told their destinations are isolated. Where would they go? How would they live? They have nothing." He finished his tea and said a sad goodnight.

The rest of the eastward voyage across the Gulf of Alaska was reasonably calm. The seas were a little choppy, but the fog was light, and the temperature rose. The white passengers discussed war, weather, and their plans once they reached Juneau, Wrangell, or Ketchikan. The Natives in the hold suffered stoically and grieved quietly.

Shortly before they neared the islands of Southeast Alaska, news came from below deck that a woman had given birth. Ensign Mark Lawson couldn't imagine it. *I didn't know anyone was pregnant. Why wasn't I informed?* He would have had the woman taken to the ship's infirmary. *What else is happening in the hold that I don't know about?*

He grinned when he was told she had given birth to twins. With the missing boy on the island and the dead elder, his tally sheet was off by two. Now, it would balance. A moment later, he bit his lip and turned away, disgusted with himself. He shoved his hands into the pockets of his peacoat and circled the ship's deck twice, berating himself and imagining a young teenager trying to survive alone on an island the Japanese might invade. He thought about the old man taken from his home and dying en route to safety. *What kind of a person am I that my first thought was the twins' birth would balance my tally sheet? How could I have put the mission above the people?*

When they heard about the babies, Miss Ruth and Haven Ray immediately went to the galley, badgered the cook for nourishing soup, and made their way to the hold. They returned with the babies in their arms. Right behind them, the father carried his wife wrapped in a blanket.

"You can't be out here," a crew member yelled across the deck.

Another said, "Go back to the hole you just crawled out of!"

Miss Ruth stopped mid-stride. "You hush, or I will report you to Captain James."

"He doesn't want none of them Indians topside neither."

"They are Aleuts." Haven Ray glared at the disrespectful crew members, "People like you and me."

"Captain ain't going to like it."

"Then I'll report him too." Miss Ruth grinned, "I'll report him to Bozhe."

"Who's that?" The younger of the two asked his shipmate.

The old seaman shrugged his shoulders. "Must be some important Admiral or something. I'll be glad when this war's over and the Navy stops ordering us around. Dang interfering government." He spat tobacco juice over the side. The wind blew it back and smacked the young crew member in the face. He swore. The old sea dog laughed and slapped him on the back. "Well, there, young fella, you made me feel better."

Miss Ruth ignored them and walked on, her little entourage following. The new family was installed in Haven Ray's room, where she could monitor the health of mother and babies. Angel moved in with Miss Ruth.

"I want to stay with the babies, funny little things. I never saw nothing so tiny, so alive."

"You may help Haven Ray whenever she calls you, but new mothers and babies need lots of rest and sleep.

CHAPTER TWELVE

The steamship plowed through the Gastineau Channel. An abandoned fish cannery at Funter Bay near Juneau was the designated living quarters for the Pribilof's villagers. They were settled there, and the ship continued through the islands of the Alexander Archipelago. The Aleut villagers were deposited at six different locations. One as miserable as the next.

Several hundred of them were to be housed in a derelict herring plant. The buildings had been empty for years and were in disrepair. Wind and weather had taken their toll. The rodents and other vermin didn't seem to mind. There was no water or source of heat. No cookstoves or bathroom facilities.

Territorial officials with clipboards hustled families into their living areas without apology for the dismal conditions. Filling out numerous forms required by the involved agencies seemed to be their priority.

"Excuse me," Miss Ruth addressed a group of workers, "who's in charge?"

The men looked at each other, shrugged, and continued checking items off their lists as each family passed. Miss Ruth tugged on the nearest man's arm, introduced herself, and repeated the question.

"My job is to count the people, make sure the numbers match my paperwork, and assign each one a living space. Now, if you'll excuse me." He walked away, motioning for a family of five to follow him.

The next official said, "I've been instructed to set up food distribution. I have some C-rations and several barrels of flour, coffee, and canned cheese. Not nearly enough."

"Did you know an adult Aleut eats up to four pounds of seal meat daily? It's a staple of his diet," Miss Ruth said.

The man glared at Miss Ruth, "Nothing I can do about that." He shook his head and walked away cursing. The person she talked to next was in charge of sanitation. He swore and threw his clipboard on the ground. "Sanitation! There's no water and only two outhouses down on the beach. High tide cleans out the refuse, but it's an unsanitary mess when it is low. This is ridiculous."

Miss Ruth approached the lone woman with a clipboard and asked what she had been tasked with, "I'm here from the Territorial Education Board. These villages were part of the school system. I can't have white teachers live here under these conditions. I suppose we'll have to send the children to Indian boarding schools. The Wrangle Institute is the closest."

"These children have been removed from the only home they have ever known. You can't rip them away from their parents." Miss Ruth's disgust was evident on her face.

"The conditions here aren't going to improve. If I had a daughter here, I'd send her to Wrangell in a heartbeat. At least she'd have decent food and a bed with sheets and a blanket." She glared at Miss Ruth, "Don't tell me how to do my job—a job I didn't ask for." She walked away, muttering, "And a job I'm going to quit as soon as I return to Juneau."

Mark came out of the building frowning, "I wouldn't let my dog stay here. Just now, a woman and her child fell through the rotting floor."

"Are they hurt?"

"The mother sprained her ankle. She was holding her little boy. He's more scared than hurt."

"I should go to them," Miss Ruth said.

"Haven Ray is with them. She's the nurse, remember?" Mark tried to laugh but couldn't, "There has got to be something better. Haven Ray is beside herself. Captain James is ready to leave, and she refuses to board."

Miss Ruth dusted her skirt and sighed, "I'll talk to her. She has no more leave from her job and must think of Angel."

"What about you, Miss Ruth?"

"I'm staying.'

"The territorial workers are being picked up this evening by bush plane. Are you leaving with them?"

"The priest is staying for a month to help the people settle. I'll remain as well and then report to the governor."

"You can't stay here, the conditions are intolerable."

She laid her hand on his arm and peered into his face. "I've been in Alaska for fifty years. I've survived many intolerable situations and conditions."

"But you were much younger," Mark gulped, then apologized.

Miss Ruth laughed and then surprised the ensign by kissing him on the cheek. "I'll send Haven Ray and Angel to you. Godspeed, my boy."

"I can't imagine Miss Ruth in that God-forsaken place, but I'm glad she's there," Mark shuddered.

"Wherever Miss Ruth goes, Bozhe goes before her," Haven Ray said.

"I'm not sure what can be done. Those who claim to be in charge seem confused and have no resources."

Haven Ray and Mark stood at the ship's rail. Neither the calm seas and bright evening light nor the pod of orcas raised their spirits. Still, they stood and watched the family of whales.

"Do you know much about Aleut culture?" She stared at the water as the ship's wake fanned out, leaving a frothy trail of vanilla foam.

He shook his head.

Haven Ray sighed, "It's difficult to put into words. The people we have evacuated, and I understand it is for their own safety, will pay a high price for leaving their islands. For many, the price will be too high."

"What do you mean?"

"Their souls are still in the islands."

"I know it's difficult," Mark said, "but they will adjust. They have to."

Haven Ray leaned over the rail and stared into the dark sea. "They believe their essence is attached to their home island."

Mark scratched his head. "You're right, I don't get it."

"We have split them in two. I fear some elders will die."

"Just by being separated from their villages?"

"Separated from everything they believe themselves to be. I think the younger ones, those who have been to school, will fare better. School for the Natives has its pros and cons. It enables them to live in a more integrated way but strips them of their language and culture." Haven Ray shook her head and sighed, "I heard a couple of young men say they would enlist in the military instead

94

of rotting away in these camps."

"I don't know what to think. Have we done a horrible thing to these people?" Mark rubbed his forehead and hoped the tension there would not become a headache.

"Yes, but with the best intentions. And at least we saved Angel."

"What will you do with her?"

"She'll stay with me for the summer and probably attend a boarding school in Anchorage this fall. If I can find a way to keep her with me, I will."

The churning water, the screech of seabirds overhead, and the ship's engines were the only sounds they heard as they fell silent, each lost in their own heartache.

Ensign Mark Lawson dreaded the debrief. His father knew him too well. *Keep it together; don't get emotional, just recite the facts.*

His father sat in silence as Mark delivered a verbal report. Elly leaned against the closed door and absorbed every word. His face grew grim as he heard the details of the mission. The commander uttered curses under his breath. Elly prayed silently and stuffed his mouth with chocolates.

"That's all of it, son?"

"Yes, sir."

The commander shook his head and shuffled some papers. "All things considered, good job. Take a few days leave. Get some rest."

"I'd rather keep working, sir. Keep my mind off things."

"I'm ordering you to take a forty-eight-hour leave. See Yeoman Richardson on your way out. Dismissed."

Mark closed the door softly, "The old man looks aged and tired, Elly. What's gotten into him?"

"This evacuation business was a fiasco, and I think it grates on him, but even more so is the fact that you're being reassigned. It's hit him harder than he's letting on."

Ensign Lawson grabbed the papers from Elly's hand, "Hot dog! This is great."

"He'll miss you. We both will." Elly sniffed and handed Mark a peanut cluster from a Whitman Sampler, the ensign's favorite chocolate, and a bag of the new treat, M&Ms.

"Wow! I know how hard these M&Ms are to get. Thanks, Elly." Mark looked into the yeoman's eyes and wondered how old he was. Godfather. Confidant. Mentor. Yeoman Richardson had always been a part of his life. "I'm still mad at you for letting me believe Heaven Ray was on the evac team."

Elly just grinned. "God will use those experiences to change you. At least, that's my prayer."

"This ill-fated mission has shown me things I'll never forget."

"Remember everything you saw and heard."

Mark ignored the advice. He knew he would do his darndest to put the whole Aleutian experience behind him. "I'll miss you too, but this is my chance to make him proud."

They shook hands, and Elly grabbed him in a fierce hug. "I'll pray for you, my boy. And you'll meet Miss Turner again, I'm sure of it. Godspeed."

"Yeoman, get in here," the commander called. Elly found him writing furiously.

"Sir?'

"Here's a check. Make sure it gets to Mrs. Turner. I assume she and Miss Ruth will be helping the Aleuts however they can."

"This is from your personal account, sir."

"Yes, and there will be one every month. And find some way to make it anonymous."

"Yes, sir. I assume Mark knows."

"There is no need. Dismissed."

CHAPTER THIRTEEN

Standing at the rail of the troop transport, gazing into the cool blue water of late summer, was a peaceful way to pass the hours. Amid all this natural beauty, it was hard to imagine the United States had been at war for nearly nine months. The Gulf was choppy during the entire voyage, but the weather held, keeping the storms at bay. It rained a time or two, and the wind, gusty and always fickle, often sent everyone inside. But when the wind died, and the sun appeared, watching the terns, murres, and ospreys competing for the abundance of fish entertained all who stood on deck. Seeing the ice-blue mountains of Glacier Bay and the mottled greens of the timberland brought a yearning to stay in this land. Vast forests and abundant wildlife on the shore and in the water showed the immense variety of the Creator's hand. What was it about Alaska that touched the heart?

After making port in Sitka and Juneau and offloading cargo and passengers, they continued south through the Alexander Archipelago and the Queen Charlotte Islands. The most hazardous part of the voyage would be through the tricky Seymour Narrows, that three-mile stretch of water between Vancouver Island and the British Columbia mainland. According to those who traversed the Narrows, it was one of the vilest stretches of water in the world, perhaps because of its strong currents and Ripple Rock.

Shortly after midnight, the engines vibrated, ground down, and stalled. The vessel groaned as it slowed and then stopped dead in the water. The ship's whistle blew several short blasts, and crewmen yelled as they ran to their stations. Heaven Ray, jerked awake by the sound of a thousand fingernails scraping a giant blackboard, pulled her clothes on, including a heavy jacket and boots, grabbed a flashlight, and went on deck. She saw sailors in various stages of dress running fore and aft. New recruits milled about and wondered if the ship had been attacked.

"What's happening?" she called to the nearest seaman.

"We hit something, or something hit us."

"The Japanese?"

"I don't know. Go to the officer's mess, ma'am. They'll tell you what to do or where to go."

Several large platters of sandwiches and a cake were nestled on the sideboard next to three large coffee urns already steaming. Two officers poured over sea charts of the Inside Passage. Two of the crew ran in, grabbed a cup of coffee and a sandwich, and left as quickly as they came. Some sat and smoked. Heaven Ray tip-toed through the sea of officers, poured herself a cup of coffee, and chose a seat in the corner where she could observe and listen.

"I told the skipper we needed an Alaskan or Canadian pilot to guide us through these Narrows, but the Navy said it was too expensive." The lieutenant's voice was quiet as he looked around the room. It wouldn't do for word to get back to the skipper that he had repeated their conversation.

"They sent divers down to assess the damage," another said.

The same lieutenant announced. "My uncle once tore up his fishing boat on Ripple Rock. It's a double-peaked underwater mountain in these Narrows. In some places, it's just nine feet under the surface. I bet we hit it."

And so they had. The ship was leaking fuel, and the divers had to work through the night in the cold, black water. The underwater lights gave a limited murky visibility. By the following afternoon, they had managed to weld a patch over the hole, and the vessel shuffled through Discovery Channel past Quadra Island and made its way to Vancouver, where a stronger steel was welded over the ship's wound. Much later than expected, the vessel crawled through the San Juan Islands of Puget Sound to its final destination, at Bremerton, Washington.

CHAPTER FOURTEEN

The ship's crew remained at the Bremerton Naval Yard, while those drafted or enlisted were bused to the train station in Seattle. Three coach cars were set aside for the military; one had several tiny sleeping compartments for officers. The train stopped at Ft. Lewis, Washington, and dropped off the newly enlisted GIs. On its way to Camp Pendleton and Naval Base San Diego, the train made numerous stops and picked up more recruits and draftees. Most were young, awkward, and shy. Rather than sitting alone in her tiny compartment, Heaven Ray spent most of her time in the crowded club car. The "no-fraternization" rule between officers and enlisted personnel did not sit well with this Alaska girl. Several other nurses on their way to San Diego felt the same, and the hours passed pleasantly.

The train seemed to stop in every hamlet and small town once it left Seattle. The smaller the town, the larger the crowd as families said goodbye to their newly enlisted or drafted sons. The American Legion Auxiliary and local church women often came with large urns of coffee and baskets of sandwiches, fruit, and cookies. The hungry boys devoured the hot coffee and food and thought of their mothers' home cooking. They would fight for home and country—mom, apple pie, and baseball—all that was good about America. Some swallowed around the lumps in their throats, and others couldn't eat at all. Seeing the homesickness on their faces caused Heaven Ray to think of her own mother and the Alaska village she called home.

The reality that many of these boys would return broken and battered squeezed Heaven Ray's heart. Some of them wouldn't return at all. She blew her nose, wiped her eyes, and asked the Lord to help her, help these boys. *Please give us the strength and faith we need for the coming months and years.* She wiped her eyes, blew her nose, and began to sing "Amazing Grace" softly to herself.

"Please, ma'am, could you sing it again, only louder?" a young draftee asked.

"Yes, sing to us," another begged.

Heaven Ray sang until she ran out of songs. The other nurses joined her, and when they finished, the GIs demanded they start over. One of the recruits pulled out a harmonica and accompanied them. Another had brought his guitar. The train clacked over the rails through the night, and the women sang, often accompanied by boys on their way to becoming warriors. She could only see them as their mothers' sons. Her heart was forever changed. It ached even as many maternal hearts across America hurt for the boys who were taken and trained to kill.

Early the following day, there were sounds of a scuffle in the next car.

"Get him!"

"Hold him down, boys!"

Heaven Ray jumped up, and the quiet nurse beside her pulled on her arm. "You better stay out of it. You don't know what's going on.

"I'm going to find out," Heaven Ray looked at the others, "Anyone coming with me?"

"It's none of our business. The officers will take care of it."

"I know someone is being hurt, and it doesn't sound like a fair fight," Heaven Ray snapped. "I'm going to stop it."

One of the nurses followed Heaven Ray but stayed at the entrance to the car. The others shook their heads and felt virtuous for minding their own business. Cheers and jeers from the men watching the scuffle greeted Heaven Ray as she pushed her way toward the scuffling men. "What's going on?" she hollered, but the commotion muffled her cry.

The Devil Dogs, as the Marines called themselves, encircled two men grappling in the aisle. Heaven Ray continued to push her way through the sea of Marine uniforms. The men were unaware that a woman was trying to move past them. She jumped onto a seat and peered over their heads. One man was on his back, the other straddled and pounded him repeatedly. Heaven Ray gasped, "Leave him alone! Let me through!" She climbed over several seats and jumped into the fray, shouting, "Anak! Leave him alone! Anak!"

A stray elbow caught her in the eye, and she crumpled. The crowd parted like the waters of the Red Sea as Heaven Ray fell to her knees, moaning, her hands covering her face. A shocked silence fell over the men, and they stepped back. As the initial shock and pain receded, Heaven Ray crawled toward the unconscious Marine. "I think you've broken his nose, and his shoulder is dislocated."

"He shouldn't be wearing that uniform," one of the crowd growled.

"He ain't no Jarhead, not with that yellow skin and slanty eyes," another said through clenched teeth and fisted hands.

"He's some kind of spy."

"Probably stole that uniform."

Heaven Ray, still on her knees, turned and faced them. "You stupid idiots. He's an Alaskan."

"Sorry, ma'am. He's as Japanese as they come. Just look at him," the nearest Marine, a corporal, said. "Sorry about your eye, ma'am, but you shouldn't have interfered."

"Never mind my eye," She said, although it was beginning to swell and her face hurt. "How could you?"

The corporal blushed and said, "Maybe we got a little carried away, But gosh, ma'am, just look at him."

The man on the floor groaned and opened his eyes, "Heaven?"

"Yeah, I bet he wishes he was in heaven," one of the jarheads smirked.

"The likes of him will never make it past the pearly gates," another said.

"But we can send him to the other place!" They all laughed. The door to the car opened, and the laughter stopped abruptly. A Navy lieutenant strode through the car, eyes surveying the scene. "What's going on?" He saw Heaven Ray on her knees. Who attacked this woman?"

"No one, sir." The Marines backed up several paces.

"Maybe it was that Marine next to her," another said.

"Liar!" Heaven Ray's head jerked around, and a sharp pain shot through her head. She covered her face and moaned.

The Marines shuffled back to their seats. The ones who had rumpled uniforms and bloodied knuckles tried to fade into the crowd. "I'll deal with you men later," the officer snarled.

He knelt beside Heaven Ray, lifted her chin, and examined her face. "I think it probably looks worse than it is, but I imagine it hurts like hel—hurts a lot." He rubbed his knuckles across her cheek, "Hmm. Still pretty."

Heaven Ray stared into his light gray eyes. After a moment, she stammered, "He...he's the one who's hurt."

"I'm much more concerned about you." His eyes never left her face.

She blushed, "Please."

The lieutenant looked closer at the man lying on the floor, then stood and asked the now quiet Marines. "Who is this guy?"

"A Jap."

"A spy."

Heaven Ray shook her head, then moaned again.

"Easy, my dear. Try to be still," The lieutenant said, holding her chin and examining her face again. "Who are you?"

She wondered whether she should salute but didn't. "I'm Heaven Ray Turner, and this is Anak. Apparently, these hooligans, I refuse to call them Marines, thought he was Japanese and started their own war."

"An easy assumption to make," the lieutenant said softly, then stood and addressed the Marines. "Stay in your seats, men, and no more of this nonsense."

"I'd hardly call it nonsense. They were brutal." Heaven Ray helped Anak to his feet. He swayed, and she put her arm around his waist to steady him. The lieutenant glared.

Anak shook her arm away. "I'm fine," he said, then turned to the Lieutenant, "Sorry for the commotion, sir."

"We'll take him to my compartment so I can check him out," Heaven Ray said.

"Are you a nurse?"

Heaven Ray grinned, and this time, she did salute, "Newly commissioned Ensign Heaven Ray Turner, Navy Nurse Corps."

"We'll take him to my compartment, Ensign," The lieutenant's voice was firm, and she couldn't read the look in his eyes. Did he disapprove of her concern for the injured man or that she intended to take him to her private compartment?

Heaven Ray followed as the lieutenant half-carried the moaning Marine, signaled the steward to make up the bed, and lay the Marine on it. As Heaven Ray examined him, the lieutenant said, "Did I hear you call him by name?"

"Anak. I thought he was still at the University of Washington. He's a graduate student of linguistics, or at least he was."

"I wonder how he ended up a lowly Marine. He probably could have applied for a commission. Maybe he didn't think he'd get it because, well, because…"

"Because he doesn't look like a white, middle-class American?" Heaven Ray snapped.

"You can't blame the men. He looks like the enemy."

"Well, he's not, and I do."

"Life is what it is, Ensign Turner. Now, why don't you continue to examine your very foreign-looking patient?"

Heaven Ray ignored the lieutenant's crass remark and wondered why she had thought him handsome and personable. She wiped away the blood from Anak's face, packed his nose, and then examined his shoulder as the lieutenant attempted to make small talk. She grimaced, "As I suspected, it's dislocated. I will need help to put it back in place. Lieutenant?"

"Phillips. Gary Phillips."

Once the shoulder was back in place and the color had returned to Anak's face, Lieutenant Phillips ordered, "How did you cause this fight, Marine?"

Heaven Ray bristled, "I hardly think he was the cause."

Lieutenant Phillips glanced at the pretty nurse and then returned his attention to Anak. "Why did you allow yourself to be attacked?"

Anak did not answer.

"Explain yourself."

"Can't you give him some time to recover?" Heaven Ray asked.

"Don't get in the habit of questioning my orders," the superior officer's soft voice carried a steely authority, and Heaven Ray clamped her lips together.

"No excuse, sir." Anak stood and tried to salute but fell back on the bed.

Heaven Ray felt the heat rise to her cheeks at the officer's critical tone. Being in the Navy was more challenging than she had thought. She gnawed on her lower lip.

"Don't do that."

"What?" she said.

"Your mouth is lovely; don't spoil it." His eyes never left her lips.

"Is that an order?" She felt her face flame and tried to cover her embarrassment by saying, "I'll find the steward and request a thermos of coffee. I think we could all use some."

After she left, Anak pulled his orders from an inner pocket and handed them to the officer, who read them and frowned. "It says you need to be at Pendleton ASAP. This train stops at every whistle-stop town along the way. Don't you know what ASAP means?"

"I planned to rent a car."

"Why didn't you?"

"I was turned away," Anak's face showed no expression. "Several times."

"I'll make a phone call at the next stop. These orders from military intelligence are vague but urgent."

Again, Anak remained silent.

"Alright, Marine. Get your gear. I've been ordered to rent a vehicle and drive straight to Camp Pendleton," Lieutenant Phillips ordered Anak as the train pulled into Redding, California.

"I'm going with you," Heaven Ray said.

"No, you're not," Lieutenant Phillips looked at his watch. "This train is pulling out in a few minutes, and you'll be on it."

Heaven Ray winked at Anak, whose face remained impassive. She turned and faced the lieutenant. "Apparently, this Marine is important. If you want him to arrive fit for duty, you will take me," Heaven Ray made her voice as stern as possible and hoped the lieutenant didn't realize Anak's bruises were fading and he had no internal injuries. "I'm afraid some of these lacerations may become infected."

"It was lovely to meet you, Ensign Turner. Say goodbye to this Marine," Lieutenant Phillips said.

Anak went to get his gear, and Heaven Ray followed. "You're going with us," Anak stated.

"He didn't order me to stay on the train."

"I think he did."

"Not in those words. I'll jump to the platform just as the train is leaving, and then he'll have to take me." Heaven Ray smiled. "It's a perfect plan."

Lieutenant Phillips looked into Heaven Ray's face and sighed, "I can see you still have trouble following orders. If I didn't need to deliver this Marine to Pendleton without delay. I'd set you on that bench and ensure you got on the next train. Yes, I think that's the best plan."

"Please don't do that. I'm concerned for him." She picked up Anak's wrist and pretended to take his pulse. With her back to the lieutenant, she winked again at her childhood friend.

"He's a Marine. He'll be fine."

"But I'll be worried."

Lieutenant Phillips smiled, slowly looked at Heaven Ray from the top of her shoes to the auburn hair peeking out of her military cap, and said, "Fine, but won't you be uncomfortable traveling with two men, one of whom finds you attractive?"

Once again, those hooded gray eyes focused on her, and she couldn't look away, nor could she read his intentions. Heaven Ray laughed through her discomfort and wondered why this naval officer affected her so. He was taller than Mark by an inch or two, and his hair was blond rather than dark like Mark's. Heaven Ray gave herself a mental shake and wondered why she compared Gary Phillips to Mark Lawson. Perhaps because she knew Mark's flirting was honest and boyish, harmless. The man before her did not let his real emotions or intentions show. There was an air of mystery about him, even danger. She threw those thoughts aside and grinned at her Native friend. "Anak always said I was too pretty for my own good, but he's just a Marine, so what does he know?"

"I know plenty," Anak said quietly.

"You two must go back a long way," the lieutenant studied both of them. His face showed no emotion, but Heaven Ray sensed his disapproval.

"We grew up on Kodiak, me in the tiny town, Anak in the Native village," Heaven Ray said.

"Where's Kodiak?"

"It's an island in the Gulf of Alaska. I tried to tell those men Anak was a native Alaskan, but they were too agitated to listen."

"I know hugging makes you uncomfortable, Anak. But we may never see each other again," Heaven Ray sniffed and held out her arms. The silent Marine took a step closer, allowed her the briefest of hugs, and said, "All will be well."

"The great unknown—that's where we're headed," Heaven Ray sniffed again.

"Everlasting distances separate, but not for good," Anak smiled and addressed Lieutenant Phillips. "Into the unknown, but Bozhe goes before us. Thank you, Lieutenant Phillips."

"I did my duty, nothing more," Phillip's voice was cold, and his eyes shielded his thoughts.

Heaven Ray frowned at her childhood friend's simple faith. "I'm ashamed to say I find myself doubting Bozhe," she whispered.

"Psalm 91, Heaven. Read it every day." Anak turned and saluted, then picked up his duffle bag, barely wincing, and entered Camp Pendleton's Administration Building.

Lieutenant Phillips put his hand on Heaven Ray's shoulder and said, "You mentioned he was studying linguistics?"

"He knows Russian and several Native languages. He's the smartest person I've ever met."

Gary Phillips rubbed his chin as he gazed at the door to the building softly closing. "Linguistics? Military intelligence? Top secret? He must be involved with the new code project."

"What project? How do you know?"

"I read his orders, and I'm smart enough to put two and two together."

"It hardly seems ethical, especially if they are secret or sensitive."

"He was on the losing end of a fight with several Marines and looked more like the enemy than a good American. Perhaps I should not have intervened, but I did my duty."

Once again, the frost in his voice unnerved her. Did he know his words about Anak hurt her? She took a deep breath and steadied her emotions. "We had better be on our way."

"We'll turn the car into the rental place in Carlsbad and take the train to San Diego."

"It would be more efficient to drive."

He gave her a long look, shielding his thoughts. "It would be less seemly."

Heaven Ray blushed and said, "If you say so."

"I say so, but before we board that train, I'm taking you out for a steak dinner at the fanciest restaurant in Carlsbad."

Heaven Ray inclined her head.

CHAPTER FIFTEEN

Heaven Ray pointed to the paperwork in front of the clerk at San Diego's 32nd Street Naval Station's Administrative Building. "As you can see, I have been given an exception and can be assigned to a duty station immediately, hopefully on a hospital ship."

"Ma'am, I'll say what I've said for the past two weeks. According to this note, it's been requested, but I don't have any paperwork saying it was granted."

"The Superintendent of Nurses was supposed to send my Officer Training Examination to this base."

The weary clerk rubbed his hand over his eyes and sighed, "Ma'am, I keep telling you I don't have those examinations. When you were commissioned, your orders were to attend Officer's Training in Rhode Island. Right?"

Heaven Ray pushed her hair behind her ear and sighed, "Captain Lawson, commander at Kodiak, assured me this would be taken care of."

"Kodiak? Never heard of it."

"It's in Alaska." Heaven Ray tapped her foot and refrained from giving her opinion about this clerk's lack of geographical knowledge.

"Ma'am, your paperwork is a mess. I can't find your travel orders." He looked through her papers again.

Heaven Ray said nothing about the copy of the orders she had in her handbag and hoped he wouldn't ask.

"There will be consequences if you're not in Rhode Island at the appointed time."

"It's not my fault. The ship hit a rock in the Seymour Narrows at Ripple Rock. We limped into a Canadian port for temporary repairs. That took some time. We lost a lot of fuel, and I think they had trouble requisitioning more since we were in Canada. It was complicated. We finally made it to Bremerton, but we were behind schedule. The ship needed further repairs, so they put us on a train, and then there was a fight—"

The harried clerk bit his upper lip. "This is going to take some time. I'll complete all the necessary documents to request updated travel orders to Newport because I'm a nice guy. I'll even ask again about your so-called exception. In the meantime, I'm assigning you to the base hospital Surgical Unit and billeted in Barracks C. That's the way it is and the way it is going to be."

"But it's inefficient and immoral to require me to spend six weeks on the East Coast when I could be on a hospital ship, saving lives."

The clerk's face grew mottled. He straightened to his less-than-impressive five feet, eight inches and said, "I am neither inefficient nor immoral. You are assigned to the base hospital until I receive paperwork saying otherwise."

"But Commander Lawson's note."

"Look here, Ensign, this is the Navy, and you can't make your own decisions, and neither can this Captain Lawson." The clerk stamped several forms and pushed them across the desk. "Give this to the hospital administrator. I'll send word when your updated travel orders have been processed. Next!"

"But, But..." Heaven Ray stuffed the papers into her leather handbag and sat on a bench outside the administration building.

Why hadn't the Superintendent notified San Diego about her exception? Why hadn't her exams arrived? Why wouldn't anyone listen to her?

The blue skies, absent of any clouds, would have thrilled her at any other time. She was hardly aware of the sun warming her back or the soft breeze rustling through the palm trees. She crumpled the papers, inwardly raging. She was capable and self-reliant. She always fixed everything. Why couldn't she fix this?

The presence of Lieutenant Phillips standing before her blocked the sun. Heaven Ray squinted and looked up.

"Everything squared away, Ensign?"

"No, sir. That wretched clerk assigned me to the base hospital. He's ignoring my exception."

"I admit you are exceptional." Lieutenant Phillips smiled.

Heaven Ray did not respond to the compliment or the look in his eyes. "I've had advanced training and experience in surgery and trauma."

"And you think your talents are wasted here?"

"I know they are."

Lieutenant Phillips nodded. "I get it. I'm behind a desk when I should be on a ship; however, we must follow orders."

"I tried everything I know to change the Navy's mind."

"I have a Jeep at my disposal. I'll take you to your barracks."

"I report to the hospital tomorrow morning." She glanced at the handsome man and said, "I'm free until then." *Why did I say that?*

Lieutenant Phillips chuckled, picked up her hand, and squeezed it. "Message received, loud and clear."

"I only meant..." *What do I mean?*

"Relax. I'm not the big bad wolf."

Heaven Ray tugged her hand free and rested it on her lap. "I wonder," she whispered.

He laughed out loud and cocked his eyebrow. "Keep wondering, lovely lady. Keep wondering."

Ensign Mark Lawson picked up his paperwork and glanced out of the administration building's second-story windows just as a Jeep pulled away. He leaned forward, his forehead resting on the thick glass. The passenger's profile, the way she sat, and the color of her hair—it wasn't possible, but it must be! Heart pounding, he raced down the stairs and into the street just as the Jeep turned the corner and disappeared. He sat on the bench, staring, and caught his breath. As far as he was aware, newly commissioned Heaven Ray Turner was attending Officer's Training School on the East Coast. Mark looked at his empty hands and realized he must have dropped his paperwork. Shoulders slumped, he retraced his steps.

"Ensign, are these yours?" A young-looking clerk handed him the file containing his orders. Mark nodded his thanks and proceeded to his billet. Now that he was going to the Pacific, he wondered if he should have kept his head down on Kodiak. Mark sighed and asked himself if he had the same courage as his brothers. He believed his love of country and patriotism was as intense as everyone else in his family. If only he could be as gung-ho about battles, military tactics, and strategies as the rest of his relatives. Their lives were consumed by the Navy. They loved the traditions and the opportunity to serve. The Navy had been a way of life for the Lawsons for generations. And it was a good life.

Mark shook his head and pushed his doubts and thoughts aside. He'd be on his way in a few days. Things were not going well in the Pacific, and the Navy needed every able-bodied seaman available. It was time for action, not contemplation, yet he felt the need to ponder and think. He tossed the file on his bunk, slipped out of the barracks, and went to the beach. The weather in San Diego was perfect. Not too hot or humid, the gentle undulating breeze off the ocean was salty and refreshing, without that arctic nip or wet fog that often accompanied the fierce wind in Kodiak. He was told the South Pacific could be brutal. Hot, tropical air so humid it almost seared your lungs. No matter what, he would go where he was told and do his duty to the best of his ability. Even if he couldn't serve with the enthusiasm his brothers had, he was determined to make his father proud. He'd make Heaven Ray proud, too,

He slipped off his shoes, tucked his socks inside, and rolled up his pant legs. The warm incoming waves flowing around his ankles refreshed him. The outgoing waves pulled the sand from beneath his bare feet. The sound of the surf soothed his troubled thoughts. He scanned the beach and the horizon, wondering how everything could seem so peaceful when battles raged, bombs fell, and men were blown apart.

The serenity of his surroundings fell away and left a knot in the pit of his stomach when his thoughts turned to Attu and Kiska. The Japanese were entrenched, and who knew what had happened to the Aleuts living there. His heart hurt, and his anger stirred when he thought about the fiasco that was the evacuation mission. Ill-timed and ill-planned. Why hadn't a proper place been prepared for the evacuees? He rubbed his hand across his eyes, squinted into the bright sun, and told himself to buy a pair of sunglasses as soon as possible.

When he returned to the barracks, he found a note to report to the administration building ASAP.

Mark glanced at his watch. He had just enough time to see what this Captain Wallace wanted before the mess hall closed. He grabbed his cover and flagged a passing Jeep. The driver, a freckled seaman recruit, looked like he was nine and drove like he was twelve. As they sped across the base, Mark, who was not given to much prayer, prayed the prayers he had learned in Sunday School. They were the 'Now I lay me down to sleep' and 'Bless this food, O Lord' variety. He hoped the Deity would understand. Mark hung on as the young driver nearly ran over pedestrians or crashed into whatever happened to be in his path.

"You just ran a stop sign."

"Gosh, sir, I thought it was okay to keep going if nobody else was around."

"Been driving long, son?"

"Just the tractors and combines back on the farm. They're nowhere near as fast or exciting as this baby." He patted the dashboard, pumped the brakes, and swerved to avoid hitting a hydrant. "I'm hoping they'll train me to drive the ships!"

Mark coughed and put his hand over his mouth to stifle his laughter. *This seaman recruit doesn't even know ships are steered, not driven.*

The boyish young seaman slammed on the brakes, and the Jeep skidded to a stop in front of the administration building. "Here you are, sir. Safe and sound." The driver looked at his watch and grinned, which made his freckles pop. "Hey, I beat my record by twenty seconds. Hot dog!"

The urge to lecture this immature farm boy was immense, but Mark resisted. "Carry on, sailor."

The boy saluted and roared away, honking at several new recruits trying to cross the road. They jumped aside and cursed the retreating Jeep.

As Mark opened the heavy glass doors, the usual noise and confusion assaulted him. An undecipherable voice droned over the loudspeaker. Clerks darted here and there, hands full of papers. Petty officers barked orders, and newly enlisted young men stumbled over their feet, hurrying to obey.

Mark surveyed the room and saw a directory on the far wall. He found the number and location of Captain Wallace's office. Mark avoided the crowded elevator and dashed up several flights of stairs.

"Ensign Lawson reporting, sir."

"Come in. This is Lieutenant Phillips. I have a special assignment for you both."

The two men eyed each other briefly, then turned their attention to the captain, who continued talking. "...since you're in communications, Phillips, the Brass chose you for this assignment. Lawson, you've had several classes in communications at the Academy, but you're here because of your campaign in the Aleutians."

"Hardly a campaign, sir."

"Nevertheless, you performed your duty admirably."

Mark focused on the captain, although he felt the lieutenant's gaze turn toward him. As the youngest man in the room and the one with the lowest rank, Mark kept his mouth shut, although he wanted to tell the captain that the Aleutian evacuation was a fiasco.

Captain Wallace looked up from the report he had just scanned. "After they're fully trained, you'll fly to Pearl with some very important Marines. When you arrive, further orders will be issued by the head of the Pacific sector's Office of Naval Intelligence. You must stay with your assets and keep them alive at all costs."

"Type of training, sir?" Lieutenant Phillips asked.

"Classified."

"Duration of training?"

"Unknown."

Although curious about this assignment, Mark's thoughts drifted back to the Aleuts he had relocated.

"You got that, Lawson?" Captain Wallace growled.

Mark felt his face reddened. "Sir?"

"I have four Marines from Alaska confined to quarters. They look like Japs, and the other Marines don't like it. They get into fights. You are responsible for their personal safety until further orders. You will eat with them, sleep with them, and breathe with them. Understood?"

"Phillips, after you're settled in, I have a lot of paperwork for you to work through. My yeoman has cleared a desk for you across the hall."

Mark did not understand this assignment but echoed Lieutenant Phillips, "Yes, sir."

"Dismissed."

The two men left the office and made their way to the barracks. "I can't imagine the Aleuts getting into fights. The ones I know were peaceful, even passive," Mark said.

"Didn't you hear the captain? They look Japanese. I imagine they were not the ones starting the fights. In fact, I met one such

Aleut on the train from Seattle. Some sort of linguistics student. He was beaten by several jarheads."

Mark didn't answer, and Phillips continued. "It was an interesting trip, and I met the prettiest Navy nurse. She was a little bit of heaven. Lovely, indeed."

Mark wished Phillips would cut the chatter. He was mentally composing a letter to Mrs. Turner. He wanted to know how the Aleuts were adjusting to their new environments. He also wanted to ask if she had any tips for him as he accompanied these four Aleuts to their destination.

The Aleuts were on the floor of their quarters, playing a game with small pebbles and what looked like bones. They stood to attention when Mark entered with Lieutenant Phillips. Their demeanor changed when Mark greeted them in their own language. They smiled and asked questions.

Ensign Lawson held up his hand, "No, no. I only know a few phrases, and I'm sure by the look on your faces, my pronunciation was off."

"Where did you learn?" one of the Marines asked.

"I was stationed in Kodiak for the past year."

"I am from Kodiak," Anak said.

"They don't speak our language there," another said.

Mark swallowed, and his voice was tinged with regret, "I was part of the team that evacuated several villages in the Chain."

"What evacuation? What villages? When did that happen? Where are they now?" They were full of questions that Mark did his best to answer without revealing the scope of the squalid living conditions and inadequate supplies. As he finished, the Marines nodded; most would not meet his eye, and one turned away. "We do not have family in any of those villages, but they are our people."

"At least they are safe. But to take elders from the islands is not good," said one.

Lieutenant Phillips had ignored Mark and stared at a particular Marine. "I know you. You're from the train. Aneck? Adak?"

"Anak, sir."

Hands on his hips, Lieutenant Phillips said, "Now, tell me what this mission is all about? Captain Wallace was not forthcoming with the details, just that you required further training."

The Marines remained silent. Lieutenant Phillips ran his hand through his hair. "Come on, man. We will be together, at least as far as Pearl, and I'd like to know why your lives are more valuable than mine."

The Aleuts remained silent. Their faces showed no emotion. Finally, Anak said, "We have been ordered not to speak."

"That does not apply to me."

"We will not speak," Anak said.

"Ensign Lawson, stow your gear. I'll take the officer's quarters at the end of the hall. You can bunk with these so-called Marines." They watched him stride through the room and slam the door.

"Ready to head to the mess hall?"

"We are confined to quarters," Anak said.

Mark felt like swearing but didn't, "How do you eat?"

"Food is delivered," Anak said.

"Most of the time," Another Marine added.

"I'll make a trip to the mess hall. What do you want me to bring back?"

The youngest Aleut said, "The food is not good."

Mark laughed, "Spoken like a true soldier. No one ever likes the food."

Anak motioned for the boy to be quiet. "We are Marines. We eat whatever is provided."

Mark winked and said, "How does salmon jerky, fireweed jelly, and Pilot bread sound to you boys?"

"You have such things?"

"Not as much as I would like. I don't know how long we'll be stateside, but I'll see if I can have more sent from Kodiak."

The dark eyes of the Aleuts sparkled, and after they feasted, they invited him to join their bone game. Mark decided the way to get to know these Marines was definitely through their stomachs. He wrote to the commander that night and asked the commander to send him a supply of Native food. He also wrote Haven Ray Turner and Miss Ruth with the same request. Between the three of them, he hoped to keep his new friends well-supplied.

Several days later, the Aleuts were ordered to report to Camp Elliot, California, where they would be trained with other indigenous Marines and GIs as general communication specialists.

"I thought you were trained and ready to go," Lieutenant Phillips barked.

"We were told we would finish our training at Pearl," Anak said.

"Obviously, the higher-ups changed their minds," Mark said.

"We're nothing more than babysitters," Phillips could not hide his irritation.

"We're ordered to guard them at all times. Loose lips sink ships and all that," Mark replied.

"A lowly seaman could do that," the lieutenant growled. "It's been weeks already. How much longer before we're deployed?"

"According to Anak, the Navajo code has been encrypted for super secret messages, and those who have mastered it have already been deployed. Regular messages will be translated from English to various Native languages and sent without encoding."

"You spend entirely too much time talking with these...these..."

"Marines?" Mark said.

"Indians." Lieutenant Phillips snarled.

Orders came the following week. The Aleut coders, or code-talkers as they were called, were taken to San Diego to await transport. The day before the ship sailed, Lieutenant Phillips was called to Captain Wallace's office.

"I'm sorry to inform you, sir, that your father has died. You will be granted emergency leave, of course."

"I'm due to sail for Pearl tomorrow."

"I'm aware. Because of the war, your leave will be shortened, but you will take it."

"Yes, sir."

"Once back in San Diego, we'll get you on an aircraft heading to Hawaii. Your team will be there preparing for their deployments. All you'll miss is the sea voyage and some last-minute training."

"Yes, sir."

"You're not coming with us?"

"It's nothing that concerns you, Ensign."

"Is everything all right, sir?" Mark eyed the weary-looking officer. The lieutenant threw the last of his clothes into his duffle bag, grabbed his cover off the chest of drawers, threw a file on the bed, and said, "I'll meet you in Pearl."

Mark scratched his ear as he watched the lieutenant leave the barracks. The voyage to Hawaii would be more pleasant without the contentious officer. There was no word whether another officer had been assigned to the unit or if Mark was in charge. He rifled through the file and found the transport orders. "Thanks a lot, Phillips, nice of you to let me know I'm in charge." He read the orders twice and was determined to execute them to proper Navy standards. It didn't matter whether the distracted lieutenant forgot to pass the orders on to Mark or if it was deliberate. He and the code talkers would do just fine on the ship and in Hawaii.

"Ensign Lawson?" Anak came into the barracks as the lieutenant brushed past him without speaking.

"The Lieutenant didn't say where he was going, and I don't know when he'll return. In the meantime, tell the men to pack their things. We're off to Pearl Harbor."

CHAPTER SIXTEEN

The crowded train station looked and sounded like organized chaos. Greetings, goodbyes, tears, laughter, and promises to write echoed through the cavernous lobby. The voice over the loudspeaker—incoherent. Heaven Ray asked a Red Cap, staggering under a load of luggage and following an elegantly dressed older woman, the way to track seven. He jerked his chin to the right.

A little later, she asked a young man in uniform the same question. "I'm just following that crowd of soldiers, ma'am. I figure we're all going east."

They smelled the oil and diesel fuel, heard a sharp blast from the train's whistle, and hurried toward it. The conductor confirmed they were boarding the correct train and punched their tickets. "The last four cars are reserved for military personnel. I've heard rumors that soon entire trains will carry troops."

"Wow! There must be thousands, maybe millions," the fresh-faced soldier exclaimed.

"I wish it were not so, young man," the conductor said with a sad smile.

"I'm going to be a hero... bring home some medals to my mama." He gave the conductor and Heaven Ray a snappy salute and joined a crowd of GIs at the end of the car. She followed him and saw several women in Navy uniforms sitting together.

"Rhode Island?" one of them asked as she approached.

Heaven Ray nodded.

"Scoot over, girls. It looks like we have another officer-in-training heading east."

Heaven Ray smiled her thanks, stuffed her jacket and bag beside her, and glanced around the overcrowded car. Most troops on the train were young GIs, fresh out of boot camp from California's many military bases, heading to the East Coast to be deployed to Europe, North Africa, and the Middle East.

Although there was much talk, raucous laughter, and glances thrown in the nurses' direction, the GIs kept to themselves. Heaven Ray noted the nurses blushed and giggled, especially the young blond sitting next to her, who winked and blew kisses across the aisle. Heaven Ray sighed and pulled a book out of her bag.

On this particular train, there were no private sleeping compartments. However, the railway seats could be transformed into sleeping berths enclosed by heavy curtains. A steward came through late that afternoon and apologized. The berths would not be made up because of overcrowding. He frowned and said, "Almost every car is overflowing with military personnel. Some have standing room only. Be glad you can all sit."

The nurses groaned and shrugged. The young blond said, "I guess we'll just have to spend the night with all these handsome GIs."

As he left, the steward shook his finger at the young women and said, "Remember, you are officers. I wish we had a private car for you. Perhaps you could move to the next car and sit with the civilians. Several matronly ladies would be happy to look after you."

They laughed and refused to take his suggestion seriously. The train rattled over the tracks throughout the night. By the next day, everyone's muscles ached, and joints had stiffened. Heaven Ray stretched, and even though the cars were crowded, she tried walking through them twice daily to keep herself limber. She carried her Bible and raised it when flirting GIs annoyed her.

"Well, girls, it's time to push through all these beautiful men and make our way to the dining car," the oldest of the group said.

"I'll be your dinner companion, darling, but you'll have to pay." A tall, slim GI turned out his empty pockets. His buddies laughed. Most of these young soldiers had very little money and depended on the local citizens at every whistle-stop along the way. The Red Cross, USO, churches, and other community groups kept GI's stomachs full and spirits fed as the trains were scheduled to stop in every small town and hamlet in America. There were many tearful goodbyes on the platforms as sorrowing mothers gave their sons one last hug.

Heaven Ray followed the chattering, teasing nurses, avoiding the soldier's playful stares and saucy offers of companionship. Stepping into the dining car with its soft lights, clinking silverware, and subdued conversation allowed a sense of peace to settle over her. The crystal stemware and silver napkin rings added an elegant touch to the tables covered with highly starched white linen tablecloths. In these serene surroundings, the war seemed far away.

The Negro stewards, with their white livery and tall chef hats, looked to her like winter's first snowfall on the dark rocks along the Kodiak coast. It appeared as if all the railway employees were colored, the first Heaven Ray had seen. If she closed her eyes and let her imagination run wild, they resembled the bears on her island home, strong and powerful, yet controlled—wanting no trouble.

The nurses crammed into the last available table, leaving Heaven Ray standing alone. "Sorry, Ensign Turner," one of them said.

At the other end of the dining car, Lieutenant Gary Phillips turned to the newly commissioned ensign sitting beside him, "You're done eating."

He looked at his half-eaten roast beef. "Sir?"

"Clear off!" Lieutenant Phillips motioned for the steward to take the ensign's plate. The hapless and still-hungry ensign left, grabbing the basket of dinner rolls and cursing all officers under his breath.

Lieutenant Phillips stood, and his quiet yell disturbed the serene atmosphere. "Nurse Turner!" His nod indicated the single empty chair next to him.

Heads turned in his direction, then her's. The nurses at the table giggled and teased.

"You've been holding out on us, Ensign Turner," one said.

"Who is that handsome guy?" another asked.

"You can have my place. I'll sit next to that man any time."

"All the officers at that table look good to me," the blond nurse sighed, grabbed another roll from the basket in the center of the table, and slathered it with butter.

"Hey, save some rolls for the rest of us."

"Where did they get all that butter? Back home, all we can get is oleo."

As the conversation shifted to the soft white rolls and abundance of the otherwise severely rationed butter, Heaven Ray quietly made her way through the crowded dining car. *What's he doing here? I didn't think our paths would cross again.* The officers rose as Lieutenant Phillips made the introductions. Several tried to catch her eye. One winked. She smiled, nodded slightly, and gave her order to the steward, then asked the lieutenant his destination.

"St. Louis. Family emergency." His flat tone and expressionless eyes told her he did not want to elaborate.

The others at the table tried to flirt or at least engage her in conversation. The frosty glares from Lieutenant Phillips put a stop to that. Their discussion turned to the war—logistics, strategies, and the latest news from the front. Heaven Ray let the conversation wash over her. With a nod or polite comment to Heaven Ray, each officer returned to the passenger car as they finished their meal. Heaven Ray drank the last of her coffee, picked up her book, and stood.

Lieutenant Phillips laid his hand on her arm, "Stay." He signaled the steward for more coffee. She waited for him to speak. He sighed twice without meeting her eyes and said, "How are you adjusting to the Navy?"

"What do you mean?"

"When I saw you in San Diego, you were angry about...let me see, what did you call it? The Navy's gross inefficiency and unwillingness to be flexible and efficient."

"The Navy hasn't changed," she huffed.

"Have you?"

"I'm trying."

"Surely, Ensign Turner, you counted the cost before you applied for a commission. You must have known that the Navy would own you—tell you where to go, what to eat, when to sleep. You must have realized you were giving up your independence."

"I guess I didn't think that far ahead. I wanted to save lives."

"And you will."

"But think of the lives that will be lost because I'm not there now!" The frustration caused a single tear to hover on her lower lashes. She quivered as he brushed it away with his thumb.

"The Navy has more to deal with than what you think is best. There are many things to consider when making decisions, even if they are inconvenient for any individual sailor or officer. If you want to be involved in making decisions, you must climb the ladder and become a senior officer."

She gave him a sideways glance while she dropped a sugar cube into her coffee. "Are you climbing that ladder, Lieutenant Phillips?" she asked.

He rubbed his hands over his eyes and then looked at her. "I'm going to my father's funeral and then getting my mother settled. I'll have three days besides travel time."

"That's intolerable. Your mother needs you."

"I was lucky I could get any time at all. If it were peacetime, I'm sure I could take an extended leave." He shrugged and reached for the small pitcher of cream. He held it toward her, but she shook her head. He poured a hefty dollop into his coffee.

Heaven Ray slumped back, shoulders sagging, "I guess the Navy does own us."

"Your life will be much smoother if you can embrace that. Surrender, and things will be easier," he forced a laugh. "I will admit, it's often difficult, especially for one with superior intelligence."

And you're the one with superior intelligence, are you? Oh, I can't say that. "You sound like my mother when she talks about the Lord. It's all about surrendering and yielding, trusting God knows what He's doing. Letting Him take control." Heaven Ray spoke without thinking. The last thing she wanted was to get into a tangled theological discussion with an officer she barely knew.

He spoke mildly, "Your mother sounds like a superstitious woman."

Heaven Ray bristled and spoke more sharply than she intended. "She is anything but; she's the wisest woman I know." *Don't give me your opinions of my mother. You don't know her.*

He dipped his chin. "I stand corrected," he said softly.

"It's easy for some people to submit. For others, it feels like weakness." Her face flamed.

"I know what you mean." He picked up his cover and nodded in the steward's direction, "I think he wants to clean up. We seem to be the last ones here."

She sighed, "I should return to those giggling, silly nurses."

"Please sit with me. We won't reach St. Louis until morning. I'd like to hear about Alaska. I'm sure it's worlds apart from my life."

Heaven Ray wondered if it would be a good idea to spend the night with this perplexing officer, warm and friendly one minute, aloof and acerbic the next. But when she looked into his face, she saw his grief. She took his hand and gave it a brief squeeze. "Only if you tell me a bit about your father."

He nodded, and the tension left his face. The train car was crowded, and Lieutenant Phillips stood next to the same ensign he had ordered to leave the dining car. The young man looked up, swallowed, and immediately stood. "Have a nice evening, sir, ma'am."

"Don't leave," she started to say, but the lieutenant's hand on her arm stopped her. She signaled her frustration to the ensign with her eyes. He nodded, almost smiled, and picked up his duffle bag.

Heaven Ray looked after the retreating sailor as she and the lieutenant settled on the bench seat. "That wasn't very nice."

"Rank has its privileges."

"Rank has its responsibilities. Taking care of those with lesser rank should be more important than your own comfort."

"And yet, here you are, sitting comfortably beside me, and the ensign is nowhere to be seen."

Heaven Ray felt the heat in her face and looked out the window. The rhythmic clacking of the rails through the evening proved hypnotic. He spoke little, so she talked of her childhood in Kodiak and about her father somewhere in the Pacific. She spoke of the things her father had taught her about surviving in the wilderness and their many adventures fishing in the Gulf of Alaska. How to adapt and find solutions that might be unorthodox but effective.

"What an amazing upbringing. No wonder you intrigue me. It's not just your looks." He rubbed his chin and studied her. "I'm sure your background makes it more difficult for you to adjust to orders from superiors who may not have the same perspective. How does your father handle doing things the Navy way?"

"I never thought to ask him. Thank you. That will be the focus of my next letter."

The sky darkened over America's amber waves of grain, and the stars shone through the train's window. As the quiet officer opened up, Heaven Ray listened with one part of her mind; with the other, she pondered their earlier conversation and thought about previous talks with her mother.

Surrender? Why does it seem so unreasonable? I'm a capable woman. Give up control? Why, when I have so much common sense? Trust? I trust my parents, but mainly, I trust myself. Is that the deeper issue? Can I let God decide everything? I don't have much confidence that the Navy knows what it's doing, but I've made a commitment. Which commitment is stronger, the one to the Lord or to the Navy. Why are my thoughts so muddled?

As the train streamed eastward, the background noise of the rhythmic chugging and hum of the wheels as they traveled over the tracks and his soft voice lulled Heaven away from her troubled thoughts. She yawned, and her eyes grew heavy. She yawned again.

The rising sun streamed through the train's window and warmed her face. Her eyes fluttered open. She began to stretch and realized her head rested against the lieutenant's shoulder, his arm tight around her. With the slowest possible movement, she tried to ease herself out of his embrace. His arm tightened, and she murmured, "Don't."

He chuckled softly and removed his arm. Heaven Ray gathered her sweater and bag and went to the restroom. She instructed herself to wash her face, brush her teeth, comb her hair, and concentrate on the usual morning routine. *I won't think about Lieutenant Phillips.*

He looked up as she approached, "Sleep well?" The glint in his eye told her he was aware of her discomfort. "I've been told I make a delightful pillow."

She sat as close to the window as possible, opened her book, and tried to focus.

"I had a lovely dream."

"Mmmm." *I don't want to know.*

"There was a certain nurse in it."

Why do you delight in making me uncomfortable?

"I could tell you." He slid his eyes over her and smiled, "On the other hand, I think I will leave it up to your imagination."

Heaven Ray shivered as the engineer slowed the train. He applied the brakes, and they screeched. The whistle blew as the train crawled into the St. Louis station. Heaven Ray ignored the hustle outside the window and turned the book's page, feeling the heat in her face. He chuckled and stood, gathered his overcoat, cover, and duffle bag. "Be at ease, my dear. This is where I get off. You probably won't see me again. Shame."

"Er, yes. Godspeed, sir."

He stood in the doorway and gave her a long look. "You really do have the most delightful mouth."

With a volition all their own, her fingers rubbed across her lips. He took a step closer, and her eyes widened. He laughed, gave a mock salute, and said, "Don't be frightened, little Eskimo."

Heaven Ray heard his laughter as the door to the connecting car closed and Lieutenant Phillips stepped off the train. She pursed her lips and clenched her teeth. *What an infuriating man! Sophisticated, debonair, and smooth. Did he see himself superior to this backwoods Alaska girl?* She looked out the window and saw him cross the platform and enter the station. He did not look back. She pulled her eyes away from his back, picked up her book, and noticed a folded paper beside it.

Ensign Turner,

I wish you well in Officers Training School. I know you will think of me often. Perhaps fate will bring us together in the future. This is my mother's address in St Louis. She will always know how to reach me.

Gary Phillips

Heaven Ray Turner tapped the paper against her chin. He seemed attracted to her, but was it genuine? Obviously, her Alaska upbringing had not prepared her for this man of the world.

CHAPTER SEVENTEEN
Christmas 1942

She felt the soft vanilla parchment and pondered the return address—*Natalie Lawson*—right here in Newport! An invitation to spend Christmas with Mark's mother, a plea to take pity on an old woman. Heaven Ray thought over the invitation while she put on the tea kettle and fixed herself a sandwich before facing several hours of homework.

The last few weeks had been lonely. Long days of classes and hours of homework each evening. There was little time to form friendships with her classmates; truth be told, few were interested. In a short time, they would be scattered across the world.

Still, many of them had reservations together at a popular ski resort in Vermont. She smiled when she remembered that her roommate planned to spend the entire holiday near the fireplace, drinking hot toddies and making herself available to every handsome skier who wandered into the rustic lodge. Heaven Ray was not inclined to go with them. She enjoyed skiing, but the mountains of Vermont could not compete with her Alaska. Instead, she determined to catch up on her correspondence and study for the upcoming examinations. The weeks in Officer Training school had been more demanding than she anticipated, and the final examinations were scheduled just after the new year.

Heaven Ray's eyes drifted toward the envelope while she tried to concentrate on her homework. What had motivated Mark's mother to send this invitation, and should she accept it? She slid the intriguing missive under her notebook. Mark. She hadn't thought about him since she met Lieutenant Phillips. She didn't want to think about the brash but charming party boy she had met in Kodiak.

She had one Christmas card left after mailing holiday wishes to friends and family back in Alaska. She had considered sending it to the handsome but enigmatic Lieutenant Phillips. Now, thoughts of Mark, the constant twinkle in his eye, and his little boy grin invaded her mind, pulling her away from her studies. If she accepted this invitation from his mother, she could ask for his address, which might give the woman ideas Heaven Ray didn't want her to have. Perhaps she should spend Christmas alone. She saw the words of Mrs. Lawson's letter clearly in her mind.

Dear Heaven Ray,

A few days ago, I spoke to my friend Carolyn—the Navy's Superintendent of Nurses. She mentioned that the paperwork and examination booklets she sent to San Diego to expedite your deployment arrived there a few days ago. They must have been lost in the mail. Since you were already nearly finished with your training here in Newport, she decided to have you complete the course.

With my husband in Kodiak and my sons in the Pacific, I will be alone for Christmas. Perhaps you will have some sympathy for this lonely Navy wife and mother and spend the holiday with me.

If you have plans with friends, don't change them for me, but I would love to share Christmas with you if possible.

If you decide to come, I have left instructions for the Yellow Cab Company to bring you. Do not worry about paying the fare. Their phone number is Red 374.

Sincerely,

Natalie Lawson

The tea kettle whistled. *I won't think about you, Mark Lawson. I won't.* Heaven Ray paced the room, snatched that last Christmas card, and wrote a note to the dashing gray-eyed blond—Lieutenant Phillips. Although his features had faded, she remembered how alluring he could be. She included a note asking his mother to forward the card to him. Even as she dropped it in the postal box, it was Mark's face she saw.

Heaven Ray handed Mrs. Lawson's address to the taxi driver and wished him a Merry Christmas. He whistled, "You must be very important, Miss. Your fare has been paid, including a generous tip." He waved the scrap of paper above his head. "This address is for officer's housing, and you're just an ensign. Excuse me, I meant no offense."

"I'm not offended. I've never been out this way. What's it like?"

"Oh, it's posh, like. Them officers have large houses on the water and lots of regular folks to take care of them. My wife cleans for an Admiral. Hoo-wee, but he has folk to cut his grass and cook his food. Yes siree, them admirals and captains live high on the hog."

"Most of those admirals and captains are in the middle of the Pacific Ocean fighting for us."

"Yes, ma'am. Right you is. I would rather be here driving my little yellow cab than in some big battleship. I bet all the wives in their fancy clothes in them big houses are real lonely, scared, too."

"I'm sure you're right. Big houses and fancy clothes are not what life is about. Peace and security are what matter."

"Right again, ma'am." The cab stopped in front of a spacious three-story brick home. The porch light shone on a holly wreath decorating the front door. Heaven Ray saw a Christmas tree gleaming in the large bay window. Her throat tightened when she saw the gold star displayed in the window. The Lawson's had lost someone in the war!

The driver opened the door, refused the additional tip Heaven Ray tried to give him, and wished her a Merry Christmas. She made her way up the long brick sidewalk and hesitated before ringing the bell.

Was Mark's mother as impeccable and luxurious as this house, as manicured as this lawn? Even as fashionable as the porch décor? At home, Mom would have brought in so many evergreens it would smell like a forest. The logs in the fireplace would crackle and spit. I'm sure our cabin—homey, cozy, and a little messy, could fit in this house many times over. She bit her lip, swallowed her homesickness, squared her shoulders, and rang the bell.

"Thank you for coming, my dear. Let me take your coat," Natalie Lawson's voice was as soft and cultured as Heaven Ray thought it would be. The woman was simply, yet tastefully, dressed in cream linen trousers and a white silk shirt. Tiny gold earrings and an ornate wedding band were her only jewelry. The laugh lines at the corner of her light blue eyes and brown wavy hair, beginning to gray, spoke of her exquisite style. Yeoman Richardson said that

Mark's mother maneuvered through naval society and political arenas with ease and grace. Heaven Ray took one look at her and believed it. She wondered how the woman would fare in the wilderness of Alaska. The commander's wife exuded grace and a refined manner. Heaven Ray took a deep breath to calm herself. More comfortable in the forests of Kodiak than in the Navy community of Newport, Ensign Heaven Ray Turner tried to convince herself there was no need to be nervous. She glanced past the woman into a living room furnished in creams and tans, with thick Oriental rugs in soft greens and dusty blues. Several large cushions softened the white leather sofas. Heaven Ray saw the waters of Newport Harbor through the massive wall of windows. They glistened in the moonlight and reminded her of home. Once again, a pang of homesickness hit her. *Christmas isn't supposed to be formal and elegant; it's family and friends, ice skating and snowball fights, bonfires at the lake's edge, and roasting hot dogs at midnight during Kodiak's fading light.* She pulled herself together, and her unease vanished when she saw the thick socks and fuzzy slippers on Mrs. Lawson's feet. She couldn't help but gawk.

"Let's sit by the fire. My feet are always cold. Not even these thick socks and slippers will warm them."

"You need mukluks," Heaven Ray was instantly comfortable with the woman's relaxed demeanor.

"What are those?"

"A soft boot made of seal or reindeer skin lined with fur. They can be worn indoors or out."

"Would my husband be able to find them in Kodiak?"

"I'll take a pattern of your foot and send it to my mom. Some of the Natives sell them. She'll have a pair custom-made and mail them to you." Heaven Ray handed Mrs. Lawson a small jar tied with a Christmas bow.

"What is this?" The older woman's face crinkled into a smile.

"Fireweed honey. My mother slipped several jars into my suitcase when I left home. Merry Christmas, Mrs. Lawson."

Heaven Ray dabbed her lips and set her napkin aside. "That was a lovely dinner, Mrs. Lawson. Thank you."

"I'm sure it wasn't what you would have in Alaska, although my husband assured me his sailors would have their turkey for Christmas dinner, and please, call me Natalie."

Heaven Ray's eyes misted as she thought of past Christmases. "Frozen turkeys are usually brought in by steamship and are very expensive. We always tried to buy one before they ran out. Mom stuffs it with reindeer sausage dressing. King Crab legs with drawn butter is a yearly favorite. My Mom's halibut cheek casserole is the best. And whenever Miss Ruth comes, she brings striped shrimp and scallop ceviche."

Natalie said, "That sounds wonderful. Do you think your mother would send me some of the recipes?"

"I'm sure she would."

They took their coffee into the living room and settled before the large windows. "The Christmas boats should be passing by soon. I love the lights," Natalie said.

"There is always a Christmas parade in Kodiak Harbor if the water is calm and no storms are predicted. I bet your husband and Yeoman Richardson will be watching."

Natalie smiled, "Dear old Elly. Now, my dear, tell me everything about Alaska and Mark, both of my Marks."

The evening passed pleasantly as Heaven Ray shared the news

with Mrs. Lawson. She mentioned the commander several times but did not talk about Ensign Lawson until she said, "I have a letter from my mother. Let me read a portion:

...The evacuation was a troubling experience. I'm so glad Mark Lawson was with us. He tried to appear unmoved, but I could tell the Natives' plight disturbed him. The children swarmed around him, and although he tried to be a stiff naval officer, his tender heart came through. He seemed embarrassed by the children's attention but responded with patience and love. I truly think he would have been an excellent teacher or some kind of social worker. Both Miss Ruth and I admired him throughout the evacuation process, especially during our excursion to Pleasure Island.

"Pleasure Island?"

After Heaven Ray told Mark's mother about Angel, both women fell silent. Natalie dabbed at her eyes, "Sometimes I think Mark should have been a medic or, like your mother said, a teacher. He has such a heart for people. But he was determined, or perhaps, pressured to follow the family tradition."

Heaven Ray remained silent but pictured Mark's happy-go-lucky-anything-for-a-laugh-ways. She couldn't shake the fact that he had dated almost every girl on Kodiak Island. Her mother's letter and Natalie's comment gave her pause, and she wondered if she needed to reevaluate her opinion of the dashing Mark Lawson.

The Christmas boats streamed past. Natalie opened the windows so they could hear the carolers from the Newport Yacht Club who stood aboard the lead boat.

"Thank you for the afghan," Heaven Ray said as Natalie pulled a couple of blankets from a cedar chest. The two women nestled on the sofa and sang along with the carolers. As the last boat passed,

Heaven Ray stood. "May I use your phone to call a cab?"

"It's so late, my dear. Stay over."

"I only signed out for the evening and don't have my things."

Natalie Lawson eyed Heaven Ray. "We're about the same size. You can borrow a nightie. I keep a supply of new toothbrushes and whatever a guest might need. Besides, I would like you to come with me tomorrow. It's a special Christmas tradition of mine."

"I don't know if I can get permission at this late date."

"Let me make a few phone calls. I'm quite well-known in the naval community here. But first, let's pray."

Heaven Ray sniffed and brushed the back of her hand across her eyes.

"Are you all right, dear?"

Heaven Ray sniffed again and nodded. "Just a pang of homesickness. You reminded me of my mother. She prays about everything."

"I'm sure we would be great friends."

Heaven Ray looked at the stylish woman in her elegantly furnished living room. "My mother lives in a small cabin filled with second-hand furniture that she recovered herself. She dresses plainly, chops wood, and spends much time in Native villages."

Natalie Lawson laughed. "I definitely want to meet her! And these," she indicated her surroundings, "these are just trappings."

"Beautiful trappings."

"In God's eyes, they mean very little. It's all about heart and soul, character and compassion. And I suspect your mother excels in those areas."

"Yes, ma'am. She does."

CHAPTER EIGHTEEN

The guest room of the Lawson home was lovely. A soft green car-pet and bed linens made Heaven Ray think of spring. The ruffled curtains framed the view of Newport Harbor and reminded her of home. The adjoining bathroom was filled with all the toiletries she might need. Heaven Ray enjoyed a long soak in the massive bathtub. The lavender-scented bath oil relaxed her but did not alleviate the bout of homesickness she experienced as she crawled into the cano-pied bed. She shed a tear or two and then gave herself a stern talking-to. She spent the next hour praying for her mother, father, and all the boys from Kodiak who had enlisted or been drafted. She prayed for the Natives that had been evacuated and hoped her mother and Miss Ruth could find ways to help them. She also thought of Lieu-tenant Phillips and how he helped her with Anak, but it was Mark's confident grin she saw when she closed her eyes. *Drat you, Mark, leave me alone. You are not for me, although I quite like your mother. I feared she would be formal and stiff, but she was gracious, friendly, and personable. She made me feel at ease, and I'm sure my presence here helped to relieve her loneliness on Christmas. I respect your father and can talk to him man to man, as it were. But you, Mark Lawson, are another story. I don't want to be attracted to you.* Heaven Ray tossed and turned, punched her pillow into a more comfortable shape. She found herself praying more for Mark than anyone on her list. It was past midnight when she finally fell into a restless sleep.

Heaven Ray, groggy from an uneasy night, hesitated at the kitchen door. She saw Natalie Lawson in a faded, nondescript house dress and sturdy brown oxfords. The mousy woman filling the percolator with choice coffee grounds did not look like the elegant Navy wife of last night. Heaven Ray took a deep breath of the fragrant grounds and thought it impolite to mention the odd dress. She made small talk over breakfast.

"My three sons all attended the Naval Academy but didn't talk about it with dear old mom. Can you share with me how your training is going?" Natalie said as she poured orange juice for both of them.

Heaven Ray took a moment to collect her thoughts. She found herself comparing Natalie Lawson to Miss Ruth. The women were vastly different in style, personality, and age. Both seemed to have a serene spirit and interest in people. Both were easy to confide in. She set her coffee cup down and turned to face Mark's mother.

"I was furious when I found myself on the train. I thought this officer training a terrible waste of time when I was needed elsewhere..." Her voice faded away, and she stared at her empty breakfast plate.

"And now?"

Heaven Ray smiled slightly, "I thought nursing in Kodiak prepared me for whatever I would face in the Pacific. Alaska is still somewhat primitive, and we had to be creative with limited resources. There were many hunting, fishing, and mining accidents, not to mention loggers and trappers who found themselves wounded, so I've learned a lot about injury and trauma. A man mauled by a bear and brought into our clinic more dead than alive is about the worst thing I've seen. He was strong and pulled through. Some don't."

Natalie's eyes sparked with sympathy, "It sounds like you've seen things and made decisions that a nurse here in the States wouldn't be allowed to make," Natalie said.

Heaven Ray shuddered and swallowed the last of her coffee. "I thought I'd seen men as torn up as they could me. But the battlefield slides they showed us in triage class were horrible. I had to force myself to keep watching. The nurse next to me kept her eyes shut the whole time. My desire is to do my job efficiently without falling apart."

Natalie Lawson sighed and patted Heaven Ray's shoulder. "You must guard your heart. With your permission, I'll give your name to my prayer group. We meet weekly to pray for our loved ones scattered across the world's battlefields."

Heaven Ray nodded her thanks, "If I am deployed on a hospital ship and assigned to triage, I must make life and death decisions quickly. I don't know if my diagnostic skills are as good as I thought they were. We've been told everything will happen quickly; I hope I can keep up. There will be little time to assess each patient, much less to comfort and console."

"You will be in dangerous waters, my dear."

"Although I've enjoyed my classes and learned more than I thought I would, I'm still frustrated that I'm here in Newport. I'm anxious to be where I will do the most good."

"God is preparing you. Remember how He prepared Moses? The poor man chased sheep in the desert for forty years, although he did acquire a spouse."

Heaven Ray laughed, "I don't need a spouse, and I don't have that kind of patience. I've struggled these past few weeks; I can't imagine years!"

"That will be our first prayer for you. Elly always told me to never pray for patience because then I'd miss the bus." Natalie Lawson laughed, put the dishes in the sink, and said, "Come, I have an old dress for you, and then we are off to my favorite part of Christmas."

The two simply dressed women entered the basement of the YMCA, set down armloads of packages, hung their coats, and donned crisp, white aprons. The yeasty smell of freshly baked dinner rolls competed with the large pots of turkey gravy bubbling on the stove. The roasted birds were carved and ready, and the vats of mashed potatoes were presided over by a large man in a gravy-stained, once-white apron. Natalie greeted the director of the soup kitchen and introduced Heaven Ray. "Thank you for coming. Would you help Nat serve the Jello salad? The tables are set, and we are ready to open the doors."

Heaven Ray agreed, then turned to the other woman, "Nat?"

"They only know me as Nat. I don't want them to see me as part of the elite society of Newport. To them, I'm just another Rhode Island housewife, and I'd like to keep it that way. Otherwise, they will be formal and strictly polite. They will defer to me, and I don't want that. I'm here to serve."

"That's why you wear the older clothes and the plain watch. You even changed your large wedding ring for a thin band."

Natalie Lawson held out her hand and admired the ring, "It was my mother's," she whispered, "I think my father bought it at Woolworth's. My parents, although poor, always cared for those who were even less fortunate."

Heaven Ray thought of her own mother and of Miss Ruth, who had no children but was a mother to many.

"Let's put the presents under the tree before they open the doors," Natalie said.

"So, this is your favorite part of Christmas?"

"I love to see the children when they dive into their dinners, then open their gifts. For some, it's all they will receive. The joy on their faces is the biggest gift they could give me. We brought the boys here whenever we were stationed in Newport, and their happiness as they served blessed me. As they got a little older, they saved their allowances and bought their own gifts for the people here—the staff, too."

"Thank you for bringing me."

Natalie put her arm around Heaven Ray and grinned, "You will work long and hard today, young lady. Then we'll return to the house and have Christmas leftovers, and I have a special gift for you. One I wasn't planning to give you but which I feel you deserve."

"I can't wait. What is it?"

Natalie Lawson's eyes twinkled, "You are just like the kids. It's hard for them to wait until the dinner and caroling are over to open their presents. But anticipation is half the fun, don't you think?"

"No, I don't think that at all."

Natalie laughed again, sang a few lines from 'All I Want for Christmas,' and handed Heaven Ray a large serving spoon. "Let's get busy. That Jello will not serve itself."

Dressed in warm pajamas, cozy bathrobes, and fuzzy slippers, the two women sat on a davenport in front of the fireplace in Natalie's elegant Newport home. The Ethan Allen side table held a plate of Christmas cookies, two dainty tea cups, and a china teapot filled with hot chocolate.

"I hope you're not saving those cookies for Santa," Heaven Ray laughed, "He's not coming back until next year."

Natalie held out the plate, and Heaven Ray selected a Russian teacake. Natalie chose a lemon bar and said, "Now for that special gift." She picked up a large, well-read Bible from the coffee table and slipped a letter from between its pages. "I want to read part of this letter from Mark. Just as the letter from your mom was a gift to me. This is my gift to you, but it will break your heart." At Heaven Ray's look of concern, Natalie quickly said, "Everyone you know is fine. It's about the evacuation."

Heaven Ray's hands were clasped firmly in her lap, and the more she listened, the firmer she gripped them.

Dear Mother,

This is a difficult letter to write, and I don't know if I can put into words all I have seen and experienced in the past few weeks. The orders I carried out were a punch in the gut to express it crudely.

I can't believe how unorganized, chaotic, and even cruel this whole campaign was. Everyone knew something must be done, but nobody wanted to be responsible.

Too many government agencies were involved and nobody seemed to have ultimate authority. Of course, all this buck-passing led to poor planning and chaos.

Alaska is massive, and the people in the far islands have adapted to the brutal environment quite well. I can't imagine living in such a place, but to them, it's home, the only one they have known for thousands of years. Most have never left their small villages on these tiny, isolated islands.

Now, they are being moved over a thousand miles away to Alaska's Southeast rainforest, which does not provide their traditional foods. An alien environment, for sure. Perhaps they will never return to their homes. They appeared passive and stoic for the most part, but I could sense their hearts were broken. Many of the sailors on my evacuation team had tears in their eyes as they destroyed homes and reluctantly herded the people aboard the ship.

Resettling them in abandoned mines and canneries, with many of the buildings rotten and rodent-infested, was unconscionable and inhuman. There was little foresight to ensure appropriate food, household goods, and tools were available. These people lived by fishing, hunting, and gathering. We have stripped them of their subsistent livelihood and have not replaced it with anything.

Father was beside himself as portions of this campaign were dumped in his lap. Oh, he never verbalized his disdain and disagreement and did the best he could amid conflicting orders from various commands. But Elly says it's been hard on the old boy.

I understood these poor people needed to be kept safe. In fact, a couple of nearby islands were bombed and occupied right before the evacuation. (I imagine the censors will black out that last sentence) and the islanders were taken prisoner. We do not know their fate. The consequences of this forced move, though unintended, are immoral. I have no words to describe the whole operation.

Pray for me, mother. I feel personally responsible for displacing these people and perhaps even destroying their lives. It's such a moral dilemma for me.

Natalie's voice faded. She folded the letter and replaced it in her Bible. She saw the tears on Heaven Ray's face, handed her a box of tissues, and said, "It's so sad."

"I've met some of those Natives." Heaven Ray wiped her eyes and blew her nose. "Mom only wrote the barest details. I had no idea it was that bad. I'm sure she didn't want me to worry or fret. I know Mom and Miss Ruth are working with several churches in Alaska to collect food and supplies, and Miss Ruth has organized education classes for the kids. Still, they said it was difficult to enlist enough volunteers." Heaven Ray crumpled her handkerchief and turned her tear-stained face to the older woman. "I hate this war, and I'm frustrated that neither Mom nor Miss Ruth trusted me with the details."

Natalie took her hand, "Don't judge them too harshly, my dear. You have your own area of the war to fight. I'm sure they wanted you to concentrate on that. Now that you know, you can pray."

"I was always better at jumping in and doing something more practical than praying."

"Praying is the most important and practical thing you can do in any situation."

Natalie poured more hot chocolate into the delicate tea cups, but neither woman picked them up. "I know how frustrating it is. I've had great difficulty enticing anyone to this cause, especially those in government."

"Anyone important?"

"I know two Senators and a Congressman. This is such an insignificant issue for them. They are caught up with larger causes. The war in Alaska and its effect on the people are of little consequence to them."

"That makes me so angry."

Natalie's calm demeanor unsettled Heaven Ray. "Another thing to pray about, my dear. I'm sorry this evacuation was necessary, but I'm grateful for the turmoil it's caused, Mark."

Heaven Ray's head jerked up. "What?"

"I admit it doesn't sound very motherly," the older woman chuckled, "But this tragic campaign has caused Mark to do some soul-searching. I believe it's caused him to shed the shallow, irreverent parts of his personality."

Heaven Ray didn't know how to respond, so only murmured, "Hmm."

Mark's mom continued, "He has always felt he had to hide his tender heart to compete with his brothers. And like many young men, he wanted to live it up in case, in case..." Natalie reached for the box of tissues.

Heaven Ray thought of the Gold Star in the window. She didn't want to cause Natalie further pain by mentioning it. She leaned toward the older woman and hugged her.

"Thank you, my dear." Natalie blew her nose, stuffed the tissue in her pocket, picked up the delicate china cup, and sipped the hot chocolate.

Heaven Ray thought of all her interactions with the good-looking and devil-may-care Mark Lawson IV. She hadn't seen the depths in him that her mother and Miss Ruth had glimpsed. Perhaps she needed to take a closer look. She mentally shook off the thought. He was back in Kodiak, and chances were they would not meet again.

The women were silent for several minutes, and then Natalie took her address book from the desk in the corner of the room. She scribbled Mark's address on a notecard. "The last letter from Mark said he'd been assigned to a classified mission and couldn't write for a while, but I still write to him. My letters are probably piling up at an NPO somewhere, but I'm sure he'd like to hear from you. He has spoken highly of you in his letters, but I won't share those." She chuckled, seeing Heaven Ray's red face, "So has my husband, and he is hard to impress."

"I thought Mark was still in Alaska. Classified mission? Is it dangerous? Do you know where he is? Is he okay?" Heaven Ray's voice rose an octave, as did her anxiety.

"My husband said he is somewhere in the South Pacific, but I don't know where."

"You seem so calm."

"I learned to pray a lot, especially since I've already lost one son."

"The gold star in your window. I didn't want to ask."

Natalie reached for Heaven Ray's hand, "My firstborn. On the Arizona."

They said their goodbyes the following morning.

"I hope you will come to my graduation, Natalie."

"I wouldn't miss it, although I wish you were going to be here much longer. I feel that we could become great friends."

"We already are," Heaven Ray smiled and hugged the older woman.

The graduation ceremony was simplified because of the war, and the nurses scattered to their various deployments. Heaven Ray felt fortunate to be on her way to San Diego and the Pacific. Most of her classmates had already left for Europe and a few for the Middle East.

The sun spread through the pale blue sky as Heaven Ray walked on the cement tarmac to the airplane. She turned to the older woman. "Natalie, I can't believe you did this." They settled themselves into the stripped-down military aircraft and fastened their seat belts.

"What use is it to have a little influence if you don't use it? Besides, I've been considering a trip to Kodiak for a while, and now seems like the perfect time."

"I thought Alaska was closed to tourists, to everyone, really."

"It is. Remember those important people in Washington I told you about? I talked one of them into giving me an assignment, a fact-finding mission, as it were. I hope to interview your mother and Miss Ruth."

"I almost wish I were going with you."

"I will try to get you on a flight to San Diego once we land at Bremerton National."

"I thought you said we were going to Seattle."

"The Navy doesn't use Seattle's civilian airport."

Heaven Ray nodded, and although it was challenging to have a conversation over the roar of the propellers of the large aircraft, she said, "I miss my Mom, and I miss Alaska."

"I've heard our Last Frontier has that effect on people."

"Alaska has a way of becoming a part of who you are," Heaven Ray fell silent, settled back, and closed her eyes. The cross-country flight would take over eight hours. Natalie had brought a couple of magazines and the latest bestseller, but Heaven Ray was deter-mined to catch up on her sleep.

They said their goodbyes at the airport coffee shop.

"I'm anxious to meet your mother."

Heaven Ray hugged the older woman, "Give this to her, a large Alaska bear hug."

True to her word, Natalie had found an outgoing flight for Heaven, but to Honolulu, not San Diego. Boarding passes were issued to Heaven Ray and several other nurses. Also on the aircraft were executives and engineers from the Boeing Company and their Naval Liaison Officer. The rest of the airplane was filled with military personnel.

The announcement that they were approaching the Islands had a sobering effect on everyone. This is where it all began. The Brass had arranged a tour of the devastation that remained at Pearl Harbor. Heaven Ray had seen photographs of the destruction and had no desire to visit the site. Still, all military personnel were required to do so before continuing on to the administration building. She stood with the others, including the Boeing executives, and gazed into the now-placid waters. Their tour guide, a captain who had been on duty last year when the Japanese attacked, pointed out the resting place of the Arizona and the Utah. He turned away and wiped his eyes. The only sound breaking the stillness were throats clearing, noses sniffing, and feet shuffling. Emotions ranged from hatred and a thirst for revenge to great sadness and grief.

Heavy machinery manned by military and civilian operators worked continuously to repair the damaged ships and raise the sunken ones. "Will all the ships be raised, sir?" a sailor asked over the noise of the machines.

"We will bring to the surface what ships we can. We will salvage and repair whatever is possible. We have engineers, divers, welders, pipefitters, and all kinds of industrial workers on this project." He slammed his fist into the palm of his hand. "We will defeat the enemy, no matter how long it takes."

Heaven Ray stepped forward. "What about the bodies?" She pulled a handkerchief from her purse.

"We've been recovering our servicemen for the past year. We

could not identify many but buried them with respect and honor. Others, especially from the Arizona, will never be recovered, nor will that ship be raised."

Heaven Ray's heart constricted as she thought of Mark's oldest brother, Brad. The Arizona was his grave, and Pearl Harbor his final resting place. Tomorrow, she would follow the Hawaiian tradition of putting a lei on the grave. She ordered the most elaborate lei from the nearest florist and tossed it into the harbor to honor Mark's brother.

Three days later, Heaven Ray joined her fellow nurses as they boarded a Navy cargo ship bound for New Caledonia. The vessel transported medical supplies, construction materials, and a large contingent of Seabees to that country controlled by the Free French once the Vichy government officials had been thrown out.

Conversations in the chow line and during dinner were lively, and everyone talked simultaneously. Heaven Ray sat alone at a corner table and listened to snippets of conversations as she ate.

"Where's New Caledonia?" a short, stocky nurse with Shirley Temple curls asked as she moved quickly through the chow line.

The sailor dishing out the liver and onions said, "It's a tiny dot north of Australia."

"I believe it's east of Australia and north of New Zealand," someone several places behind the Shirley Temple curls yelled.

Daisy Dunton pushed the curls from her face, turned, and addressed the chow line, "Well, you know what Mark Twain said, 'God created war so Americans would learn geography,' although

I believe that's an insult to both God and Americans. Then again, I've never heard of New Caledonia or Old Caledonia, for that matter. I hope it's livable. We will make the best of it, I'm sure. Are there bugs and snakes? I'm from southern Ohio. We have bugs and snakes. Live and let live is my motto. What about coconuts? I love coconut pie. My mother's coconut pie is to die for." All this was said in one breath as she plucked a dinner roll from her tray and nibbled it.

"New Cal is like Hawaii, only better. It's a French colony," the cook said as Daisy Dunton opened her mouth to continue.

"Oo la la. That's great. I took French in high school but didn't get a good grade. Better a few words than none, I suppose. Does anyone else here speak French?" She looked around, but few, if any, of the sailors paid attention to her. "I know how to ask where the bathroom is or to tell someone I'm hungry," she laughed, "That and a dime would get me a cup of coffee."

"I heard we were assigned to Mobile Hospital Number Five in Dumbea Town," the nurse standing behind the curls said.

"No, we're to be on a hospital ship," another insisted.

"There's no use listening to scuttlebutt. We'll know when we get there," the head nurse said.

"Since the government on the island is held by the Free French, Americans are barely tolerated," A chief petty officer stated.

"Gee, that stinks, Chief." A cook's helper said as he loaded the officer's plate. "I don't mean the food, Chief. Those Free French, or whoever they are, should be grateful we're protecting them from the Japs. Don't they know there's a war on."

"Actually, the liver does stink, and I hate onions. I'll have a steak."

"Sorry, Chief. We're out of steak."

"I've had steak every night since we left San Diego."

"That's why we're out. I can make you a ham and cheese omelet."

"Make it two," another chief ordered from across the room

Requests for chicken and grits, meatloaf, tuna noodle casserole, and other favorites bombarded the poor server, and he hid behind the grill. "This is not a restaurant, and I'm not a short-order cook. You'll eat what the Navy provides," he lamented.

Heaven Ray let the talk drone on around her.

"Excuse me, want some company? You look lonely. Two's company, they say. My name is Daisy Dunton. I've noticed you ever since we left Pearl. You're a watcher," Daisy said, balancing her tray on the table as the ship rolled. "I'm not a very good sailor, even if I am a Navy nurse. I'm from a little landlocked town in Ohio. I guess that's why I can't find my sea legs."

"A watcher?" Heaven Ray said, ignoring the rest of the chit-chat.

"Hmm," Daisy said around a mouthful of liver, "This meat tastes like mud. My mother can make liver so good you'd think you were dining at the Ritz. What? Yes, you are a watcher, seeing everything and listening. But you don't talk much, do you? That's all right, I can fill in for you. I bet you are a deep thinker. I am, too, but nobody realizes it because I talk so much; that's what people say anyway. My mom said a church mouse wouldn't get a word in edgewise around me." She laughed, took another bite, and continued, "What's edgewise, anyway? Never mind. If people only knew everything I could say and didn't—" Daisy tossed her head, and the ship's lights caught her curls, "Why, you'd think I was reserved and restrained, just like that church mouse."

Heaven Ray sat amazed as Daisy kept a steady monologue and polished off the liver and onions.

"I'm going for dessert. Sweets for the sweet, I say. Do you want anything?" Daisy asked. "Never mind. Of course, you do, I'll bring pie and cake, maybe some cookies we can save for later."

"But I really don't want..." Heaven Ray said.

"Of course you do. If not, I'll eat everything." Daisy patted her ample hips and weaved through the galley to the dessert counter. She returned with a full tray. "Where was I?" she asked. "Oh, I was going to ask about Alaska. Somebody said you were from the frozen North." She shook her head, "I think I did ask, but you didn't answer. Never mind, I will be quiet now and let you tell me about your exciting life with the polar bears. Did you live in an igloo and eat raw fish? I can't begin to imagine."

Heaven Ray smiled, "I like your Shirley Temple curls."

Daisy patted the curls and smiled, "It took me a long time to enjoy my hair. Do you think it makes me look too young? I have a devil of a time keeping these babies tucked into my nurse's cap." She patted several errant curls. "Believe me, the South Pacific will not be good for my hair, the humidity, you know. Did you say the curls were young-looking? At least I don't have freckles. That would put the kibosh on my sophisticated good looks." She laughed and rubbed the end of her nose. "Never mind. Now tell me about Alaska."

Each time Daisy paused, Heaven Ray asked another question. It became a game to see how long the other girl would talk without realizing Heaven Ray hadn't answered. She relaxed with a second cup of coffee and enjoyed the one-sided conversation. The call for lights out came all too soon. Daisy yawned, "Don't think I don't know what you did, Heaven Ray. It's okay, but I'm determined to know your story. Next time, it will be your turn to tell all. Tit for tat, and what's good for the goose is good for the gander. That's my motto."

As they said their good-nights and headed to their quarters, Heaven Ray realized she had a nasty headache. It was probably caused by all of Daisy's chatter, although she had thoroughly enjoyed it.

Heaven Ray's flight from the West Coast to Hawaii had been uneventful. The voyage across the South Pacific was pleasant due to the fine weather, safe seas, and Daisy Dunton. But the closer they sailed to their destination, the more anxious everyone became. The news was scant, rumors flew, and tempers flared. The crew and everyone else spent time watching the horizon. Heaven drew into herself and spent hours in the sunshine at the ship's rail. The serene ocean and gentle breeze calmed her mind and spirit. She refused to think about battles raging on several small islands in this vast ocean.

The only disturbance to her serenity was when Daisy appeared by her side. "I like you, Heaven Ray Turner." She started to sing 'Don't Sit Under the Apple Tree with Anyone Else But Me.' "You're restful and pleasant to be around—easy to talk to."

"Thank you, Daisy." Heaven Ray smiled, although she wished she were alone.

Daisy stared into Heaven's eyes. "They say the eyes are the windows to the soul. The curtains are drawn in yours, but I can see through them. You struggle. Am I right? Of course, I'm right."

Heaven Ray stared at this personable chatterbox. Daisy rested her elbows on the ship's rail. "The sea and sky are so vast, so beautiful—hard to imagine the world is at war."

Heaven Ray squirmed, and Daisy lifted her guileless eyes to Heaven's. "What?" she asked softly.

"Nothing," Heaven Ray turned her attention back to the ship's wake.

"It's not nothing. People think I'm ditzy and write me off, but I know things. I can see below the surface."

Heaven Ray laughed and said, "Alright, Daisy Dunton, what do you think you know?"

"Still waters run deep and all that. I believe you want everyone to think you have nerves of steel, but you don't. You're trying to figure out the war and everything we're sailing into. A world at war doesn't make sense. It's nuts, and you will go crazy trying to understand it." Daisy turned her back to the rail and leaned against it. "You're unsettled, and you don't like it."

Heaven Ray shivered and looked away. "How can you know such things?"

Daisy shrugged and said, "I read between the lines, but my great-grandmother claims I have second sight. You know, clairvoyance—a sixth sense. She was always getting her knickers in a twit about something. I don't have any kind of special sense or sight; I just look for the handwriting on the wall."

Heaven Ray's mouth fell open. Daisy said, "Close your mouth, girlfriend. My mama always said to keep your mouth closed, or you'll be eating mosquitos."

CHAPTER NINETEEN

The hospital at New Caledonia was a thrown-together make-shift building that wouldn't have passed a health inspection in any mid-sized American city. At the present time, there was no running water. It was hauled in by the truckload, and the electricity was supplied by several diesel generators. The Navy assured the incoming medical staff they were working with the local government to up-grade the facilities.

"I've given quality casualty care to our men in worse conditions," the head nurse said after inspecting the building. "But I hope we don't run out of diesel."

"Negotiations between the Navy and the Free French are stalled. We will have to make do for a while longer," the hospital administrator answered.

The other nurses, fresh from the States, were aghast. Heaven Ray remembered her experiences in Kodiak before electricity and running water. "Does the town have a supply of lanterns and kerosene? Can we access local resources without going through government bureaucracy?"

The head nurse nodded to Heaven Ray, "We will do what we can with what we have until the Navy provides more. Heaven Ray, I want you to do an inventory of supplies. I'll speak to the captain about procuring resources not under government control."

After a tour of the hospital, the nurses were shown to their quarters.

"They can't expect us to live in these cramped and squalid huts," a young nurse complained.

"When I raised the blind, several large bugs scattered into a crack in the wall. I'll never be able to sleep in that room," another nurse wailed, "I hate bugs."

Daisy Dunton laughed, "Well, doesn't this just take the cake. Nursing school and officers' training did not cover anything like this. There's nothing to be done but roll up our sleeves and get on with it. If you're nice to the bugs, they'll be nice to you. Don't let them get you down. We'll shoo them out of here and get down to brass tacks. Oh, and can someone give me a scarf? My curls are going wild in this heavy humidity."

The head nurse handed Daisy a thin, silky scarf and scowled at the complaining nurse. "Your comfort is not more important than caring for our casualties. You will spend most of your time in the hospital, so don't worry about your quarters. Get settled and meet back at the hospital."

She left, and the grumbling increased. Daisy Dunton put her hands on her hips and whistled. "Now, girls, it's time to put our noses to the grindstone and our best foot forward. The sun is shining, so come on, get happy."

"Do you always talk in clichés?"

Daisy laughed, "Whenever I can. It's a wonderful way to communicate, don't you think? You know exactly what I mean when I say—he's behind the eight-ball, a bird in the hand is worth two in the bush, or his business went belly up. I think I might write a book about clichés after the war. Wouldn't that be the frosting on the cake? So, girls, save your clichés for me."

The grumbling stopped, and the mood lightened. Heaven Ray stepped close to Daisy and whispered, "Thanks."

"For what?"

"For just being you. For a moment, you've distracted them from the, ah, less than perfect accommodations."

"Nothing can get you down unless you let it. Look on the bright side. Silver linings and all that."

"What if there isn't a bright side?" the bug-hating nurse asked.

Daisy laughed, "Look harder. It could be worse."

"Do you think everything is all sweetness and light?" another nurse muttered.

"If you look for the good, you'll find it," Daisy answered.

One of the other nurses called across the room, "You're a regular Pollyanna, aren't you?"

"Thank you. That's the nicest thing anyone's said to me today."

"I didn't mean it as a compliment."

"I know," Daisy grinned, "but I took it as one. Have you read the book *Pollyanna*? Have you ever played the Glad Game?" The nurses shook their heads. "Never mind. I'll teach you. In any situation, look for something, any little thing to be glad about. There is always something, even if it's just that you're still breathing."

"What a stupid game, especially with the job we're doing. In the middle of a war and all this carnage, you want us to be glad?"

"Believe me girls, it will do your souls a world of good if you practice the Glad Game. I admit it will be difficult for some of you, but you'll get better with practice."

"I'm sure I won't," a cranky voice said from across the room.

"Time will tell. Practice makes perfect is my motto," As she talked, Daisy unpacked her duffle and arranged things in the locker next to her bunk. "I'll start. I'm glad my grandmother met an Irish woman many years ago."

"How is that relevant to our present situation?"

Daisy Dunton held up a large bag of lemon drops. "This red-headed Irishwoman showed my grandmother the power of lemon drops and how they can help when you're feeling down. They're like little bits of sunshine. It's been a custom in my family for generations to give each other lemon drops."

Heaven Ray gasped as she took a few lemon drops from the bag Daisy passed around. "Daisy, did your grandmother ever visit Alaska?"

"What a silly question. She was born and raised in our little Ohio town and never left it."

As far as Heaven Ray knew, Miss Ruth had never been to Ohio; she wasn't Irish, and her gray hair had never been red. She looked at the lemon drop in her hand and then at Daisy. This didn't make sense. It couldn't have been Miss Ruth. However, all thoughts flew from her mind as a corpsman yelled from the hallway that they needed to assemble at the hospital cafeteria immediately.

General orders were issued, and specific assignments were given. Nurses stifled their complaints and did not grumble in front of the senior officers. And Daisy Dunton continued to play the Glad Game.

CHAPTER TWENTY

Casualties were transported by several hospital ships to the New Caledonia hospital at Dumbea for long-term care, which kept the nurses busy. Injuries were massive; gaping chest wounds, hemorrhages, limbs that needed amputation, and severe burns from exploding shells. Broken bones, shrapnel wounds, blunt head trauma, and spinal cord injuries were common. The risk of infection was significant. The mental anguish these young men faced brought on by the unimaginable combat experiences was inexplicable. It also took a toll on the nurses.

Malaria was a constant threat, as was tropical dengue fever. Beriberi was also rampant. An inadequate supply of nutritious food only added to everyone's misery.

However, on the plus side, the sight of the nurses reminded the men of their girls back home. It made them feel less alone. Daisy kept a chattering monologue as she cared for each sailor and Marine. She talked about the latest movies and music. She read aloud the letters from her mother, aunt, Sunday School teacher, and the students from Mrs. Maloy's fifth-grade class. She made all the men honorary residents of her hometown and invited them all to visit after the war. Almost all of the injured sailors were in love with her.

"Nurse Dunton!" The head nurse yelled.

"Ma'am?"

"When I'm on the ward, cut the chatter."

"Yes, ma'am. I'm just doing my best to cheer up the men. They seem to like my ramblings, and I don't think my prattle interferes with my duties. Does it, ma'am?"

"Keep talking, Nurse Dunton." The man in the closest bed responded with applause and a whistle, and the others cheered. "We love your chatter, Nurse Dunton."

Daisy whispered to him, "In for a penny, in for a pound. I guess I'll chatter till the cows come home."

The head nurse rubbed the back of her neck as she looked around the ward. "I admit you are one of my best nurses, but I get a headache whenever I work with you."

"I'm sorry, ma'am. My grandmother always said lemon drops helped headaches. I always pop one into my mouth before my shift. A stitch in time saves nine and all that. Would you like one? I think they are better than aspirin. In fact, when I give the men their medicine, can I include a lemon drop? Better than an apple a day, which is good because we don't have any apples. My family sends the drops to me by the bagsful." Daisy Dunton noticed the head nurse's scowl, "Really, ma'am, you should try them. It's good for what ails you, as they say."

"Carry on, Nurse Dunton. I'm going for a smoke," the head nurse left.

Daisy looked at her back, "She never said if she wanted a lemon drop. How about you, men?"

After several months, Heaven Ray was called into the hospital administrator's office.

"Nurse Turner, you have done an excellent job and are to be commended."

"Thank you, sir." *I've had to push myself every minute.*

"I'm sure you've heard rumors about the building across the field?"

"Yes, sir." *I never want to step foot in that evil place.*

"I'm transferring you there."

Heaven Ray's stomach lurched, and her eyes widened. "Sir?" *Please, don't make me go there.*

"You're level-headed and capable. I don't think the fact that these men have maimed and killed our boys will in any way determine your level of care for them. We are required by the Geneva Convention to treat the wounded Japanese prisoners as we would any of our boys." He shuffled papers on his desk and refused to make eye contact with her. "Any questions?"

Heaven Ray whispered, "When do I start?" *I think I'm going to throw up.*

"In the morning."

It took everything in Heaven Ray to set aside her trepidation as she walked across the field that first morning. Her interpreter, a sturdy young New Caledonian with a thin mustache and a French accent, warned her not to make eye contact with the prisoners.

"I'm not sure how to approach them, Vincent. My mother would want me to show them kindness and God's love. I don't think I can." *I know I can't, and I don't want to.*

"They don't deserve it, ma'am."

"My mother would say none of us do."

"Pardon?" His lack of understanding thickened his French accent.

"Deserve God's love," Heaven Ray replied mechanically. The sweat dribbled down her back as they neared the hastily built prison that had several wards for wounded prisoners. When Heaven Ray and Vincent entered the ward, all heads turned toward them. The dull, vacant eyes of the prisoners unnerved her, and she shuddered. The room was thick with tension, as hot and humid as the air outside. Heaven Ray was vaguely aware Vincent had continued their conversation. She turned to him, "I'm sorry, what did you say?"

"I wanted to warn you, ma'am, that some of the more volatile men have a wrist handcuffed to the bed. The ones that might try to escape. Be careful when you approach them."

Heaven Ray whispered, "I can't do this." She quickly left the ward, followed by Vincent. She was allowed to stay in the office and file reports for the next three days. She also prepared the medicine carts. She occasionally peeked into one of the wards and shuddered. Most of the men lay silent and stared at the ceiling. The ward nurses did their jobs without a word, although Vincent was there if needed.

"Nurse Turner," the lead ward nurse said, "I think you're ready for nursing duty."

"I think my skills would be more suited to surgery, ma'am." *At least the casualties would be unconscious, and I wouldn't have to face them.*

"I need you on the ward. You can start with afternoon rounds." She handed Heaven Ray a clipboard that listed the men's names, injuries, and medications.

Heaven Ray plastered a smile across her face and entered the ward. Vincent stood at her side. "How are you feeling today, Mr.—" she looked at the chart but couldn't pronounce the prisoner's name. She tilted the clipboard so Vincent could see it. "Kasuma," he pronounced it slowly several times, and Heaven Ray repeated it until it no longer felt awkward.

"I speak Japanese with a French accent, so these men do not think much of me." He gave a Gaelic shrug, "It does not matter. I think even less of them."

She saw Kasuma's wrist shackled to the bed and slipped a blood pressure cuff around his upper arm. He jerked her forward with his other arm, and she sprawled across the bed. She yelped, dropped the cuff, and pushed against him to get her balance, but he held her firmly. She felt a fierce pain and shrieked. Vincent pulled her upright and paled when he saw the rip in her uniform and the blood seeping through. "Did that yellow devil bite you?"

The two guards in the hallway rushed in with pistols raised. One of the guards swore and shackled the patient's other wrist to the bed rail.

"I'm alright." Heaven Ray bit her lip to keep the hate in her heart from exploding into the room.

"You're not," Vincent said.

"What's he saying?" Heaven Ray turned her attention to Kasuma. The guard who had restrained him could not keep him quiet. The other had his firearm trained on the rest of the ward. The prisoners stared without expression.

"You don't want to know, ma'am. Curses mostly." Vincent shook his head. "I don't understand the way they think."

"Explain." Heaven Ray held a gauze pad on the bite and tried to ignore the pain.

"First, let's see to your wound. That Japanese dog might be rabid."

Heaven Ray grimaced, "I hardly think so." *He might be; he's mean enough.*

He led her out of the ward. A nurse washed her wound, applied a pressure bandage, and then gave her a tetanus shot and two aspirin. She was warned to watch for signs of infection. She was given the rest of the day off. As Vincent accompanied her across the field, she said, "Now explain why you don't understand the Japanese people."

"They aren't like us."

"People are the same the world over." *Do I still believe that?*

"No, ma'am. Bushido, the way of the warrior, defines them. They cannot imagine defeat. In fact, they would rather die than surrender. It's considered disloyalty to the Emperor."

Heaven Ray thought of the impassive, soulless look on Oriental faces in the prison ward. "No wonder they look so numb."

"Kasuma harangued the others about their great shame and dishonor. It was worse than death, he said. They must fight until the Americans kill them. The only way to retrieve their honor."

Heaven Ray exclaimed, "We're not going to do that!" *Maybe we should.* She shuddered—horrified at the thought.

"I think the others consider themselves as good as dead."

Heaven Ray stopped and stared at Vincent. "That is the stupidest thing I ever heard. They must think their Emperor's a god if they expect to die for him."

"Yes, ma'am. Japan's religion is Emperor worship."

Heaven Ray shuddered. *I almost feel sorry for them. No! They are the enemy, and I hate them, and I hate myself for hating them. Mom would be so disappointed in me.*

Heaven Ray continued to be wary of Kasuma and with good reason. Just yesterday, as she changed the dressing on his wound, he raised his head and spat in her face. She stood, frozen in shock. Vincent pushed Heaven Ray away from the bed and pulled a handkerchief from his back pocket. Anger started in the soles of her feet, and she felt it rise through her body. That rage screamed for release, and she pictured herself slapping his hate-filled face. Instead, she let Vincent wipe the spittle from her face.

Hostility emanated from Kasuma. Heaven Ray had never experienced such indignity, never felt so humiliated and violated.

Vincent touched her elbow. "Ma'am?"

She walked past him without expression, without a word.

That afternoon, Daisy found Heaven Ray on her cot, with her face shoved into the pillow. She knelt on the floor and rubbed her friend's back. "I'm here, Heaven Ray. I'm here."

Heaven Ray remained silent, and for once, so did Daisy. Several moments passed, and Heaven Ray whispered, "Daisy."

"Yes?"

"Talk."

Daisy laughed, "Well, that knocks my socks off. No one in my entire life has ever asked me to talk. Dad said I could talk the hind legs off a donkey, but right now, I don't know what to say. Hmm, what shall I talk about?"

"Just talk," Heaven Ray whispered.

Daisy talked of inane things until Heaven Ray relaxed, sat up, and smiled slightly. Daisy sat on the cot, took Heaven's hand, and said, "It's time to get serious. I'm so sorry this happened to you, Heaven. First, the bite, and now the spit. You must feel, I don't know, crushed at the indignity."

"I am so angry. And don't ask me to play the Glad Game with them."

"It's not for them." Daisy squeezed Heaven Ray's hand. "This is a tough situation, but you're tougher."

"I'm not tough at all." Heaven Ray choked back a sob and wiped her eyes with the edge of her uniform. "I thought I was, but all I feel is a gut-busting rage."

"Who are you raging against? Kasuma? He's just continuing the battle, doing his duty."

Heaven Ray pulled her knees to her chest and rested her chin on them. "If not him, who?"

"I think you are angry at whatever God you believe in. He's not running the war the way you think He should. Protecting the good guys and eradicating the bad ones. He's letting innocent people die, and that tears you apart. Am I right? I think I'm right." Daisy said.

Heaven Ray sighed, "I don't know. I can't think."

"Are you smarter than this God of yours? Wiser? Are you more powerful? Stronger? Do you know how all of this will end?"

Heaven Ray sniffed, "You don't know what you're talking about."

"I've seen you reading that Bible of yours. You frantically flipped through the pages, searching for something. If God is God, then you're not, so leave the running of the war to Him. I imagine He'll sort it out eventually, and then we'll all live happily ever after, pie in the sky and all that."

"And if He doesn't and we don't?" Heaven Ray choked back tears of frustration.

"We can only handle what is in front of us. We can't grasp what's beyond our reach. Do what you can where you are and leave the rest to your Deity. Am I right? Right as rain, that's me." Daisy laughed and said, "I'm glad we had this talk. Now it's tea time. Tea for two." She stood and pulled Heaven Ray to her feet. "Oh, and I talked to the commander of the prison. I'll take your shift for the next few days, maybe longer."

"You don't have to do that. And believe me, they won't play the Glad Game."

Daisy's look of indignation was almost comical. "Do you think I'm stupid?" She stood tall and thrust her chest out. "I am a woman wise beyond my years. Owls are jealous of my mental prowess." She laughed and said, "At least I have the gift of gab and a plan. You know, the best-laid plans of mice and men. Wait, that one doesn't fit."

Despite herself, Heaven Ray grinned, "Plan?"

Daisy laughed, "Be prepared, that's my motto," She put her finger on her temple and cocked her head. "Hmm, that's the Boy Scouts. If it's good enough for them, it's good enough for me."

"Daisy! Focus!"

"Right. Anyway, among all my many accomplishments, you will not find one iota of musical ability. So, I am going to sing the entire time I'm in the prison hospital. Those poor Japanese prisoners will wish they had never been born, much less captured. I'll sing everything from nursery rhymes to hymns from my gramma's church to the latest from the Big Bands. I will sing in my loudest voice, and you know how loud I can be. They are going to stuff their heads under their pillows and wish they were dead. I'd give you an example, but I like you too much. Now, let's go get that tea."

"You've been in the prison hospital for seven months, Nurse Turner. How are you doing?"

"I do my duty, Doctor White." *I don't know how much longer I can last.*

"I've had you reassigned to the hospital ship, Solace."

"Isn't the Solace based in Noumea?"

"It is, but has been reassigned. Rumor is a major push is coming. The Navy has new nurses assigned here, and you experienced ones will be reassigned to hospital ships."

"Yes, sir."

He fiddled with his stethoscope and refused to meet her eyes. "The ship will sometimes be within thirty miles of the battle zone. Are you prepared for that?"

She nodded. "When do we leave?"

"Pack your gear and be ready. The Solace will depart when her current casualties have been transferred to our hospital."

"Do you know anything about the Solace, Nurse Turner?" Lieutenant Doris Malone, the ship's head nurse, asked as Heaven Ray reported for duty.

"No, ma'am."

Doris patted the ship's rail and smiled. "She was at Pearl during the attack. Of course, she had no weapons, but she immediately sent her motor launches to the Arizona with stretcher parties. Her crew also pulled men out of the harbor, which was covered in burning oil. Horrible! Since then, she's been all over the South Pacific."

Heaven Ray shuddered and said, "I'm surprised the Japanese didn't bomb her."

"So far, our hospital ships have been safe from enemy attack. I doubt that continues throughout the war." Doris sighed, "The Germans have already attacked our hospital ships. Never mind. Stow your gear and report to the ready room. We'll be getting underway soon."

As Heaven Ray stowed her gear and listened to the inevitable grumbling from the other nurses sharing the quarters, she heard Daisy Dunton long before she saw her.

"—at least there won't be any lizards on this ship. I'm glad for that. Bugs don't bother me, or snakes, for that matter. But lizards, ugh. Walking little dragons. Hello everyone. For those who don't know me, I'm Daisy Dunton, at your service. I'll probably forget your names as soon as you tell me, but that's all right. I'll ask again. Tippecanoe and Tyler, too, I'm glad to be here." She shook her Shirley Temple curls and looked around, "Attending to our boys as soon as they are transferred from the battlefield will be so helpful. Time and tide wait for no man; a stitch in time saves nine and such."

They all made their way to the ready room, poured coffee, and sat. The day was hot and humid, and the metal folding chairs were warm.

"Welcome to the Solace, ladies. As you saw, the ship is painted white with several huge red crosses to let the enemy know we are an unarmed hospital ship. So far, so good. Nevertheless, we will be close to the fighting, and no one can say what will happen. There is no guarantee the Japanese will continue to honor the Geneva Convention regarding ships of mercy." He cleared his throat and assured them the good Lord was watching over them.

"I'll leave you now in the capable hands of your head nurse, Lieutenant Doris Malone."

"Thank you, Captain Withers," Doris said, "Ladies, you will see your assignments posted on the bulletin board at the back of the room. Take the next two days to acquaint yourself with the layout of the ship as we sail closer to the battle area. You will be on the run for more hours than you can count. Every minute you spend trying to determine where you are or where you need to be may cost one of our boys his life." Lieutenant Malone's eyes clouded for a moment. She shook off her despair and said, "You'll also see a large map of the South Seas. I have kept a list of all the places this ship has taken me. I've been to Samoa, the Tonga Islands, New Caledonia, New Zealand, Australia, and Fiji. I am determined to return after the war. I want to lay on the sandy beaches and relax. I want to swim in warm seas and meet the people of these lands in peace. I want to sail these waters without seeing enemy aircraft or hearing the big guns of the battleships." Doris sighed and shrugged, "You are all compassionate and competent, or you wouldn't be here. As I said, familiarize yourself with the ship. I don't want any of you losing your way."

Daisy leaned over to Heaven, "Isn't that a grand idea? Wouldn't you like to return after the war and see these islands and their people? Around the world in eighty days or at least the South Seas. Oh, look, you're assigned to the surgery unit. That's your favorite, isn't it? I don't think I'd like it at all. I'd much rather the men were awake. If I'm going to talk, and I am, I do need someone to listen. Why use one word when ten will do? That's my motto."

Once the intensity of the battle subsided, the seriously injured were ferried to the Solace in small boats. Heaven Ray was reassigned to triage. The casualties were laid on the deck, and many were unconscious. Others moaned or screamed in agony. After evaluation, corpsmen placed those designated for surgery on stretchers and carried them to the ship's operating rooms. Heaven Ray longed to go with them. It was easier to be with the men after they had received anesthesia. It silenced their screams. She saw Daisy apply a thick coat of lipstick to her mouth and kiss the forehead of a nearby patient, "Daisy, what are you doing?"

Daisy stepped over several men and knelt beside Heaven Ray. She leaned close and whispered in her ear. "You know we've been issued bright red lipstick to mark the foreheads of those who will not make it. I suppose because it's easier to wash off than ink," she whispered.

"I know, but why are you kissing them?" Heaven Ray spoke as low as Daisy, but she doubted the wounded could hear anything past their pain.

"Some know they are going to die. Others are longing for home. The least I can do is hold their hand and seal it with a kiss. These poor boys."

Heaven Ray gulped and nodded. Trust Daisy to find a way to give the best comfort possible. Heaven Ray asked to be relieved from triage. She was denied, but thirty-six hours later, they finished triage, and after a short and restless sleep, she was in the operating room.

The compact surgery unit became her world. Men wounded in battle, as well as fleet casualties, were treated. Those who could not be returned to duty immediately had been brought to the Solace and other hospital ships or evacuated to Pearl Harbor or the States for long-term care.

The Solace was constantly in motion, in good weather and foul. The ever-shifting sounds at sea, the wind and the waves, and the ship's engines drummed in Heaven Ray's ears. Just over the horizon, low-flying aircraft released their bombs, battleship guns fired, and exploding vessels added to the chaos of sound. Heaven Ray, grateful the echoes of war were muted by the ship's engines, became immune to the battlefield cacophony.

Because of the ship's pitch and roll, she used all her energy to stay balanced and upright in the operating room. Restless nights filled with dreams of the wounded—images of battered men floating on the sea—drained her. Water, coated with battleship fuel, burned everyone who came in contact with its hot flames. She heard their screams and death cries. She smelled the hot oil and burning flesh. Japanese swords slashed at the poor men, and no one came to their rescue. Sea monsters grabbed the men and pulled them underwater. She dreaded sleep and often woke with tears staining her pillow and screams locked in her soul.

"Heaven Ray, let's have coffee. I haven't seen you in an age. Absence makes the heart grow fonder, definitely not out of sight, out of mind." Daisy grabbed her arm and led her to the nearly empty galley. "We are birds of a feather, my friend. We need to flock together." She poured each of them coffee and grabbed a couple of stale donuts from a greasy cardboard box. "Today, I am the listener, and you are the talker. I mean it. I'm all ears. In fact, I am going to bite my tongue."

Heaven Ray smiled, but it didn't reach her eyes. "I'm so tired."

"You look emotionally exhausted." Daisy threw up her hands,

"So help me, I will zip my lips or button them if you prefer."

Heaven Ray smiled, reached across the table, and squeezed Daisy's hand. "You're a good friend. Seeing the newly wounded, some maimed beyond all hope, breaks my heart. The carnage man can do to man numbs me. I wish the world was the way it used to be."

"If wishes were horses, beggars would ride. That's what they say, and I think it's true. The world will never be the same, and we must make the best of a bad situation. Do what you can, where you can, the best you can. That's what my mother always said."

"Does she like clichés, too?"

Daisy laughed, "She's the cliché queen. I could never rise to her level of expertise." She pulled a rubber band from around her wrist and trapped her frizzy hair into a braid. "I mean it; focus on the casualties you have. Do not let your mind dwell on those you could not save."

"I see their faces, even when I'm asleep."

"There is no future in the past. And didn't I read in that Bible of yours that it's appointed unto man once to die? I think that's what it says. So we all have an appointment." She shrugged, "Seems to me it's up to that God of yours."

"You're right, my friend, but it's senseless."

Daisy took Heaven Ray by the shoulders and gave her a gentle shake. "We will stop this evil. Some day, somehow, Lord willing, and the creek don't rise," Daisy said. "Now I'm dragging you to the newest John Wayne movie they're showing in the wardroom. No arguments, and we need to hurry. We've already missed the first few minutes. It's a good thing the bad guys wear black hats; otherwise, we might get confused."

"Lieutenant Malone, things seemed pretty quiet this past week. We haven't picked up any new wounded," Heaven Ray stood next to the lieutenant in the chow line.

Doris laughed. "Where have you been? We're on our way to San Diego, almost there in fact." She turned to the server, "More mashed potatoes, please."

"What?"

"We'll deliver our casualties to the new wing of the naval hospital and then turn around and make our way to the Gilbert Islands after refueling at Pearl."

Heaven Ray pushed her hair back under her nurse's cap. "I must admit I haven't paid attention to where we are. It seems all I've done is one surgery after another."

"And when you aren't in the operating room, you visit the casualties. You hardly take time to eat. You need to pace yourself, Ensign Turner."

"I've forgotten how to do that." *I don't know why I force myself to visit the wards. Seeing all those boys in pain drains me.*

"You need a break from active war zones. It's taking a toll on you," Lieutenant Malone advised. "I have half a mind to transfer you, but we are so short-staffed that I can't."

"I'm fine, ma'am." *I thought I was hiding my fatigue.*

Doris patted Heaven on the shoulder. "We'll talk once we reach the West Coast. I'd like you to ask for a transfer to Yosemite Park's Naval Convalescent Center Hospital. It's for mental stress and battle fatigue, as well as serious physical injuries. Being in the park surrounded by nature is thought to be healing."

"I thought you said we are short-handed." *Does she think that's what's wrong with me? Mental stress? Battle fatigue? There's no way I'm going to hide in the States with the war raging in the Pacific. I'm a trained surgical nurse, not a babysitter for those who can't handle their emotions.*

Lieutenant Malone shrugged and said, "We're short-staffed everywhere. You'll have a few days leave in San Diego. Make the most of them."

"I'm going to miss you, Daisy, but I'm sure you'll be great helping the men recover." Heaven Ray and Daisy packed their bags and prepared to leave the ship.

"I thought at first I was transferred to the San Diego hospital, which would have been fine, but Lieutenant Malone says my prattle will be more effective cajoling and badgering the men who need to do their exercises and physical therapy, so they are sending me to a rehabilitation center somewhere in Southern California."

"Whatever you put your mind to, prattle or not, you do a great job."

"Thank you, Heaven Ray. I only wish I could have coaxed you into facing your inner turmoil. You know, turning wounds into wisdom, lemons into lemonade." She lifted the candy bag from her pocket, "Or, in our case, lemon drops."

Heaven Ray ignored the wounds into wisdom comment and laughed as she reached for a lemon drop. "Coaxed? Is that what you call it?"

"I'd do more than that if I thought it would help. What kind of skeletons do you have in your closet that I could pull out and use to blackmail you? Never mind, you're good through and through. I shall miss you terribly. Opposites attract and all that. Sugar and spice, Mutt and Jeff, that's us."

"Do you think you will enjoy your new posting?"

"It'll be a piece of cake. Several men on this ship have promised to marry me if I follow them to the rehab center. Isn't that a kick? You know what they say about marriage. I think it was Ben Franklin. 'Keep your eyes wide open before marriage and half closed afterward.' Isn't that funny? Anyway, I don't care where I'm posted or what I'm doing. I'll play the Glad Game and make the men play it, too. As long as I've got a bag of lemon drops, I'll be fine."

"The nurses on New Caledonia sure resisted your efforts."

Daisy put her hand over her heart in a dramatic fashion and, with drawn-out syllables, said, "Grouchy old bats, one of the few failures in my life. But every strikeout gets me closer to the next home run, that's what I say. But I'm sure my rehabilitation boys—."

"Boys?"

Daisy grinned, "I don't care how old they are. They are all-American boys, red, white, and blue. I will make sure they take their medicine, do their exercises, and crunch lemon drops. I want to send them home to their mamas healthy and whole."

Heaven Ray felt a pain pierce her heart. She pictured all the men who had died in triage and on the operating table. Young men who would never return to their mamas or their wives. The physical pain in her chest caused her to gasp.

"What's wrong?" Daisy asked.

"I just need a couple of lemon drops. That reminds me, who was that Irish woman who told your grandmother about them?"

"When Granny was a young girl, a passenger train jumped the tracks at the junction east of town."

"Ohio, right?"

It was as if Daisy didn't hear the question. "Everyone went to help. The conductor, along with a fiery redhead and her son, had separated the wounded into those not too seriously hurt and those who needed to be taken to the hospital. I think Granny said this redhead's name was Molly, Maureen, Mauve, something typically Irish. Anyway, she asked my grandmother to help pass out a large bag of lemon drops. Her thick Irish brogue made it hard for my granny to understand her, but she said the Irish lass learned about the value of lemon drops from a priest in the Emerald Isle. Erin Go Braugh, the Luck of the Irish and all that."

"Hmmm," Heaven Ray smiled and held out her hand for another drop. *It's a mystery!*

CHAPTER TWENTY-ONE

The weather in San Diego was pleasant, and the base personnel efficiently handled the transfer of casualties to the Navy Hospital at the Balboa Center. They would be further evaluated, and some would be sent to a rehabilitation center. The doctors, nurses, and crew of the Solace were given leave while the ship was resupplied and refueled.

Daisy locked arms with Heaven Ray as they descended the gangplank. "Come along, my friend. After we stash our gear at the barracks, we are going to paint the town red. And by that, I mean we are going to the latest movie. I want a romance, not another John Wayne, shoot 'em up saga. We are going to buy make-up, and we are going to eat tacos and burritos."

"All I want to do is sleep. I don't have the energy for anything else."

"You can sleep on the return trip."

"How did you know I was going back?"

"I told you I pay attention, but I wish you would take everyone's advice and ask for a transfer to the States. It would be good for what ails you, as my granny always said. Wait, that was about cod liver oil. You could probably use some of that, too," she laughed. "Seriously, Heaven, I worry about you."

Heaven Ray sighed and said, "You're going to drag me to a movie I don't want to see, buy make-up I won't wear, and eat something I never heard of."

"It's an uphill battle, but I'm no fair-weather friend. A friend in need is a friend indeed, and you, my dear, are desperately in need. So let's grab the bull by the horn and find those tacos."

"What am I in need of?" *I'm going to regret this. Why didn't I keep my mouth shut?*

"Fun, relaxation, and a deep distraction. The fact of the matter is your mind and heart are still fixed on the dying. You can't carry that."

Heaven Ray drew in her breath and stumbled a little. She clenched her jaw and wondered how this frothy little nurse saw the well-hidden parts of her soul. The beginnings of a headache were making themselves known, and she rubbed her forehead. Heaven Ray pulled a small bottle of aspirin from her pocket—one she carried since becoming friends with the ever-chatty Daisy Dunton. Heaven Ray choked down several tablets and tried to keep the irritation from her voice. "You really are the most annoying little person, aren't you?"

"I am, but only because I love you, and I know you return the favor. All's fair in love and war."

"It's not! Nothing is fair in war!" Heaven Ray threw up her hands as a taxicab screeched to the sidewalk in front of them. "I give up," she said, pressing her despair into the deep recesses of her soul. She climbed into the yellow vehicle and, with a false cheerfulness, asked, "What are tacos?"

"My cousin had leave here last year and found this little Mexican taco stand on the corner of, wait—I have the address written down somewhere," She patted her pockets and looked in her pocketbook. "Here it is." She gave the address to the cab driver, asked how far it was to the Mexican border, and then looked at Heaven Ray.

"Don't even ask."

"We have enough time for a little trip. They say nothing develops intelligence like travel, broadens the mind, and all that. How about it?"

"We just crossed an ocean."

"That's not the same. I bet the tacos in Mexico are out of this world, or at least out of this country."

"I can drive you to the best food in Mexico," the driver offered, "My cousin Jose has a fine taco place built onto the side of his house. Very cheap for pretty American girls."

"You stay out of this," Heaven Ray snapped. He turned back to the steering wheel but glanced in the mirror, clearly interested in their conversation.

"Don't push it, Daisy! I'll do make-up, a movie, and tacos! American tacos! That's it! I mean it!" Heaven Ray sucked on her bottom lip. Her voice was louder and harsher than she intended.

"Okay. Okay. I can take a hint. No need to bite my head off."

Heaven Ray saw the stricken look on Daisy's face and reached for her hand.

Daisy pulled away, turned her head, and looked out the taxi's window. She sniffed, took a tissue from her pocketbook, and blew her nose.

"Come on, Pollyanna. Let's play the Glad Game."

"Even Pollyanna gets her feelings hurt."

"You're always cheerful. Nothing bothers you," Heaven Ray realized how foolish she sounded. "Sorry. I didn't think. I'll miss you, but I'll write often."

"Well, you can bet your bottom dollar I won't write back!"

Heaven Ray frowned and whispered, "Daisy?"

Another sniff and the tissue was stuffed back into the purse and a nail file pulled out. Head bent, Daisy sawed at her fingernails for a long minute. Sniff. Sniff. "When I have a pen in my hand and a blank paper in front of me, the words in my mouth fly out the window, and I can't find them."

Heaven Ray chuckled, "Most of the time, I don't know what I think until I write it down."

"I wondered where all your words went. You certainly don't share them with the rest of us. It's not fair, Heaven. I thought we were friends."

The cab pulled up to the corner next to the taco stand. Heaven Ray handed the fare to the driver and said, "My treat. We are going to have a good day, right?"

Sniff. Sniff. Hiccup. "There's a saying back home, anger is like a tornado. We have to go into the storm cellar until it blows over."

"And has it blown over?"

Sniff. "Just a minute." Daisy pulled out the soggy tissue again and blew her nose—a tremendous honking sound. The taxidriver cringed, seagulls overhead squawked and flew away. Two alleycats quit fighting and ran behind a garbage can. "Can I borrow a tissue?" Daisy asked.

"I don't have one."

The driver handed a crumpled and slightly used bandana to Daisy. One more fierce blow. "Now it's blown over!"

When Daisy tried to return the bandana to the driver, he shook his head, and a stream of rapid Spanish followed. He motioned for them to get out of his cab.

These two young nurses discovered they loved tacos, burritos, and all things Mexican. They bought extra to eat later that night.

"Tomorrow, we'll go to Coronado, swim in San Diego Bay, rent an umbrella, lay in the sand, and eat hotdogs," Daisy said. She gulped and stammered, "I mean, if you want to."

"I don't have a swimsuit."

"I'll lend you one of mine. Any port in a storm." They looked at each other and laughed. Short, stocky Daisy and tall, slim Heaven Ray could never wear each other's clothes.

Heaven Ray sighed and said, "It doesn't matter. I can't swim."

"Of course, you can swim. Everybody can swim."

"I'm from Alaska. We don't swim!"

Daisy shook her head, and her confused Shirley Temple curls bobbed and swayed.

Heaven Ray continued, "The water's too cold. People die."

"What do you mean, people die? Never mind. I don't want to know. Doesn't your city have a public pool?"

Heaven Ray tried to imagine a swimming pool in her hometown. "My town has less than four hundred people. Some of us don't even have electricity or running water yet."

Daisy sputtered, "I don't get it; you're in the Navy. Aren't you afraid you'll drown?"

"My friend Rita is a bush pilot in Alaska."

"What's she got to do with anything?" Daisy opened her mouth as if to say more, but Heaven Ray held up her hand and continued.

"She flies to all sorts of remote and isolated places in all kinds of weather. She might be forced to land if something goes wrong with the plane, provided she can find a suitable place. She could be several hundred miles from another human being."

"What if she can't fix the airplane or is injured when she lands? What if the radio goes out or nobody's close enough to hear her call for help? What if she crashes? I'd be terrified."

"I asked her about it once. She feels completely at peace in the air. It's as if she's cocooned in her own little world. She has absolute trust. No fear."

"Is that how you feel on a ship?"

"I grew up on the water: canoes, kayaks, small fishing boats, even an oomiak. My father knew the currents and could read the weather. He had absolute faith the Lord watched over us. I felt the same as Rita, peaceful, content, safe, even during fierce storms."

"You don't anymore."

Heaven Ray's sad smile and slight nod signaled the truth of Daisy's statement.

CHAPTER TWENTY-TWO

"Daisy Dunton, I shall miss you terribly. You're like a breath of fresh air." Heaven Ray's chin rested on the shorter girl's Shirley Temple curls as they hugged.

"Look at you, a cliché at last. I must be rubbing off on you." Daisy pulled a bag of lemon drops and a box of raisins out of her oversized pocketbook. "Vittles for the journey."

"Thank you for dragging me all over San Diego during our leave."

"It did you a world of good, if I say so myself, especially the dance at the USO. Who knew you could jitterbug with the best of them? And like I said, all work and no play..."

"You're right. I got lost in the music and enjoyed myself immensely."

"I enjoyed the Red Cross donuts!"

They giggled and hugged once more. Heaven Ray picked up her duffle and walked up the gangplank backward, waving to her friend.

"Eyes in the same direction as your feet, Heaven. That's what my mama says," Daisy yelled as she stood at the end of the pier. She waved a white handkerchief until she could no longer see the ship.

Heaven Ray soaked in the peace and calm of the ship's crossing. *Smooth seas and fair winds. Godspeed.* She reveled in the Pacific's fair weather. The sapphire sky by day and the Milky Way by night soothed her soul in a way she could not articulate. The dolphins and whales brought her great joy. *If Daisy were here, she'd say it was good for what ails me—that joy and laughter are the best medicine.* She struggled to hang onto that joy the closer they sailed to Hawaii.

"Ensign Turner," Lieutenant Malone called, "come into my office."

"Yes, ma'am."

She picked up a paper from her desk, "You and all the nurses returning on the Solace are being transferred to the Navy Hospital at Pearl Harbor, and nurses from Pearl will be assigned to the Solace. You have done an excellent job. I want to personally thank you. I am requesting a commendation for you."

"Ma'am?"

"I was worried about you a while back, but you pulled yourself together and developed some much-needed backbone. I wish all my nurses had become as unemotional, detached, and unfazed by all the carnage as you."

The cords in Heaven Ray's neck tightened. The faces of mortally wounded young men who died on the deck while being triaged flashed through her mind. Their cries for their mother, their pleas that Heaven Ray would remember them, pray for them, or hold their hands as they breathed their last haunted her. Those who stopped breathing on the operating table and could not be revived and those who didn't live long enough to reach the hospitals in Australia, New Zealand, or Hawaii filled her with guilt and grief. *I will not break down. I will not admit weakness.*

She blinked rapidly and refused to let the burning in her eyes develop into tears. She felt beads of sweat on her upper lip and longed to wipe them away. Instead, she stood rigid, her gaze fixed on the wall behind Lieutenant Malone's desk.

The other nurses were excited as they packed their belongings. Heaven Ray was the only one who seemed to be conflicted.

"It will be great, Heaven Ray. Liberty in Honolulu. Waikiki beach, swimming in the ocean, going to the movies in town, not aboard the ship. We'll hardly know there's a war," one of her fellow nurses said.

Another chimed in, "We won't see enemy planes overhead or hear the bombs explode."

"Shopping in Honolulu. That's the first thing I'm going to do. I'd kill for a pair of silk stockings."

"It will be like working in a peacetime hospital."

Heaven Ray's smile did not reach her eyes, "I hope you're right."

CHAPTER TWENTY-THREE

Twelve metal hospital beds lined each side of the long room and faced each other. The white paint on the window sills chipped and flaked, and the mattresses sagged. The drab green walls, cement floors that amplified every footstep, and antiseptic smells of the hospital clashed with the royal blue sky and the ocean's turquoise water. Once-white curtains adorned the two tall windows opposite the door, letting in the tropical light. Lush palm trees, rustled by soft sea breezes, sounded like a mother's lullaby. The middle-aged ward nurse, Lillian Rushmore, opened the windows every evening to catch that breeze, and the sweet smells of plumeria and gardenia filled the room.

On Tuesday nights, she approached the radio that sat on a short metal cabinet between the windows. With the skill of a surgeon, she twisted and turned the dial. If the atmospheric conditions were right, she could pull in a radio station from San Francisco, and the men listened to The Pepsodent Show with Bob Hope.

"Hey, Joe, what's with the new guy?" No one knew the Marine gunny's name, and his cropped hair, slightly graying, showed him to be older than the others. He asked again.

"Quiet, I'm trying to listen to Bob Hope." Roy Rogers Wilson, who resembled and was named after the singing cowboy his mother loved, threw his pillow at the gunny, "Bad enough, I have to listen to you snore all night!"

Joe, the curly-haired Italian, grinned at Roy Rogers but answered the gunny, "They brought him in during the night. You were snoring so loud I couldn't sleep."

"Aw, nuts! I don't snore." gunny put the pillow behind his head and nestled into it. "Thanks for the pillow, Trigger."

"Trigger was the horse. My mama didn't name me after no horse."

"She should have. You look more like the horse than the cowboy," Gunny said.

"He doesn't look like Trigger," Joe yelled, "at least not the front end."

Walt said, "I listened to Roy Rogers on the radio in my granny's living room. Happy trails to you, Roy."

"Thanks, Walt, you're the only civilized guy in this joint," Roy Rogers called.

"The new guy doesn't look like a Marine; must be one of you Navy boys," Gunny said.

"Just because you're a gunny doesn't mean you know everything," Joe yelled. "And how do you know he's not a Marine?"

"First, we have a certain look. Second, being a Marine doesn't mean I know everything." He sat up in bed and saluted. "I'm a Marine because I know everything, Ooh Rah! And I don't snore!"

The other guys laughed and good-naturedly harangued Gunny about his opinions and snoring.

"Aw, nuts," Gunny said again. "Nurse Rushmore—what about the new guy?"

She checked the chart hanging from the foot of the bed. "Name's Mark Lawson. Ensign. In a coma, but his vitals are stable." She sighed and chewed on her bottom lip. "He's in pretty bad shape."

"What ship was he on, ma'am?" Walt, a skinny, red-headed farm boy from Georgia, asked, his voice barely above a whisper.

"She's not a ma'am," Joe yelled, "She's a nurse."

"They're all ma'ams in the South," Walt mumbled.

"As well as the military," the Gunny snorted, "You should know that Joe."

Nurse Rushmore raised her voice and quickly answered, hoping to quell the ongoing bickering in the ward, although it was usually good-natured. "Not a ship. The ensign was rescued from some uninhabited island," the gray-haired nurse answered.

"Was he marooned or a deserter?" Joe hollered.

Nurse Rushmore frowned, "You always think the worst, Joe. Rumor is he was a lookout somewhere in the Solomon Islands."

"I heard they had lots of lookouts in the New Georgia Sound. That area was brutal for our boys," Joe yelled, running his hand through his dark hair.

"The ensign probably warned the Brass about Japanese whereabouts in the Slot and saved a lot of lives, maybe even yours."

"Do you really think so, ma'am?" Walt asked as he raised himself and looked at the bed where the ensign lay motionless.

The tired nurse looked at Lawson's chart again and then at the men in the ward. "From the many bullet wounds in his body, I'd say he was strafed."

"Probably from a Japanese fighter," Joe's eyes flashed. "I wish I'd been there. I'd have taken care of those –"

The gunny growled, "You Italians think you can do everything."

"Not me, Gunny," Joe yelled, laughing, "but my mama and Nonna could rule the world if anybody would listen."

"What's a Nonna?" Roy Rogers asked.

"A grandmother, you idiot," Joe yelled, "If I had an extra pillow, I'd deck you."

"When he comes out of his coma, take it easy on him." Nurse Rushmore, plump and eternally cheerful, waved goodbye to "her boys" and left the ward. "I'll see you all in the morning." She hurried down the hall but turned when she heard another nurse ask, "How are you doing, Lillian?"

"Better than you, I think," Lillian answered gently, then lifted her wrist and checked the time. "I'm off duty and going for a swim. I wish you'd come with me sometime. It would do you good."

"Have fun." The attractive but harried nurse took a deep breath and resolved to get through her shift without breaking down. Her work here in Hawaii was calmer and more peaceful, but her pent-up and denied emotions had caught up with her. It had become more challenging to barricade them and do her job without letting them spill over. *I can do this. Nobody is dying, at least not in this room. Not today. I won't think of the last three surgeries. We did everything we could.* She stood straight, threw her shoulders back, braced herself, entered the ward with a false smile, and greeted the men. Roy Rogers pointed to the metal bed nearest the door and whispered, "New guy."

When she saw the name on the chart, her heart stopped. The clipboard fell from her fingers and clattered on the pitted cement. Several casualties looked her way, but the man in the bed did not stir. "Oh, Mark," she whispered and stepped closer.

His eyes were swollen shut, his lips dry and cracked. Purple bruises and deep cuts spread across his face. Beneath the wounds, his face was ashen, nearly unrecognizable. A jagged laceration started at his right temple and nicked his eye, which was sewn shut and then continued across his cheek. The chart informed her it took nearly forty stitches to close the wound. It would leave an ugly scar, but that was the least of his worries. Both legs were heavily bandaged, and his right arm was encased in plaster.

For the next several weeks, Heaven Ray slipped into Mark's ward whenever she had the chance. She watched the shallow rise and fall of his chest and ached for him to wake up. She often did not return to the nurses' quarters but slept fitfully in the metal chair beside his bed.

As soon as she arrived in Pearl, she volunteered for double shifts. Because they were short-staffed, she was assigned to a surgical team as well as a ward. The lack of rest and double shifts added to her fatigue.

The metal chair was uncomfortable, and sleep was elusive. Heaven Ray tried to pray for Mark, the others in the ward, and all those fighting battles across the Pacific. But her prayers often ended in tears and angry despair. Soon, she ceased praying and, instead, held Mark's hand and gazed at his face. A great tenderness grew in her as she made these daily visits. *I must write Natalie, but what can I say? I'll wait until he comes out of the coma or until all hope is gone. I will write to Mom and Miss Ruth. God always answers their prayers. Please, Lord, give me hope.*

Heaven Ray sagged against the corridor's wall. When did she last sleep or stop long enough to eat a decent meal? When did she last take a few hours to walk on the beach, read a book, or spend time in Honolulu with the other nurses shopping or going out to dinner? She yawned, closed her eyes, and then jerked them open when she heard a deep male voice.

"Nurse Turner?"

Heaven Ray pushed an errant lock of hair under her nurse's cap and turned. "Yes, Doctor."

"I've been told you spend all your spare time—what there is of it—with a certain patient."

"Is that a problem, Doctor?"

"It is when you're not taking care of yourself. I have had several complaints from the head nurse and one of the surgeons."

Heaven Ray stiffened but made no reply.

He shifted from foot to foot, cleared his throat, and gentled his voice, "Take care of yourself, my dear. We need all the nurses we can get."

"Yes, Doctor. Is that all?"

"Actually, I wanted to tell you that your ensign is awake."

"When?"

"This morning."

Heaven Ray spun around but was restrained by the Doctor's hand on her arm. "Just a minute. I want to talk to you about him."

"I read the chart. I know what he's facing."

"Your young man doesn't know the extent of his injuries, and I don't want him to know."

"I understand."

"Fortunately, he hasn't asked any questions."

Heaven Ray stifled a nervous laugh and said, "That doesn't sound like him. Did you tell him about the scars on his face and that he'll have a limp from the shrapnel left in his thigh?"

"It's more severe than that. I don't know if he'll walk again, which I did not tell him. I only said he had a long way to go, and there would be scars and a long stay at a rehabilitation facility. He was silent for a few minutes and then said it would be refreshing to be liked for himself, not how he looked. He started talking a lot of religious nonsense, but I cut him off."

"That definitely doesn't sound like my Mark, er, Ensign Lawson."

"I'm confident sight will return to his left eye, but I'm afraid the right will remain impaired."

"Oh, no! Poor Mark."

"As soon as he is able, we will send him to the States."

"When will that be?"

"Weeks, maybe several months. Infection is still possible. He has more healing to do before I'm comfortable letting him travel."

Heaven Ray's heart ached for Mark and all the young men wounded in this awful war.

"I had hoped once the swelling went down, I could remove the rest of the shrapnel." The doctor shook his head and gave Heaven Ray a long look. "It's too close to the femoral artery, at least for me." He shook his head and sighed, "Perhaps an expert surgeon in the States will attempt it."

"Is his Navy career over?"

The doctor's voice roughened, "Nurse Turner, aside from the fact that the shrapnel will affect his mobility, he's blind in one eye. His ability to track moving objects or judge distances will be skewed. His depth perception and balance will be affected." The doctor huffed, "Besides, I just told you I don't know if he will walk again. No one knows how long his rehabilitation will take or what level he will attain. I don't think the Navy will want him. He may sink into a deep depression."

200

Heaven Ray's eyes widened, and she said, "I must see him."

"After visiting your young man, Nurse Turner, I want you to sleep for eight to ten hours." When she didn't respond, he barked, "That's an order!"

Ensign Lawson moaned when she took his hand, "My eyes are swollen. It's hard to open them. Who are you?"

She cleared her throat but did not speak. The man on the bed shifted but could not get comfortable. He groaned and said, "A nurse? Well, my dear, feel free to hold my hand as long as you like."

"Just checking your pulse," she whispered, "How do you feel?"

He turned his face in her direction, but still, his eye did not open. "I know that voice. Heaven?"

"Yes, it's me," she squeezed his hand.

"Last I heard, you were heading to New Caledonia."

"That was over a year ago. I arrived in Pearl in time for the 1944 New Year's party, but I didn't go."

"I had a letter from your mother before I was sent to the island." He sighed and said, "She let me know where you were heading."

"Your's writes to me, but I haven't mentioned that I've seen you. I wanted to wait until...until..."

He struggled but failed to raise his eyelids as he patted her hand. "Dad would have been notified, and he'll keep Mom in the loop. I'm sure Elly calls regularly for updates. There are some advantages to being a commander's son." He licked his cracked lips and winced, "Water?"

She held a glass, and he sipped slowly through the metal straw.

She grabbed the jar of Vaseline Petroleum Jelly from a nearby cupboard and smeared his lips with it.

"I don't remember a thing," he said.

"That's not unusual. You had a severe concussion, and your body is full of pain-killing drugs. It muddles the brain, but the doctors are confident your memory will return."

He attempted a smile. "My face hurts. Thanks for the sticky stuff on my lips. They seem to split whenever I try to talk or smile." He squirmed again. "Everything hurts. Sorry, a good sailor doesn't complain."

"Try not to move; it pulls at your stitches. There are so many. I'm afraid it's not pretty."

Mark was silent for a moment and squeezed her hand. "You won't mind, will you?"

Heaven Ray Turner burst into tears. She laid her forehead on the side of the bed. He let go of her hand and rested his on her hair. "I know you're not weeping because I've lost my rugged good looks. What's the matter?"

"He means his pretty boy face," Joe yelled.

"Give them some privacy, you idiot," Gunny snarled.

"There's no privacy here," Roy Rogers said, humming the theme song from the Roy Rogers radio show, 'Happy Trails to You.'

"Quiet guys, I can't hear," Walt raised himself and leaned forward, "This is better than the Helen Trent show my mama listened to."

"My mama and Nonna listen to that soppy love show, too." Joe sat up in bed, used an empty juice glass as a microphone, and recited the opening lines of the popular radio soap opera in his best radio announcer voice. "...the real-life drama of Helen Trent who when life mocks her, breaks her hopes, dashes her against the rocks of despair, fights back bravely, successfully, to prove what so many women long to...." A pillow smacked Joe in the face.

"Hey!" he yelled.

Gunny laughed, "Sounds like you're a fan of that sissy soap opera."

Mark tried to grin as the others started their good-natured bickering. He knew it helped relieve their frustrations and boredom, but he wanted to concentrate on Heaven Ray. He remained still and let her weep. She hiccupped, pulled her handkerchief from the deep pockets of her nurse's uniform, blew her nose, and spoke softly so the others wouldn't hear. "I'm fine."

"You're not."

Heaven Ray spoke slowly as she tried to put her chaotic thoughts into words. "It's everything, Mark. The world has been bashed and broken. Everything good has been desecrated."

"Like me, huh?" he joked, "Bashed and broken, but hopefully not desecrated."

"I'm serious." She wiped her eyes with the back of her hand. "There's an empty bed near the windows. There was a sweet boy in it yesterday. From Iowa, I think. Now he's gone." She stuffed the messy handkerchief back in her pocket.

"Look out the window, Heaven. What do you see?"

She didn't respond for a moment, then sighed and said, "The bluest sky. Palm trees swaying in the breeze. Tropical flowers looking to the sun."

"The world is still beautiful."

She smiled sadly, "You're right, Mark." *How can I tell him all I see are mangled bodies—young men who should be playing baseball and buying sodas for their girlfriends.*

"You sound like you don't believe it. Where's your faith?"

"I don't know." *It lies bloody on the battlefield. Mortally wounded like the men I see every day.*

"Heaven?"

She continued as if he had not spoken. "The world is lost, and I'm beginning to think I am, too."

"Nurse Turner! A plane load of wounded has arrived." A gruff voice yelled from the hallway. Nurse Rushmore entered the room and softened her voice when she saw Mark was awake. "On your way to triage, stop at the cafeteria and eat."

"I'm not hungry. I'll stay here a bit longer."

"Nurse Turner! Take your lunch break now, or you won't have a chance until Lord knows when. We're expecting two more planes full of injured."

Heaven Ray took a deep breath, stifled a yawn, and nodded. *I guess I won't get the sleep the doctor ordered.*

Joe yelled, "What ship are they from?"

"What battle?" Roy Rogers called.

"Were any of our planes shot down?" Walt whispered, then turned his face away, not wanting to hear the answer.

"I'll just grab a sandwich," Heaven Ray said.

"How many lives were lost?" Gunny asked.

"You will take a full break, sit down and eat, then go for a short walk. I will need you in top form. Don't disappoint me." She turned to the ward. "Sorry, men, I don't have much information. When I know, you'll know." She stomped out of the ward to inform the other nurses to prepare for the onslaught.

Mark squeezed her hand. "I'll pray for you, Heaven."

She nodded but did not leave his bedside despite her orders.

The gunny threw back his blankets and hobbled to the radio, wincing with every step, hanging on to each man's bed and pulling himself along. He fiddled with the dial, but all he could pull in was Big Band music. He kept trying until he heard the sultry but mocking voice of Tokyo Rose.

"Shut that thing off, Gunny. I don't want to hear anything that foul woman says," Roy Rogers shook his fist at the radio.

Gunny shuffled back to his bed, leaving Tokyo Rose spewing her propaganda. "Sometimes we learn more from her than through official channels," Gunny muttered.

"Heaven," Mark whispered and nodded toward the radio. She strode through the ward and turned the dial, and soon, the Andrews Sisters' latest hit, 'Boogie Woogie Bugle Boy of Company B' filled the room. Gunny complained, "Nobody wants to know nothing about what's happening in the world."

Mark mouthed his thanks as Heaven Ray left and Nurse Rushmore reentered the ward.

After her lunch break, Heaven Ray trudged toward the staging area with feet as heavy as her heart. Other nurses ran past her, urging her to hurry, saying the second plane had arrived and the third was expected momentarily. But Heaven couldn't make her feet go any faster. She was last to enter the triage area, and the pungent smell of alcohol and disinfectants, combined with the iron odor of congealed blood and the putrid smell of gangrene, assaulted her. Sweat and urine also fouled the air.

A triage nurse's first responsibility was ascertaining whether the wounded still breathed. If not, she marked his forehead with lipstick. She also marked those who would not be breathing long.

They were moved to the side. The lipstick was easy to remove before the body was prepped and sent home. Heaven Ray thought of Daisy and how she held the hands of the dying and marked their foreheads with a kiss. She tried hard but could not follow her friend's example. Heaven Ray steeled her heart against all she saw. She worked mechanically, feeling nothing.

While sailing from San Diego to Pearl Harbor on the Solace, Heaven Ray seemed to recover her sense of self. She felt her anger and despair drain away as the nautical miles of the voyage increased. She began her assignment at Pearl by praying with the men who would let her, joking with others, singing to some, and responding kindly to those who cheerfully flirted. After a few weeks, much to her dismay, those bleak emotions resurfaced. *Now, I can't look them in the eye, especially the ones I know aren't going to make it. I have to think of them as cases, not men. What kind of a nurse does that make me?*

Yesterday, a Marine officer grabbed her hand. She tried to shake it off, and his grip tightened. "Please, ma'am, I know I'm a goner, and it's okay. My battlefield letter is under my pillow. Will you make sure it's mailed to my sister?" He coughed, and she wiped the spit-up blood from his chin. "Besides the Corps, she's my only family. I've been married to the Marines for nearly 30 years." He coughed again. "Some of my boys are here, ma'am. Remind them I prayed for them every day and will continue from heaven." His eyes locked on hers, pleading. She pulled the letter from under the pillow and stuffed it into her pocket.

Tension in the ward increased over the next few days as the nurses scurried to and fro. They had little time to visit as they cared for the newly arrived casualties, most severely wounded. Gunny cursed the military news service every time he turned on the radio. He found the news vague and lacking in detail. He usually twisted the dial to the voice of Tokyo Rose, which generally caused an argument among the men.

Mark used his good arm to push himself up in the bed. It did not ease his discomfort. Nurse Rushmore put an extra pillow behind his back. "Do you have any more information?" he asked, "If I have to listen to Tokyo Rose one more minute, I cannot guarantee Gunny's safety."

Nurse Rushmore chuckled, "You are in no shape to take on the gunny, verbally or otherwise. I'll take care of this."

Mark frowned and mentally cursed his broken body. Nurse Rushmore fluffed his blankets and said, "You have a long journey ahead of you, Ensign Lawson. You need to pace yourself."

"I'm having a hard time accepting that."

She nodded toward the other casualties, "The others have the same problem. Be an example."

Tokyo Rose continued her tirade, and Mark looked pleadingly at the nurse.

"I don't know much, but I'll try to make it sound like something." She grabbed a bedpan and hit the end of Mark's metal bed. "Attention, fellas! Gunny, turn off that radio."

He cursed under his breath and made no attempt to do so. Nurse Rushmore took a step toward his bed. "Gunny! Don't make me come over there! Radio, now!" she barked.

He shuffled to the radio, muttering that she'd make a great drill sergeant. He cursed the war, the radio, the weather, and everything else he could think of.

Nurse Rushmore met him next to the radio and whispered. "I brought the radio into this ward, and I can take it out."

Three of his favorite cuss words escaped before he clamped his lips together.

"That's right, Gunny. Eat those words. I'll have no swearing or cussing in my ward."

"But, it's the Marine Corps way. I don't know any military man who isn't proud of his, er, vocabulary."

"This is my ward, and I make the rules," Nurse Rushmore said as she unplugged the radio.

"Wait! I'll do my best."

"Ooh Rah, Marine." She handed him the cord, and he bent down to plug it in. She turned to the men and then looked toward the open door of the ward. "I'm not supposed to pass along information. Doctor's orders."

The men groaned, and Joe threw his comic book on the floor. "Nuts!"

She placed it on the end of his bed. "I said I wasn't supposed to, Joe. I didn't say I wouldn't."

Several men clapped, but Walt pulled the covers up to his chin and closed his eyes. Nurse Rushmore hurried to his bedside and whispered. "I can bring you something to help you, a sedative."

"I'm fine, ma'am." He barely opened his eyes.

She reached deep into her starched white uniform, pulled out two packages of M&Ms, and placed them in his hands. "Take these one at a time and let them dissolve in your mouth. They are called M&M because they bring miracles of mercy."

"I don't know if I believe in miracles."

Nurse Rushmore whispered, "I've been a nurse long enough and have seen things that can't be explained. The human spirit is unfathomable."

Walt sighed, shutting his eyes, "Not mine."

"Don't let anyone see, and don't share. Let me know when you need more." She patted his shoulder and strode to the middle of the room. "Where was I?" She tapped her index finger on her eyebrow, and the men groaned. "I remember. This is off the record, and you didn't hear it from me. Our newest arrivals said they were in a fierce battle on a small island."

"Where?" yelled Joe.

"What's the name of the island?" Roy Rogers asked.

"No one will say, but I can tell you the battle was long and intense."

"Did we take the island?"

"We did."

"Not according to Tokyo Rose," Gunny muttered, "she says we haven't won a battle yet."

Joe's comic book flew across the room and smacked him in the head.

"That's a fine way to treat a USMC gunny," he muttered, putting the comic under his pillow. The others laughed.

"I believe our guys over Tokyo Rose any day. We took that island but didn't take many prisoners," Nurse Rushmore said.

"Those Orientals are tough. They'll fight to the bitter end," Roy Rogers said.

"It's an honor for them to die fighting. They lose face if they are captured or surrender," Mark added.

"All I know is, our guys feel pretty good about it. We are one island nearer to Japan, one island closer to the war's end. Now, I've got to make my rounds." Nurse Rushmore shook her finger in Gunny's direction, "Mind what I said about the radio."

As Lillian left, Heaven Ray entered.

"I thought you forgot about me," Mark smiled. "Walt said you cared enough to sit by my bed day and night when I was in a coma."

"Nobody could love your ugly mug that much," Joe yelled to Mark across the ward. "No offense, sir."

Ensign Mark Lawson IV grinned, "This one could. She's special."

"Mark!" Heaven Ray felt the heat rush to her cheeks. *Love? Who said anything about love?* She pushed away the thought and the emotion she saw on Mark's face. She forced a light-hearted laugh. "You must be feeling better. I see that irrepressible twinkle in your eye."

"The one eye I can open. The other still has stitches and hurts like heck."

"Oh, Mark." She bit her lip and thought about what the doctor said.

Mark gripped her hand. "I've been worried about you."

She looked away. "Sorry for my outburst last time; I'm usually more controlled."

"You can share anything with me. You know that."

"Thank you, Mark. But I'll break if I don't stay in command of myself."

"You know it's the Lord that's in control."

Heaven Ray gasped, "If I didn't know better, Mark, I would say you've seen the Light."

"Yes, yes, I have."

"You? The Casanova of Kodiak? The young officer without a serious bone in his body?"

He laughed and said, "That was the old me. Now, I want whatever God wants. That includes all of this." With the only limb not immobile, he indicated his various wounds.

Heaven Ray shook her head slowly, and doubt flooded her face. "I don't believe it."

"It's true, and you can blame your mother, Miss Ruth," his voice softened, and he almost choked, "and an Aleut named Anak."

"My friend Anak? From Kodiak? Unbelievable." Heaven Ray gasped, then checked her watch. "I want to hear everything, but I can't be late for my surgical shift. I'll be back as soon as I can."

As Heaven Ray left, Nurse Rushmore came and took temperatures, checked blood pressure, and dispensed medications while flirting and teasing the men. Mark watched with gentle amusement. There was a time when he would have been the loudest and most flirtatious man in the room, even though Lillian Rushmore was well past dating age. He noticed the tired lines around the nurse's eyes and the fatigue on her face. When she put the thermometer in his mouth, he prayed for her. When she took his blood pressure, he asked how she felt. When she gave him the pain medication, he thanked her for everything. His voice broke, and he whispered, "I will pray for you daily."

She nodded, and her face softened, "Thank you, Ensign. It's hard to be continually upbeat in front of the men. Sometimes, I pretend."

Mark's trademark grin appeared as he said, "You're doing a good job. I don't think these guys realize how tired you are. Take care of yourself."

She lifted his wrist and took his pulse. "I must say you are sensitive and caring, Ensign Lawson. It's refreshing."

"I didn't used to be. When you have time, come and visit, and I'll tell you what, or rather who has changed me."

She laughed and exclaimed, "When I have time? That won't happen until the war's over!"

"Hey, you two, stop whispering," Joe looked their way, "Let the rest of us in on the conversation."

"All the nurses stopped by your bedside every day. Why do you get all the attention?" Roy Rogers asked.

"Don't blame me. I was in a coma," Mark laughed.

"Doesn't matter, sir," Walt said.

"Aww, Lawson's got the bead on every nurse in the place," Gunny complained, "And he's not even a Marine."

"He probably gets extra meds for the pain," Roy Rogers sighed.

"Even the old and chubby nurses favor the ensign."

Mark didn't know which one of the guys said that, but his face reddened, and he hoped the nurse hadn't heard. Lillian chuckled, turned, and shook her finger at them. "You could learn a lot from Ensign Lawson. And Roy, I asked the doctor to prescribe stronger pain meds for you."

"Thanks. It's the pain that's making me..."

"As cranky as Gunny?" yelled Joe.

"As mean?" Walt asked, his eyes wide in his young freckled face.

"Aw, Gunny's always been bad-tempered," Roy Rogers winced and tried to laugh despite the pain. "I'm as pleasant as the day is long."

"I think it's a rule that every gunny must be cantankerous." Nurse Rushmore said, "And Roy Rogers, you are a nice boy. I'll get the doctor to hurry up with those meds."

Joe yelled, "Giddy up, nice boy." The others made horse noises.

"Behave yourselves! I'll see if I can confiscate some ice cream. I happen to know several cartons were delivered this morning. And I have a jar of Hershey's chocolate syrup stashed in my quarters."

Joe yelled, "The real thing? Not that powdered stuff?"

"The real thing, honey," Nurse Rushmore said.

"I love you, Nurse Rushmore." He reached for another Superman comic from the pile under his pillow.

She laughed again. "Two scoops for you, my boy."

The men whooped and hollered. She winked at Mark, then turned again to the ward, "And, if you continue to behave yourselves, I will add whipped cream and macadamia nuts."

"What kind of nut is that?" Gunny asked.

"My new favorite. Trust me, you'll love them," the chubby but cute middle-aged nurse laughed again.

"Not as much as we love you," Roy Rogers shouted as she left.

Mark leaned back on his pillows and gazed around the ward. How precious all these young men were. And how surprised he was that he cared. *You continually amaze me, Lord. I hardly recognize myself.*

"Tell us more, Ensign Lawson," Roy Rogers begged.

"The whole story," Joe ordered.

"I want details about what you did on that uninhabited island," Gunny said, "Tactical details."

"I don't get how you survived," Walt muttered.

"It was that Injun that done it. They know how to live in the wild," Joe yelled with a smirk.

Mark sat up and spoke sternly, "He was an Alaska Native, an

Aleut, and I owe him my life."

"Why did the Navy jerk him out of Alaska and throw him into a jungle island in the middle of the Pacific," Gunny said, "That's the part that doesn't make sense."

"Shut up and listen," Joe shouted.

"Didn't your mama ever tell you to pipe down? You are so loud." Roy Rogers frowned at Joe.

"Loud? If you want loud, listen to my ma. She's Italian!" Joe yelled, "And from New Jersey!"

"That's a lethal combination," Gunny laughed.

When the laughter subsided, Mark said, "I've repeated my story several times. Surely you don't want to hear it again?"

"Start with the dragons and monsters that nearly took you out," Roy Rogers shuddered.

"Yeah, that was weird," Walt said.

"I'm not sure I believe that part," Joe hollered.

"Everything I've told you is true, but it was snakes," Mark said quietly.

"Snakes that turned into dragons," Walt shuddered.

"Tell us again," Roy Rogers settled back and closed his eyes. "Anything to distract me from the pain," he murmured.

Mark gathered his thoughts. "There are still some things I can't recall, but every day my memory improves. This is what I remember."

CHAPTER TWENTY-FOUR
Somewhere over the Solomon Islands

The roar of the airplane's propellers precluded their ability to communicate. The other code-talkers had been deployed to their designated coordinates.

The co-pilot left his seat and motioned to Mark and Anak to prepare to jump at his signal. A high mountain with sheer cliffs covered most of the atoll below. The pilot circled and approached from the south.

Mark and Anak eyed each other after scanning the small sandy beach. If they landed in deep water—broken bones, concussion, shock, and possible death awaited them. The thick jungle was equally dangerous. They must hit their target—that tiny strip of sand.

The co-pilot tapped the Aleut on the shoulder. Anak smiled, made the sign of the cross on Mark's forehead, and leaped out of the airplane. Before Mark jumped, he was handed a packet of letters. "Mail came right before we took off, sir. Nothing for the Native, though."

Mark stuffed the letters inside his jacket, nodded his thanks, and leaped into the blue. *I'm not sure you're there, God, and even if you are, you don't owe me any favors, but please don't leave Anak alone on this island.*

Anak landed on the beach and fell to his knees as he felt something snap. For a moment, there was no feeling from the bulge he saw in his lower leg. Then he screamed. He bit his lip as he noticed the wind shifting and saw Mark drifting toward the water. The pain briefly blinded him, and he lost sight of Mark.

Mark grabbed a riser and pulled, hoping to turn the chute's direction. It wasn't going to be enough. He drifted farther out to sea. Sweat blurred his vision. Mark saw the devout Native on his knees. *I know he's praying, God. Please listen to him.* Mark sensed he was falling faster and shuddered, fearing the worst. At the last moment, a strong gust blew him away from the water and toward the jungle. He grabbed the opposite riser and pulled with all his strength.

"Good landing," Anak tried to smile through the pain.

"Almost in the water, which would have been disastrous, and then nearly crashing into the trees, which wouldn't have been any better. I wouldn't say that was good."

"God put you in between. He is good." Anak grimaced.

"I saw you fall to your knees, and I knew you were praying for me," Mark said as he crouched beside Anak.

Anak shifted and showed Mark his injured leg.

"It's busted! Either your God is not good, or you forgot to pray for yourself."

The stoic Marine clamped his jaws together as he tried to stand, but a small moan escaped, and he collapsed on the sand. He motioned to the mountainous center of the island. Mark pulled a map from his pack. "According to recon, there are caves on that mountain overlooking the Slot, and that's where we need to be. How to get you there is the problem. I saw our equipment's parachute tangle in the brush about half a mile north. I hope the radio didn't land in the creek."

"I am sorry, Ensign Lawson."

"For what? Your lousy landing? Don't be stupid. How did you make it through jump school, anyway?"

When Anak didn't answer, Mark frowned, "They didn't send you to jump school, did they?"

"It is of no consequence."

"The consequence is your broken leg. I'll drag you into those trees and retrieve our equipment after I set your leg. There should be splints in the medical kit." Mark settled Anak at the base of a tree. The island's dense canopy concealed him from any enemy planes. "I'm leaving you both canteens and my morphine syrette. Don't be afraid to use it."

When he returned, Mark gave Anak more morphine. "We'll camp here tonight. The light is fading fast. Tomorrow, I'll climb that mountain and find a suitable cave."

"You will have to drag me."

Mark unpacked the radio. "Radio Lieutenant Phillips and let him know we landed safely. No need for him to be concerned about your little mishap. I'll open the C-rations."

Mark took the machete and hacked a trail through the dense underbrush. After finding a cave, he made several trips slogging up the mountain with the remainder of the equipment.

"Rest," Anak said.

"I'll rest when we're settled in the cave," Mark said, lifting the canteen to his lips. "The light is fading, and I'm afraid we'll have to camp here one more night."

The following morning, Mark laid his parachute on the ground and settled Anak on it. "Riding with the blankets underneath should shield you from some of the bumps."

Anak pushed away from the tree and crawled to the makeshift travois. "The air is heavy. It sears my lungs."

Mark wiped the sweat from his face and neck. "It is hot and humid."

"The air on my island is without weight. It is not burdened with trees. The wind smells of the sea, not rotting vegetation."

Mark sniffed, "I smell damp ferns and sweet flowers."

"This place burdens me, but I'm a Marine and will overcome."

"Once we settle in our cave, you will quickly heal."

The primitive trail was rougher than Mark anticipated, and the Native was heavier than he looked. Pulling him up the mountain was more intense than either man expected. Anak lost consciousness after the first mile, which was fortunate for him but not for Mark. The Aleut seemed much heavier, and Mark stopped often to wipe his sweaty face. He emptied both canteens before reaching the cave.

The mouth of the cave was small and partially hidden by a sizable boulder. Mark fixed a pallet for the still unconscious man near the entrance and refilled the canteen at a nearby stream. He wanted the Aleut to see the ocean when he awoke and not feel any kind of claustrophobia. Radio reception was also stronger near the cave's entrance.

The mid-sized cave had enough room for a sleeping area and all their equipment. Mark set up the primus stove and piled their foodstuffs nearby. He arranged his sleeping area at the rear of the cave. Once he had everything in place, Mark laid the packet of letters on his sleeping bag. "Home, sweet home," he said.

Anak awoke several hours later, thirsty and hungry. He volunteered for the evening shift, scanning the seas under the bright stars. The moon graced the water with its shimmering light. Anak hummed and sang.

"What is that?" Mark asked.

"Whale song," Anak continued to sing quietly.

Mark sat on his cot and reread the letters using his military flashlight. Much to his disgust, he fell asleep, still clutching a letter. The day's activities, plus the extreme heat and humidity, had exhausted him.

Anak crawled the short distance to Mark and shook him awake just after sunrise. He handed him a tin mug of coffee and reported that everything was quiet.

"Looks like you only spilled half of it. Even so, thanks." Mark gulped it down, gathered the scattered letters, and settled in the mouth of the cave. He scanned the waters of Georgia Sound. The sun glistened off the water as far as the horizon. He squinted against the brightness and cursed the nasty flies and the humidity. He swatted at a tropical flying insect buzzing around his head. He picked up an envelope and used it to fan the insect away.

He separated the letters according to who had written them. He could almost recite them but knew he would read them over and over. Nearly of their own volition, his fingers pulled the letter from Haven Ray from its envelope. The fate of the Aleuts sat heavy on his heart, and he was sure Anak would want to know the news. How much should he share?

Dear Mark

By now, I am sure you are on your way to your assignment. Please know I pray for you daily as I do for Heaven Ray. She has finished officer's training and is on her way to Pearl Harbor. I don't know where her permanent deployment will be. She said it will be somewhere in the South Pacific.

When I have her address, I will pass it on as you requested. When you write to her, please be vague about the details of the Aleutian evacuations. It will break her heart, and since there is nothing she can do, I'd rather she not be distracted.

I'm sure Miss Ruth will write you all about her work at the camps although she can do little. Heartbreaking.

I've been busy here in Kodiak. Angel is still with me. I couldn't bear to send her to the boarding school in Anchorage; to tell the truth, she was not ready. I've been teaching her to read and write. She's very bright and enjoys learning. She clings to me and is timid around others. Perhaps cautious is a better word. Poor little thing. I am determined to find a way to keep her as my own. She has no family that she knows of, and I believe I am morally bound to search for them. In my heart, she is already mine.

You would not believe the progress on the base. Your father has pushed the construction, and everything is ship-shape and on a proper war footing. It makes us all feel safe.

Take care of yourself, dear boy.

Haven Ray Turner

Mark opened the next letter. The old-fashioned Spencerian script was tiny, and the words were closely spaced. He chuckled. Miss Ruth was determined to cover every inch of the single sheet with as many words as possible. She had obviously used an old-fashioned fountain pen, and at some point, moisture had created several splotches obscuring the words. He had to guess what she had written. He tilted the paper toward the sun and held it close.

Dear Mark,

It's been three weeks since you and Haven Ray sailed away from this wretched encampment. Of course, it may be months before this letter reaches you.

The longer I am here, the more frustrated I become. In the old days, before all these government regulations, things were easier. Actually, that's not true. There were just as many regulations back in the day. I was younger, had more of my wits about me, and could circumvent some of those rules to do what was right. This situation is so convoluted, and few seem to care.

Two federal agents from the Bureau of Indian Affairs have resigned over the conditions here or, rather, their inability to change things. I am as frustrated as they are and wish I could stay longer. I have responsibilities back in Sitka that I can no longer ignore.

I am so grateful to your father. I am sure you know how he and Yeoman Richardson have helped us financially. They have helped in ways I dare not mention—rules and regulations, you know. He is an honorable man. I respect him greatly. You have the same depth of character.

Mark raised his eyes to the cloudless blue sky. He had no idea what his father and Elly had done. His mother would know. He'd read her letter next and see if she mentioned anything.

> *... I grieve at the grave injustice of this situation, and I pray for each one sequestered here. These people are precious in Bozhe's eyes. They are resilient and will survive. Even as their culture suffers, I am sure they will adjust and adapt. I also pray that someday justice will be done and this wrong will be righted.*
>
> *Praying Psalm 91 over you, my dear boy. Even though you have not yet realized it, you are one of God's chosen children.*
>
> *Sincerely,*
>
> *Miss Ruth*

Mark found another letter from Miss Ruth and tore open the envelope, hoping for better news.

> *My Dear Boy,*
>
> *I'm back in Sitka, but my heart is still with the Aleuts. I realize how unreliable the military postal service is; all the information may be old news by the time it reaches you. Please know that my prayers are with you.*
>
> *I have increased my efforts to collect food, clothing, and bedding for those in the camps. With strict rationing and limited resources, everyone concentrates on himself. I can't blame them for being concerned about their families. There is usually nothing left to share with others. People are also anxious about their loved ones overseas; it consumes them, and they have little energy or compassion left, especially for a group of Native villagers. The local churches also focus on their own congregations.*
>
> *I admit I am saddened that I have been unable to stir up any*

sympathy for those relocated. Many say I'm an addled old woman making up stories.

As we suspected, the Aleuts at Funter Bay are not faring well. Many of them have slipped into Juneau, where they can find work. That's a good thing. The bad thing is instead of taking care of their families, some spend their wages on alcohol, which is easy to come by. I think they want to numb themselves to the strange and miserable world they have been forced to live in. Others have become active in the Alaska Native Brotherhood, and I encourage them whenever possible. Several of the young men have joined the military as a way of escape.

Nevertheless, I do what I can, which isn't much. I have never been so angry or heartbroken. Only God knows what the future holds for these poor people.

Take care, dear boy. I hope to have more news, better news, in my next letter.

Miss Ruth

Mark searched through the packet. Unfortunately, there were no other letters from Miss Ruth. He wiped the sweat from his face, took a long drink of water, and scanned the horizon. No sign of any Japanese ships.

Dear Marky,

I know you think you've outgrown that silly childhood nickname, but mothers are afforded some rights, and that's one of them. I'll probably call you Marky until the day I die.

It isn't easy not to know where you are, what you are doing, and if you are safe. Yesterday, the mailbox held a letter from your brother. I do wish he wrote more often. He said to send along his greetings and to tell you the Hornet is the best ship in the fleet, and maybe one day, when you are all grown up, you can be on a ship too. I almost didn't include that part, but I know how you boys kid around. I'm sure you'll have a snappy comeback for me to pass along.

Your father could not secure a leave and join me for Christmas, but I was not alone. That girl from Kodiak who ignored you and made you a little crazy spent the holiday with me. She was just as lovely as you said. I didn't find her at all reserved or standoff-ish, as you claimed. She fit right in, especially at the soup kitch-en. Oh, and she's having her mother see that a pair of authentic Alaskan mukluks are custom-made for me. No more cold feet for this mama.

I'll write more tomorrow and pray that my letters reach you sooner rather than later, but I suspect they won't. However, the Lord will deliver all my prayers when they are needed.

Love,

Mom

Mark's face softened, and he smiled as he thought of Heaven Ray in his parents' Newport home. How he wished he could have been there. He folded the letter carefully and placed it with the others under his pillow. He knew he would read them every day, probably more often. He swallowed the lump in his throat, wiped the moisture from his eyes, and put all thoughts of family and friends aside. He had a mission that needed his full attention.

After several weeks of tinned beef and C-rations, Anak said, "I brought hooks, lines, and lures."

"We have to stay hidden."

"I cannot yet walk well. You must fish." Anak held the fishing gear toward Mark, who refused to take it.

"It's not a good idea."

"Ensign Lawson. You will fish on moonless nights. We will eat well."

Mark laughed, "Who has the highest rank here?"

"I'm a Marine."

Mark laughed again, "You Marines think you outrank everyone."

"Ooh-Rah," Anak answered with a gleam in his eye.

"On this mission, I consider us equals, rank not-withstanding. You translate our reports into your Native language and encode them. I keep the radio in working order. We both watch for the enemy and nobody fishes."

"You fish. I cook."

That night and many nights thereafter, Mark fished in several of the island's streams. They settled into a routine, taking turns watching the ocean for signs of Japanese vessels. Even if the enemy was in the range of transmissions, they wouldn't recognize the language, much less how it was encoded.

The two men were grateful for the nearby creeks and streams. It was almost impossible to stay hydrated with the onslaught of the hot weather. Heat and humidity drew moisture from their bodies and often weakened Anak. Mark did not tell him about the approaching monsoon season.

"Freezing rain," he said as he lay on his mat almost naked. "I miss the cold wind."

"Speaking of home, didn't you once say you were from Kodiak?"

Anak nodded.

"I met a girl there."

Anak did not respond.

"A lovely girl. Maybe you knew her."

The Native remained silent.

"Her name's Heaven Ray."

Mark saw the barest flicker in Anak's eyes. "You do know her. Tell me about her."

"What?"

"Tell me what she is like. She barely talked to me. I couldn't get her to open up."

"She speaks when she has something to say."

"Like you, huh?" Mark said.

Again, Anak nodded. Mark couldn't hide his frustration. "Come on, man. Tell me something. What does she want out of life?"

"She struggles."

"What does that mean?" Mark ran his hand through his hair and frowned.

Anak sat up and leaned against the entrance of the cave. He looked over the placid ocean. "She is a seeker."

"But what is she seeking?"

"She is unaware."

"Huh?" Mark ran his hand through his hair. "I don't get it."

"She seeks the man of the Book." Anak glanced at his Bible.

Mark turned away from the conversation and poured a canteen of water over Anak's sweating body. "I feel for you, man. As soon as the sun goes down. I'll help you to the creek; you can immerse yourself in it."

"Good."

Anak eventually tolerated the weather but was happier when it rained, although the muggy aftermath drained him. Once a week, they checked in briefly but otherwise maintained radio silence.

Mark became restless and complained, "Once again, the war is passing me by. I'll never do anything to make my father proud."

"Be content."

"Trapped in a cave on the side of a mountain," Mark exploded.

"We are watchers."

Mark paced the cave. "I'm sick of fish and tinned meat. I want a steak." He picked up his binoculars, stood at the cave's entrance, and mumbled, "I wish something would happen."

"You are bored."

"I'm a military man, far away from the action."

Anak pulled out his Bible. "I will tell you a story about a great warrior and his battles."

Mark eyed the Bible warily. "I told you no religious talk."

"I will read."

Mark had no idea about the battles narrated in the Bible. Soon, he and Anak discussed the tactics and strategies used by Joshua, Gideon, David, and others. After many weeks and stories, the talk turned to the world's battle between good and evil, right and wrong. The present forces aligned with goodness, and those with evil seemed reminiscent of the biblical narrative.

Mark thought of his talks with Heaven Ray's mother and Miss Ruth. He reread all the letters he had brought with him. They were several months old, and he longed to have fresh news from everyone. He also wondered how long they would be left in this lonely lookout post. Undoubtedly, the threat had moved on.

"I'm going for a run, Anak."

"Too dangerous. The sun is high."

"I can't settle. I'll be careful. We've been here for months and sighted nothing."

"It's not a good idea, Ensign Lawson."

Mark sighed and slung a canteen over his shoulder. Anak always addressed him by rank when he disagreed. "I won't be long."

Mark clambered up and down the atoll's mountainous cliffs, trying to wear himself out. He couldn't outrun his thoughts. *Anak insisted the Bible was true. And the other things they talked about, man's rebellion against God and the consequences of that—were they also true? Anak believed everything was made right by trusting Jesus. How could that be? None of it made sense.* Mark stumbled and slid down an embankment. *Anak, you're giving me a headache."* He laughed out loud as he pulled himself together and climbed up the steep hillside to the hidden cave.

"I'm back safe and sound."

"Do not do this again."

"I'm going to hike every day. It clears my head and keeps me in shape."

Anak turned away and mumbled, "Stupid Navy. You need Marine discipline."

Mark fell back against the pillows. "That's all for today, fellows, I'm tired."

"Please, Ensign Lawson. What happened next?"

"Mail call." An orderly pushed a squeaky cart into the room. He called out names and delivered the envelopes to the appropriate man. Several times, there was no answer, and a pall fell over the room. The orderly cursed, "Why don't they check the casualty lists before they give me the mail?"

Joe ripped open the envelope from his mom. "I don't believe it! It can't be true."

"What's the news, Joe?" Roy Rogers looked over his newspaper.

"Did something happen to your family?" Walt asked.

"Baseball! They've ruined baseball. What are we fighting for if not baseball?" Joe had tears in his eyes as he read a portion of his mother's letter, "...and so dear boy, since all you men are scattered across the world keeping us safe, America's women have formed a league of their own. My favorite team is the Racine Belles, but the Rockford Peaches are pretty good too." Joe crumpled the letter in his fist and moaned, "Belles and Peaches! How can you play baseball with bells and peaches?"

"Women in baseball!" Gunny groaned, "What is the world coming to?"

The conversation looked like it would continue for hours. Mark ignored it and read his letters. A long one from Elly with a note from the commander. Three from his mother, two from Haven Ray Turner, and one from Miss Ruth. He raced through them and reread them slowly, savoring each word. He set the ones from Mrs. Turner and Miss Ruth aside. He'd share them with Heaven Ray.

"Ensign Lawson, after supper, can you tell us more about your time on the island?" Joe yelled over the top of his comic book.

"I wish I had spent the war on a deserted island instead of in the middle of a fierce sea battle," Walter bit his bottom lip, but the words slipped out.

Mark almost felt guilty for the peaceful yet tense and tedious days on the island. "Sorry, Walt."

"I'm not a coward, Ensign Lawson. Really, I'm not." His eyes scanned the room.

"Of course not." Joe yelled, "You're the bravest freckle-faced red-headed farm boy ever sent to sea from the state of Georgia." The others agreed and gave Walt a soft round of applause.

"I heard there's a John Wayne movie in the cafeteria tonight. They'll push the tables back after dinner and fill the room with wheelchairs. The nurses can roll our beds in if we can't get into a wheelchair," Gunny said.

"Aw, they've been showing that cowboy flick for two weeks. I want to know how the ensign was strafed but still got off the island," Roy Rogers said.

"I want to know about the dragons," Walt said.

"Snakes," Joe yelled, "Those dragons are pure fiction."

Mark laughed, "Okay, boys. I'll continue my saga right after dinner."

Heaven Ray entered the ward just as Mark promised to continue his story. She had asked him several times to tell her about his experiences, and he reluctantly gave her a sparse outline of events. Whenever she pressed him for more, he turned his head away. The camaraderie in the ward made it easy for the men to laugh, joke, and share their stories, no matter how tragic. It helped them cope. She longed to be part of their inner circle.

Lillian had confiscated more of the longed-for ice cream. Heaven Ray helped her serve sundaes that evening and took the empty dishes to the cafeteria. Lillian waved goodbye to the ward and said, "I'll think about you boys while I'm swimming in the Pacific."

Heaven Ray brought one of the metal folding chairs from the cafeteria, quietly placed it outside the ward door where she could not be seen, made herself comfortable, and ignored the inquiring looks of orderlies and nurses as they hurried through the hallways. She put a finger to her lips whenever anyone looked like they were about to speak. She leaned toward the open doorway and heard...

"Tell us about the dragons, sir."

"I told you there ain't no dragons," Joe yelled and slammed his fist on the metal rail of his bed.

"Actually, on a few islands, they have a creature called a Komodo dragon. I read about it once in National Geographic." Roy Rogers put his newspaper down. "Were you on one of those islands?"

"I was on a small atoll, but the lizards I saw were big enough to make my skin crawl. They looked dragonish. Anak hated the snakes. He said there were no snakes in Alaska."

"What about the bugs, sir."

"Some of them had jaws like a pit bull. Adak said the bugs had nothing on Alaska's mosquitos."

Walt shuddered and tried not to listen to the ensign's story. The gruesome images of giant lizards, menacing snakes, and monster mosquitoes filled his mind.

"I don't know if I had a dream or some kind of vision, but I saw myself on an island surrounded by small children, brown children."

"What island?" Roy Rogers asked.

"Nothing like the islands around here. It was cold, dark, and barren. The wind howled, and a large snake slithered toward the kids. I spread my arms and saw they had turned into wings. I gathered the children and hid them under my feathers."

"A nightmare, just a nightmare," Walt whispered to himself, "God, don't let me have a nightmare tonight."

"The snake hissed to his friends, and we were surrounded. I panicked and tried to fly away. I couldn't get off the ground with all the kids clinging to me."

"Just a stupid dream." Roy Rogers, the youngest Marine in the ward, opened his newspaper and buried his face in it.

"Then what happened? Did you wake up?"

Mark answered, "It was the middle of the day. That's why I think it was a vision, especially after I talked to Anak."

"What did he say?" Gunny asked.

"I saw a huge book fall out of the sky. The snake had turned into a dragon and directed a fiery blast of his hot breath toward the book. It refused to burn. I grabbed the book and held it to my heart."

"What does it all mean, sir?" Walt asked despite wishing he was somewhere else.

Mark shook his head, smoothed the sheet, and rested his hand on it. "Here I was on this lush tropical island surrounded by gruesome things. I didn't need dangerous creatures swirling around in my imagination."

"What did the Indian say, some kind of medicine man mumbo-jumbo?" Joe asked.

Mark ignored the ignorant comment as he remembered his conversation with the Aleut, who had become his friend.

Anak hunched over the tiny Primus stove and boiled water for coffee. "The vision is your future."

"That's ridiculous," Mark said.

Anak poured the coffee into two tin cups and handed one to Mark. "I will speak if you listen."

"Sorry, Anak. Go on."

"The island is north, maybe the Pribilofs. The children are of my race. The book is holy, and the snakes and dragon are everything evil." The Native stared into the hot brown liquid. "You are blessed to have such a vision."

Mark scratched his head. "I don't understand."

"It is your future."

Joe rolled up his comic book and slapped his fist with it. "Indians! They never tell it straight." He laughed loudly, "I guess what they say is true; they speak with forked tongues. Just like snakes."

"Shut up, Joe. Don't let your ignorance show." Roy Rogers rattled his newspaper.

"What did he mean—it's your future?" Gunny asked.

"I don't know. It makes my head hurt to think about it," Mark answered.

"I had a dream last night. I was at our local diner with my girl. But then the bombs started falling." Walt turned away and pulled the covers over his head.

Roy Rogers left his bed by the window and sat beside Walt, talking softly. The others were quiet, recalling their own nightmares.

The men in the ward were indeed brothers, with deep bonds of commitment and trust forged by their training and battlefield experiences. A steadfast tie made strong by the life and death circumstances they shared, an unbreakable loyalty to each other, an exclusive union that surpassed rank, family background, and individual differences. This bond was a healing balm to them.

The wind whistled through the palm trees, and the rain beat against the windows. Lightning flashes and booming thunder completed the tropical storm's symphony. No one slept.

"Ensign Lawson, tell us more."

Mark raised his bed and spoke softly. "Is everyone awake? I continued my hikes down the mountain, and one morning, it was so hot and humid, and the water looked so inviting."

"You didn't go swimming, did you?" Gunny asked. "Surely, you weren't that…" the word stupid hung in the air. No one had the guts to say it out loud.

"I did," Mark said. "Stupid. A Japanese plane, obviously a scout, spotted me. I ran for the brush as he lowered the nose of his aircraft and blasted. I couldn't outrun the strafing bullets. Once in the dense jungle, he circled twice but couldn't find me. There was blood everywhere, my blood. I felt bugs and lizards crawling over me. Monkeys shrieked, and I thought I was going to die. I had been hit multiple times, flesh wounds mostly. I lost a lot of blood. After several hours, Anak was worried. He found me and helped me back to the cave. I have little memory of that. Dizzy and weak from lack of blood, I guess. He dug a dozen bullets out of me. Between the several vials of Native medicine Anak had packed and the sulpha powder in our supplies, my wounds did not become infected. I began to heal, but it took longer than I wanted."

A new night shift nurse came in and shushed the men. Joe called after her. "You don't have to shush us like little boys. We're not twelve."

She laughed, "I'm not so sure."

"Go to sleep, Joe," Walt muttered, although he himself could not sleep. Heaven Ray found him quietly weeping when she checked on Mark shortly after midnight.

"Are you alright, Walt? Do you need something to help you sleep?"

Storm clouds splayed across the open window, and Heaven Ray moved to close it.

"Don't," Walt begged.

"But it's so gloomy—depressing."

"It's how I feel." Walt squirmed and turned his head away.

Heaven Ray stood next to his bed and squeezed his shoulder. "I have just the thing for that."

"No more medicine, please. I'm so groggy all the time."

Heaven Ray grinned, "Gloomy and groggy are never a good combination. What I have is not a drug." She pulled a small bag from her pocket and jiggled it. "Ever since I was a little girl, my mother gave these to me when I had a dark day. She told me they were little bits of sunshine."

Walt gave her a half-hearted smile, "Nurse Rushmore gave me something to remind me that there are miracles of mercy. Now you are giving me little bits of sunshine." He sniffed and wiped his sleeve across his nose, then sniffed again. "Do you believe in miracles? With a name like Heaven, you must."

"Try to get some sleep." She tucked the blankets around his shoulders and patted his cheek.

As she left, Walt whispered, "Pray for me, ma'am; I don't know how."

You're not the only one. Heaven Ray nodded at the pleading look in his eyes and stumbled out of the hospital, heart pounding, legs shaking, and temper raging. She almost fell down the steps and onto the wooden bench at the building's entrance. *I will pray for you, Walt, and all the men in the ward. Do you hear me, God? I'll pray for them.* She raised a fist toward the sky. *I'll pray for my father and everyone on the Lexington! I'll pray for everybody in this war and won't stop until You answer!*

Heaven Ray stood, sat down, and stood again. She felt as if she had nothing but tears inside, welling up and spilling over. Would she ever empty herself of these sobs? Grief and despair provoked a restlessness in her. She paced the sidewalk in front of the hospital, unaware of the starlit sky above. She mentally pleaded, begged, implored, and beseeched the God of the universe. *Why is there so much evil?*

TRUST ME.

I don't understand what's happening in the world.

TRUST ME.

When will the carnage end?

TRUST ME.

Will my father make it through alive?

TRUST ME.

What about Mark?

TRUST ME.

Deep in her soul, Heaven Ray knew she did not have the strength to continue to repair broken bodies only to have them return to battle. Last week, her hands shook so badly that she dropped the forceps, and the surgeon had her removed from the

236

operating room. His stern look and pitying glances from the others humiliated her. She raised her hands, they tremored, and her whole body shook. She took several deep breaths. The tears came again, and she sagged against the bench.

I give up.

GOOD.

I can't do this anymore!

I CAN.

Exhausted and empty, she closed her eyes. She felt the prayers of her mother, Miss Ruth, and the little church in Kodiak. She pictured all the letters she had received these past months, encouraging her to trust the Lord amid dangerous waters. She rested her folded arms on the back of the bench and lay her head on them.

I surrender.

She filled her lungs with the floral air. She let the warmth of the newly risen sun infuse her.

Lillian scrambled down the hospital stairs, crying, "Heaven Ray! Are you alright? You've been missing most of the night."

"I've been right here."

"Your eyes are swollen, and your face is streaked with tears. You look spent. What's wrong?"

"I'm drained."

"Fortunately, it was a quiet night. It's not like you to neglect your duties. What's going on?"

"I've been wrestling."

"Did you fall, hit your head? Shall I get a doctor?" Nurse Rushmore came closer, her eyes searching Heaven Ray's.

Heaven Ray chuckled and said, "As long as I don't limp when I stand, I'll be fine."

"Did you fall?"

Heaven Ray shook her head and said, "My hip might be broken." She stood and walked toward Lillian.

"You can walk okay. Your hip's not broken." Lillian shook her finger at the younger nurse. "Stop this crazy talk. It worries me."

"You know, like Jacob in the Bible. God won the wrestling match, and Jacob limped for the rest of his life."

Lillian frowned, "You're worn out; it's given you some kind of nervous breakdown."

Heaven Ray patted the older woman's shoulder, "I feel better than I have in a long time. Thank you for caring." As Heaven Ray headed into the building, she reached into her pocket and, instead of her handkerchief, found a package of M&Ms. *Hmmm, miracles of mercy. Thank you, Walt.*

Nurse Rushmore stared after her and muttered, "Wrestling with God, indeed. If there was a Deity, who would dare wrestle with Him?"

Several nurses and orderlies tumbled out of the hospital, laughing and chattering. As they passed Lillian, one of them said, "Grab your suit. It's time for a swim and breakfast on the beach."

Lillian shook her head. "Not this morning. I have a special project." Nurse Rushmore squared her shoulders and marched into the hospital, determined to keep an eye on Ensign Heaven Ray Turner.

Several mornings later, Lillian and Heaven Ray delivered breakfast trays to the men. She poked her head into the ward.

"Mark, Lieutenant Phillips is here to visit. He says he knows you." Heaven Ray stood just outside the ward next to the breakfast cart.

Before pushing past her, Lieutenant Phillips said, "Relax. Nurse Turner. I won't let the ensign know we spent the night together."

Her cheeks burned. She turned away before saying something she would regret. *I never should have sent him that overly friendly Christmas card. He obviously has the wrong idea.* After a step or two, she turned back and whispered, "Mark knows me, and he won't believe anything you say."

"Are you sure of that?"

"Tell him anything you like," Heaven Ray said through gritted teeth.

Lieutenant Phillips laughed and lay his hand on her arm, "Well, well, our innocent little nurse has become a bit scrappy. I like it."

"I'm sorry, Lieutenant Phillips. I've obviously given you the wrong idea."

"About us?"

"I never should have sent that Christmas card."

"I believe you meant every word, and I might have to make time for you."

"Excuse me, I must continue serving breakfast."

He grasped her arm more firmly and said, "And if I don't excuse you?"

"I have no time for you, Lieutenant Phillips." She kept her voice quiet lest Mark should overhear.

The lieutenant's lips tightened, and he increased the pressure of his grip until Heaven Ray winced.

"Is there a problem, Nurse Turner?" Lillian asked.

Lieutenant Phillips turned and smiled in her direction, "No, ma'am, Nurse Turner and I are reminiscing about old times, good times." He winked at Nurse Rushmore, who frowned in return. Lieutenant Phillips laughed, "Heaven Ray and I go way back."

"Not far enough." Heaven Ray jerked her arm away and wondered why she had considered the good-looking officer appealing. Why hadn't she noticed the calculating look in his eye and the edge to his charm?

Frowning, Mark saw them in the hallway but did not hear their exchange. The expression on Heaven Ray's face told him the conversation was not pleasant. He filed that look and would ask her about it as soon as he could.

"Good morning, Lieutenant Phillips," Mark said as the officer entered the room. He looked around him, hoping to see Heaven Ray.

"Relax, your little nurse friend is pushing breakfast trays around, although I can think of more pleasant activities for her to engage in, especially with me."

"She is an officer in the United States Navy. Have some respect," Mark mumbled the words. It wasn't exactly the way one spoke to a superior officer.

Lieutenant Phillips glared at the man in the bed. "I'll let that comment pass since you seem to be in a bad way, or perhaps you're territorial about our lovely young nurse."

Mark's face flamed. He struggled to raise his head from the pillow. Nurse Rushmore came to Mark's bedside and glared at the lieutenant. "State your business, Lieutenant."

"Lawson. I came to see when you can return to duty."

"I'm off to the States soon for rehabilitation." Mark kept his voice even.

"Can't it wait?"

"Not if I want to walk again."

"I'm sure you're exaggerating. We all have to make sacrifices in this war." Lieutenant Phillips's voice was cold, and his words clipped.

"Surely, there are others to take my place," Mark said.

"Of course. Don't think for one minute you're indispensable, but you seem to have an affinity for the northern Natives. The ones I have in the field are doing okay, according to their handlers. The ones at the Command Center are not."

"What do you mean?"

Lieutenant Phillips twirled his cover in his hands, looked around the ward, and sighed, "Lethargic, vacant, as if they're not there. They sit all day at their radios and refuse to speak."

"When they have something to say, they'll say it. Anak often sat staring at the ocean for endless hours. He was as still as a statue and did not speak, sometimes for days."

Lieutenant Phillips jingled the change in his pocket, shuffled his feet, and growled, "I find it highly disrespectful."

"I suppose they have ten or twelve-hour shifts at the radios, with few days off," Mark said.

"There is a war on."

"I've learned the Aleuts are tied to the land and sea. Take them away from that, and they are lost. Anak had difficulty adjusting, and he wasn't cooped up in an office."

"They're Marines and need to act like it."

"My only advice, sir, is to give them a canoe and let them be on the water. Anything to make them feel at home."

"I didn't ask for your advice, and they are not here on vacation."

"Sorry, sir."

Lieutenant Phillips glanced around the ward, frowned, and

placed his cover under his arm. "If you're not fit for duty, I have no use for you."

Mark clamped his jaws together and was sure his face wore the same expression Heaven Ray had a few minutes ago.

Heaven Ray served the breakfast while eyeing the two men. She could not hear their quiet conversation over the chatter in the ward. *I can't believe I was ever attracted to Lieutenant Gary Phillips. Ugh!*

"Hey, Lieutenant, tell us about the Ensign's rescue. He doesn't remember much," Joe yelled across the room.

"I don't have the time," The lieutenant snapped.

"Please, sir," Roy Rogers asked, laying his newspaper aside. "We know so little of what happens outside these walls. I'm beginning to miss the war."

Gunny saw Joe's angry red face, motioned him to remain quiet, and spoke to the lieutenant, "Sir, I bet you know more than anybody." The gunny smiled and added, "I can tell, sir, you know how to put two and two together. That's probably why they put you in charge of whatever this project is. It sounds important."

Mark remained silent as the gunny cajoled the lieutenant, who finally faced the ward. "The ensign had one job, to guard his asset. He failed."

Mark felt as if he had been punched in the stomach. He turned his face away. His failure to remain hidden on the island led to a series of events that resulted in Anak's death. Mark knew the Lord had forgiven him, but it would be a long time before he forgave himself. Joe objected to the lieutenant's comment, but Mark shook his head and said, "What the lieutenant said is correct."

Surprised, Lieutenant Phillips gave Mark a brief nod and continued, "I've read the reports. It was a stormy night, suitable for cover, but the sub couldn't get as close to the rendezvous point as they wanted. The Aleut—"

"His name was Anak," Mark said quietly.

"Yes—Anak piloted the rubber raft as dawn rapidly approached and the sub surfaced. Anak threw a line to one of its crew. A lone Japanese fighter swooped out of the sky with guns blasting, piercing the raft. The sub's crew returned fire from the machine guns mounted on the deck. Anak threw himself across Mark and took most of the fire as the raft began to sink." Lieutenant Phillips placed his cover firmly on his head and turned to go. "All of this because Ensign Lawson behaved recklessly on the island and was spotted by the enemy."

"What happened to Anak's body?" Mark asked.

Lieutenant Phillips muttered, "Unrecovered. I really don't have time for more."

"How do you like that," Walt muttered to the officer's back, "He doesn't have the time."

Roy Rogers picked up his newspaper and snarled, "Officers, bah."

Joe stuffed his fist in his mouth so he wouldn't yell his thoughts at the arrogant officer. He turned to the Gunny and said, "You sure worked that blasted officer. I don't think he intended to tell us anything."

Gunny laughed and said, "Don't you know it's the gunnys that run the Marines, just like the chiefs run the Navy. The officers would be lost without us. No offense, Ensign Lawson."

"None taken, Gunny. It's your job to make the officers look good and keep them from making too many mistakes."

"Some officers are beyond help," Joe yelled to the room. The others looked to Ensign Lawson.

Mark laughed, "You're right, Joe, but let's not mention any names."

The account of Mark's time on the island continued to intrigue the men, but none mentioned his stupidity or Anak's death. Mark, plagued by guilt and his fragmented memory, awoke from a disturbed sleep covered in sweat. He could almost feel the small Aleut's body covering his, protecting vital organs, almost feel the bullet damaging his face, injuring his eye. Trembling, he spent the rest of the night in prayer. Mark vowed he would visit Anak's family after the war. They needed to know what a fine, honorable man their son was.

"You look tired, Heaven Ray. Sit for a minute," Mark said.

"I just finished fifteen hours in surgery. I can hardly stand," she sank into the chair next to his bed.

"Then why are you here? You need to sleep."

"I just wanted to check on you and the others before I drag myself to my quarters."

"As I said, you look tired, but there is peace in your eyes that hasn't been there in a long time."

"I took some advice from my good friends, Daisy, Jacob, and Miss Ruth." Heave Ray smiled

"I know Miss Ruth, and I've heard you talk about Daisy, but who is Jacob?"

Heaven Ray chuckled, "You know him, and you like him." She told Mark about her moment of surrender.

Mark reached for Heaven'Ray's hand, "That makes me so happy, I've been praying."

"Thank you, Mark. The Lord is working."

"Maybe this isn't the time." Mark began, then turned his face away.

"What is it?" She took his hand, but it lay limp in hers. "What's wrong, Mark?"

Mark's eyes held the questions he would not ask. "I've been having thoughts I don't like."

"What kind of thoughts?" All sleep and weariness vanished, and Heaven Ray focused on Mark.

"Lieutenant Phillips."

"That man means nothing to me."

"That's not what he says."

Heaven Ray sucked on her lower lip. *How can I admit to Mark that the lieutenant's devastatingly handsome good looks blinded me to his true character? How can I tell him I was attracted, even when it made me uncomfortable?*

"It seems like you two have some history, but it's none of my business," Mark spoke softly in the dimly lit ward. The others were quiet, and Mark assumed they were asleep. He wished he was as well.

"It's only none of your business if I mean nothing to you," Heaven Ray squeezed his hand and softened her face. "I do mean something to you, don't I, Mark?" she whispered.

"Talk louder; we can't hear you," Joe yelled.

"Shut up, Joe," Gunny growled. "Now nobody can sleep."

"Can't you see they are close to admitting how they feel?" Walt said, rubbing the sleep from his eyes. "Who wants to sleep?"

"Huh? What time is it?" Roy Rogers groped for the small alarm clock on the window sill. "Three o'clock in the morning!"

"Who's feeling what?" Joe yelled in Mark's direction.

Heaven Ray blushed, and Mark grinned at the men, "Give us some privacy, guys. This isn't easy."

"It is if you're Italian," Joe yelled.

"Semper Fi," Gunny added, "Go Navy!"

Heaven Ray pulled the curtain around the bed. "Were you going to say something, Mark?"

"I didn't like Phillips's attitude toward you. He insinuated things. Things that sounded—unlike you."

Heaven Ray looked at the hands she had folded in her lap. After a moment, she raised her eyes to Mark's. "When he helped Anak on the train to San Diego, I was grateful. He portrayed himself as an officer and a gentleman. On my way to Officer Training School, I met him again. He was sophisticated and urbane, unlike anyone I had ever met in my tiny town of Kodiak."

Mark winced and turned his head away. "And he swept you off your feet?"

"No, yes, maybe a little, at first. I finally saw him for what he was. He is nothing to me." Heaven Ray spoke softly but forcefully.

"Give her a break, Ensign Lawson," Roy Rogers called across the room.

"The woman has obviously come to her senses," Joe yelled.

Mark reached for her hand and gave it a tug. She sat on the edge of the bed. Mark frowned as he searched for words, "He irritates me. It's something under the surface that I can't quite define."

"Oh, Mark, let's forget about him and talk about us."

"That's right, Ensign Lawson, we want to know about you and Nurse Turner. The suspense is killing me," Joe yelled.

This time, Mark blushed. Heaven Ray pulled back the curtain

and spoke loud enough for the men to hear, "We're all waiting, Mark. Especially me."

Nurse Rushmore bustled into the room. "Nurse Turner, you're wanted in surgery, Code Blue."

Mark sighed, the men groaned, and Ensign Turner rushed out of the room.

CHAPTER TWENTY-FIVE

"Thank you, doctor, for everything you've done."

"Not as much as I wanted, but the Navy has a fine rehabilitation center in Southern California. You will learn, well, everything you need to."

"A few days ago, some of the guys helped me try to walk. It didn't go well. My legs crumpled."

"You shouldn't have tried anything without my permission."

"It was stupid," Mark shifted in the bed, trying to get comfortable.

"The medical personnel at the convalescent hospital know what they're doing. And I hope the surgeon there can remove more shrapnel from your thigh."

"I hope so, too." Mark grimaced, "Every time I move my legs, it pains me. But I will walk and learn to live with one eye."

"I believe you." They shook hands, and the doctor continued his rounds.

"Are you leaving us?" Roy Rogers looked over his newspaper and met Mark's eyes.

"The paperwork is done, and I'll be on the next ship sailing Stateside."

The men wished him well, and Nurse Rushmore declared they must have a going away party as soon as she could locate some ice cream.

"Better add some cake to that," Joe yelled, "I've been declared fit for duty and will soon return to sea."

Congratulations were thrown at Joe by everyone except Walt, who turned his head into his pillow.

"Ooh Rah," Gunny said and saluted Joe.

Roy Rogers cautioned, "You better keep your voice down while on sea duty, or the enemy will take bearings on your location."

Nurse Rushmore approached the young farm boy. "Walt?"

"Yes, Mom."

"You mean, ma'am."

"Sorry, Nurse Rushmore. I meant mom, if that's all right with you." He lifted sad eyes to her, "My mother died giving birth to me, and I never had anyone mother me before."

She blinked away the moisture in her eyes, reached for another package of M&Ms, and slipped it into Walt's hand. "Some of the men in the other wards call me Mama Lil. You can, too. I think of you all as my boys."

"Thanks, Mama Lil."

She leaned over and kissed his cheek, "That doesn't sound right. You are very special to me, Walt. Call me Mom."

He smiled his thanks and, for once, drifted into a peaceful sleep.

Nurse Rushmore looked at the other men, all staring at her. "No one will give Walt a hard time, understand?"

They looked at Walt and then at each other. The silence became awkward. Joe cleared his throat and said, "Thanks, Mama Lil, we didn't know how to help him."

The others nodded their agreement, and then Roy Rogers said, "Why, Joe, your voice isn't nearly as obnoxious when you speak quietly."

Mark whispered to the nurse, "That was a beautiful thing you did for Walt."

She approached Mark's bed, "It's not exactly protocol. This is a military hospital."

"The men will never tell, and if the Brass hears about our fine Mama Lil, I think they'll pretend they didn't. I'd be more worried about the ice cream you, em, confiscate and all the special treats you give us."

Mama Lil patted her ample stomach. "I'm a firm believer that food makes you feel better, and so does the base commander. I've heard he buys all those extra sweets on the sly and stores them in the hospital kitchen just so we can confiscate them."

"What a great guy. Give him my regards," Joe yelled.

"You hush, Joe, nobody is supposed to know about that."

"Mama Lil," Mark said with a wink, "Can you get me several boxes of chocolate, the good stuff?"

Her eyes twinkled, and she put her hands on her hips. "Now, why would you need several."

Mark looked at the others in the ward. Everyone seemed to be interested in his conversation. Nevertheless, he nodded toward the chair. She scooted it close to the bed and sat.

"I need to discover how a certain nurse feels about me," he whispered.

"That certain nurse is crazy about you; everybody can see it."

"I need to be sure. The chocolate will tell me."

"How so?"

"Back in Alaska, I must have given her a hundred boxes of chocolates."

Mama Lil laughed, "If you did, she'd be as plump as me."

"Oh, she never ate any."

"What?"

"She didn't really like me."

"That's hard to believe. Surely, you can see she cares. Just tell her how you feel."

Mark averted his eyes and sighed, "I can't seem to get the words out. I'm not the same guy I was back in Alaska. I was shallow." He swallowed the lump in his throat and forced himself to look Nurse Rushmore in the eye. "I was all about living it up, having fun. I've changed, but I'm not sure Heaven Ray believes that. I don't know how deep her feelings are."

"Poor boy. You look miserable, lovesick."

"Don't tell the guys," Mark pleaded.

"As if they don't already know," she winked. "I happen to know of a confectionary shop in Honolulu that makes macadamia and caramel chocolate truffles that are to die for."

She pulled the covers up to Mark's chin. "Now go to sleep. It's past your bedtime."

He laughed, "Yes, Mama Lil."

Several days later, Heaven Ray stopped by Mark's bedside. "Mark, You have to stop sending me chocolates. I've gained three pounds!"

"Holey Moley! It worked."

CHAPTER TWENTY-SIX

The men in the ward placed bets on nearly everything. The gambling increased once they saw the budding relationship between the ensign and the nurse. Who would be the first to declare their feelings? How would the other respond? Mama Lil ordered them to refrain from becoming involved. She swore there would be no more ice cream if she heard they badgered Mark or teased Heaven Ray. It drove them crazy, and Joe bit his lip several times until it bled.

"I tell you, Gunny, I have to do something. What if he leaves before he says anything? I'm about to explode."

"Easy, Joe. The guys will gang up on you if you cost them their ice cream."

"It might be worth it," Joe yelled.

"What are you yelling about now?" Mark asked.

"Aw, nuts!" Joe bit his lip again and stuck his head in his comic book.

"I'm going to miss you, Mark. More than you know."

He grinned and said, "If you tell me, I'll know and won't have to wonder."

"I'll write you every day."

He wiggled his fingers. "Now that the cast is off, I'll write daily as well."

She cupped his cheek with her hand. "I won't expect you to. Some days, your whole body will scream from the rehabilitation therapies they'll put you through. All you'll want to do is sleep to escape the pain."

"Why, Nurse Turner, how encouraging. You make me want to start as soon as possible."

She looked intently into his eyes. "I know what you're facing, Mark, and I want to be there to help and comfort you." Her voice shook, and she added, barely audible, "Love you."

Mark leaned closer and took her hand. "What was that last part? You spoke so softly I didn't hear."

"Comfort." Heaven Ray's face flamed. *Did I just tell Mark I love him?*

"Nurse Turner, look at me."

She slowly raised her eyes, focusing on his chin. *I can't look. What if he doesn't love me?*

"Look at me."

Heaven Ray forced herself to let all her love for this man show on her face and in her eyes.

"I love you too and have wanted to tell you for a long time."

"Why didn't you?"

"I wanted to wait until I knew the extent of my injuries."

"That doesn't matter."

"The doctor recently told me there's no guarantee I'll walk again, not to mention my vision problems. My career in the Navy is over. I can't ask you to join me in this long healing process."

"You don't have to ask. I'm offering. In fact, I'm insisting."

"I may never become the man I was."

"You'll be a better man, and we'll face the future together."

Mark turned his head and refused to look at her. She sighed, kissed his cheek, and said, "Lucky for you, I am due in surgery in two minutes." She faced the ward and raised her voice, "Boys, I need your help. I practically threw myself at the ensign, and he refused to propose."

Whistles and applause drowned out Mark's explanations.

"Don't worry, Nurse Turner, we'll talk sense into him," Joe yelled.

Roy Rogers sang, "Here Comes the Bride."

"Aw, nuts. I was going to propose to you myself," Gunny grinned.

"As if she'd have you," Joe yelled, "Everybody can see those two are crazy about each other." He threw his comic book at Mark. "Where's your sense of romance, Ensign Lawson? Propose to the woman! I've got ten bucks riding on this!"

"He needs some of your romantic Italian blood," Roy Rogers said, humming the wedding song.

The men in the ward showed no sign of calming down as they encouraged Mark. There was no way they would let this go. Mark tossed the comic book back in Joe's direction. It hit the side of the bed and slid to the floor.

"You win, Heaven. You don't play fair, but you win." Mark said.

She winked at him, went to the center of the ward, and said, "Mark said I won. Does that sound like a proposal?"

Gunny said, "It's time to send in the Marines." He started getting out of bed, but Heaven Ray held up her hand.

Joe yelled for Mark to act like an officer and a gentleman. Roy Rogers banged his spoon on his coffee cup, and Nurse Rushmore hurried into the ward to check on the ruckus.

Mark laughed and yelled louder than Joe ever had, "Heaven Ray Turner, will you marry me? After the war's over? After I'm completely well? After I've gone back to college and trained for a new career? After I've secured a good job?"

"No! It's now or never!" Heaven Ray smiled, but her tone was serious.

"I always wanted to be a bridesmaid," Gunny grinned.

"Dibs on best man," Joe yelled.

Roy Rogers left his bed, shuffled to the open window, and plucked a gardenia from the tree leaning against the hospital's wall. He stuck it behind his ear and said, "I guess I'll have to be the flower girl."

Walt watched the proceedings and thought about the weddings in his small farming community.

"Boys, you can plan the wedding while I'm in surgery," Heaven Ray kissed Mark on the lips, much to the delight of the men.

Walt sat up straighter and motioned for everyone to be quiet. "Nurse Turner, I propose..."

Joe yelled, "You propose? The ensign just proposed."

Walt's freckles popped as his face reddened. He waved his hands before his face and stuttered, "I mean, well, back home, I used to sing at the grange dances and the annual 4th of July picnic." He stopped, embarrassed. "I just thought—"

"Walt, that's a lovely idea." Heaven Ray smiled in his direction. "I'd love for you to sing at my wedding."

Nurse Rushmore clapped her hands. "We can have the wedding this weekend. I'm sure the hospital chaplain will be available."

Mark groaned while Nurse Rushmore told him, "You can have a big reception after the war with all your family, another after you graduate, and another when you get a job."

"Perfect." Heaven Ray blew kisses to each of them and hurried to the surgical wing.

Mark nestled into his pillows, frowning. After a few minutes, he relaxed, crossed his arms behind his head, and smiled. Apparently, he was a soon-to-be-married man. His mother would be sad she missed the wedding, but thrilled for him. The commander would be proud of his choice; he'd always had a soft spot for Heaven Ray. Mark motioned for Nurse Rushmore to come close.

"Mama Lil, I'm going to need a ring."

CHAPTER TWENTY-SEVEN

Dear Heaven Ray,

You got married without me! I hate you! I could never hate you, but how could you do this to me? Wait a minute while I catch my breath. I mustn't go off half-cocked.

As you can see, I haven't written you. One of my patients is from Los Angeles, and his parents come to visit often. His mother always brings cookies or banana bread; I help myself at her insistence. Just to be polite, you understand. Never mind. What I meant to say is it turns out the father has a small, somewhat unsuccessful recording studio and told me I could use it anytime I was in LA if I had a hankering to sing, you know, or to cut a record for the folks back home. As if! Fingernails on the blackboard and all that.

This is the result. Much better than pen and paper, don't you think? I know Nurse Rushmore has a record player. But enough about the logistics.

You! An old married lady! I can't believe it! And then your newly acquired husband is transferred to the rehab center soon after. So, no time for a honeymoon! He is settling in here, faithfully doing all his exercises and therapies. The man is motivated! We talk about you all the time.

He said the wedding was fine. You looked lovely, but typical man, he was short on the details! But you know me, I wouldn't let it go. It was like pulling teeth. All he could do was give me a sappy smile and say he had the most beautiful bride in the world. I kept at it like a dog with a bone. These are the details I pulled out of him.

He told me Joe was mad that he was returning to his ship before the ceremony. Time and tide wait for no man, they say. Poor Joe, I know how he feels.

Mark said Walt sang "Chatanooga Choo-Cho" and "Don't Sit Under the Apple Tree with Anyone Else but Me." Not your typical wedding songs, but I guess everyone applauded when he was done.

I gather Gunny, Walt, and Roy Rogers sang 'Happy Trails' when you and Mark kissed, and prior to that, all the nurses and doctors had run out of the room to deal with an emergency. I'm glad that happened after you said your vows.

I'm happy Lillian Rushmore stood up for you. She is an old sweetie. But I wish it had been me.

Are you going to put in for a transfer to the States? They say the war is winding down and shouldn't last much longer. In Europe, it's just mopping up.

Oh, it looks like my time is almost gone. I should have made a 33 and 1/3 LP instead of this 45. Never mind. Next time, I'll talk faster—as if that's possible.

In the meantime, please write and tell me all the lovely details. I constantly hum, 'Here Comes the Bride,' which annoys everyone. I guess my humming is as good as my singing.

Anyway, I love you and miss you.

Daisy Dunton

Dear Heaven Ray,

We just heard on the radio that the war is over! It's about time! You can't imagine the excitement. Of course, you can. I bet dollars to donuts; it's the same everywhere. Our boys will be coming home.

I guess it was that atom bomb that did the trick. They say all's well that ends well. How do they know? I suspect someday we'll say this didn't end well. The details are sketchy, but the newspapers say it was horrific. I guess we have to trust President Truman knows what's what. He's from Missouri, so how bad can he be? Never mind, he is a politician, after all.

How will we go back to our old lives? The war has changed us and changed the world we live in. They say you can't go home again. I wonder if that's true.

I'm sure you will resign from your commission soon and reunite with your husband. I can hardly wait. He's been talking about it nonstop. The man is obviously besotted.

He's also been having that weird dream again, although he says it's more than a dream. I'm glad my granny isn't here. She'd say it was a portent, a prophecy, or an omen—a real look into his future. I think it's indigestion, but what do I know?

I do know Mark is fixated on the children in his dream, little Alaskans that remind him of his friend Anak. I have a feeling he will find a way to live those dreams. And since you are from Alaska, it's a perfect match. A match made in heaven, as they say.

Anyway, come to us soon. We are waiting with bated breath. What is a bated breath anyway? Never mind.

Love you,

Daisy

Daisy Dunton left Mark sitting in the wheelchair at the end of the sidewalk. She dashed into the parking area before the vehicle had stopped moving. She yanked open the door and practically pulled Heaven Ray out.

"You're here! You're finally here!"

Heaven Ray embraced her friend while looking over her shoulder, "I missed you, too. What have you done with my husband?"

Daisy laughed, "I left him on the sidewalk." She saw Mark struggling to stand. "Mark Lawson, you sit down! You're still my patient!"

Heaven Ray ran to her husband. Daisy turned her back to give them a moment of privacy, then slowly approached them. She pulled an envelope out of her pocket and said, "Since I wasn't chosen as your maid of honor and couldn't spend a fortune on a fancy dress, and since I wasn't invited to the wedding and couldn't spend a fortune on plane tickets and an outrageous gift and since I love you both dearly. I mean, I love you as much as peanut butter loves jelly, as much as macaroni loves cheese, as much as hot dogs love mustard."

Mark elbowed Heaven Ray, "Notice how Daisy equates food with love."

"As I was saying, I love you both as much as, as much as..."

"Bacon loves eggs," Mark said.

"Smoked fish loves Pilot bread," Heaven Ray added.

"Huh?" the other two said.

"Never mind. It's an Alaska thing. We know you love us, Daisy. Please continue." Heaven Ray hugged her husband and then her friend.

"Everyone needs a honeymoon, and although I can see that you two honeys are over the moon, so to speak, we need to make it official. I've made a three-day reservation for the Bridal Suite at Hotel Coronado."

"Oh, Daisy, that's way too expensive!" Heaven Ray cried.

"It's done. No arguing."

"I thought about buying tickets to the zoo or the museum but decided against it."

Mark squeezed Heaven Ray's hand and said, "Good."

"But I did make arrangements for dinner to be delivered to your room the first night. A proper wedding feast."

"I can hardly wait," Mark said, "I'm so tired of hospital food. What are we having? Steak? Lobster? Salmon? Deep dish apple pie a la mode?"

Daisy Dunton put her hands on her hips. "Use your imagination, Mark. Nothing as ordinary as all that. You will hear a knock at the door when the clock strikes seven. Your mouth will begin to water. You will open the door and find a double order of tacos!"

"What?" Mark exclaimed.

Heaven Ray grinned and said, "Tacos?"

"American tacos," Daisy Dunton laughed.

Mark escorted Heaven Ray to one of Coronado's restaurants. "This is my treat, Daisy," he said, "You two gals, catch up. I'm going for a walk on the beach. I'll meet you in the tropical garden when you've finished." He kissed his wife, winked at Daisy, and left.

"I'm so glad we have a chance to catch up," Heaven Ray said.

"Tell me everything that's happened since I last saw you in person. I want all the details of your romance, well, maybe not all," she laughed.

Heaven Ray pulled Miss Ruth's well-read letter from her pocket and read it to Daisy.

"Well, shut my mouth and call me stupid. That's what my Aunt Tilly always said, but she never shut up, and nobody ever called her stupid. She was from Kentucky, after all. Someday, I'm going to go to your Alaska, and if I don't do anything else, I'm going to meet this Miss Ruth person."

"She does hit the nail on the head, doesn't she?" Heaven Ray said.

"Hey, that's my line," Daisy laughed, took the letter, and scanned it quickly. "This is the part I love."

...I've known your mother since she was a little girl and you from the day you were born. In fact, I was there! What an entry into the world, but that's a story for another day.

Your letter outlining your spiritual journey was encouraging to me. Like Jacob, you struggled, wrestled, and then surrendered. That was a fork in the road, a turning point, whatever you want to call it. I'm sure your friend Daisy will have an appropriate cliché.

It's simple, really, just like that song you sang in Sunday School when you were young—always trust and obey. We make it complicated when we insist on understanding and knowing all the whys and wherefores.

"That woman is one smart cookie, although I don't bother overthinking about struggles, wrestling, and surrendering, or who's in the driver's seat, so to speak. I just tell myself to do the next right thing and forget about everything else."

Heaven Ray hugged her friend and said, "For all your differences, and believe me, there are many. You and Miss Ruth are quite a bit alike."

"Sing that song for me," Daisy said, something about trust."

EPILOGUE
St Paul, Pribilof Islands,
1947

Dear Daisy,

I can't believe the war has been over for almost two years. Forgive me for not writing.

Shortly after I resigned from my commission and Mark was released from the rehabilitation center, we visited his mother in Rhode Island. Commander Lawson was reassigned to Naples, Italy, a month earlier, so we missed seeing him. Natalie told us she would soon join her husband overseas.

Then, we flew across the country and visited my folks in Kodiak. While we were there, Mark's discharge date came, and he was officially a civilian. Miss Ruth came to visit and suggested Mark apply for the school teacher position in St. Paul. He felt inadequate since he did not have a teaching degree, but the Territory did not require it, and Mark was the only applicant, so here we are on this bleak, isolated island in the Bering Sea.

We arrived last year just as summer began. Wildflowers filled the island's tundra with a glorious carpet resembling Joseph's coat of many colors. All too soon, summer waned, and violent weather approached. I thought life in Kodiak had prepared me for brutal Alaskan winters, but no. We learned so much, and we survived...

Heaven Ray looked up and said, " I was just writing to Daisy, telling her about the fierce beauty here." She put down her pen and picked up her knitting needles and a skein of fine baby-blue yarn.

"It's one of the harshest climates in the world." Mark gulped his coffee and frowned.

Heaven Ray looked out the window of their snug four-room house. "The wildflowers are still here."

"Winter will come quickly. I want you out of here before then." He set his coffee cup more firmly on the table than he intended. The hot liquid sloshed over his fingers and stained the white tablecloth.

"Now, look what you've done." She set aside her knitting and sponged the linen fabric.

"I'm sorry, but I want you somewhere safe before winter isolates us."

"I am safe."

"Between the storms, the heavy snowfall, and icy seas last winter, there was no traffic off-island. We were totally cut off."

"We were cocooned in our little house. I didn't mind."

"But you agree you'll be safer with your mother?"

"Safer, maybe, but I won't leave you."

"Please, Heaven."

"The baby is not due until spring."

"Spring comes late to St. Paul."

"We were so green last winter. Real cheechakos. I should have known better. I'm an Alaska girl, after all."

"These islands in the middle of the Bering Sea are as different from Kodiak as Newport is from the equator."

Heaven Ray picked up her knitting and thought about their first day on St. Paul. The barren volcanic rock with the black sand beach and thousand-foot cliffs shocked and then enchanted them. The outcroppings and ledges of the cliffs were home to hundreds of thousands of birds. The climate was too cold for trees to germinate, but the ground was covered with various grasses and wildflowers, a severe beauty. The village of St. Paul hugged the shore, and they heard the constant roar of the waves and the incessant barking of a million seals from the rookeries on the other side of the hills. Combined with the squawking of the myriad of birds, it made for a confused, chaotic choir with no apparent conductor.

Mark and several village men spent the better part of two days bringing the packing crates to the tiny house they would call home. That structure was on a rise a mile outside of the village with a tiny combination living-kitchen area, an even smaller bedroom, and a cramped bathroom. The most significant space was the storage room. At first, Heaven Ray was determined to use it as the bedroom, but she changed her mind when the men started to unload the crates. The dried and canned foodstuffs, winter clothes and gear, books, and miscellany soon filled the storage room.

Mark was appalled by the government housing. "This house is so small."

"Just a bit smaller than my folks cabin in Kodiak, but nothing like your home in Newport. It fits our needs, Mark. Be content."

"I want to give you the world. You deserve so much more than this."

"Stop fussing, Mark. You've given me everything I need or want."

Heaven Ray dropped a stitch, bit her lower lip in concentration, picked it up, and laughed as she remembered how she had learned to prepare seal meat. She surprised herself by acquiring a taste for it; seal oil is the best oil for cooking.

"Last winter was brutal, Heaven Ray, and this winter will be more of the same. I couldn't take the dark days on Kodiak, but here, the lack of light is deeper, longer, and seeps into my soul. I have to fight to stay awake," he said. "The sound of winter's wind blowing out of Siberia and crashing into the village is unnerving."

"We are safe in our little cabin, and Lady Aurora visits often."

"The Northern Lights are beautiful, but I missed daylight."

"You are enjoying summer's light now, and you have a lot of energy."

"I'll try to get everything done before the weather turns."

The men of the Pribilofs were hunters and fishermen, and Mark asked them to teach him. Heaven Ray remembered how frustrated Mark was that he couldn't keep up with them. He still carried shrapnel in his leg, and his limp was pronounced, although he constantly pushed himself. The villagers never mentioned it, and Mark didn't either.

"Life slows down in winter. I'm glad we have these diesel generators and that our fuel cans are kept from freezing in the storage room. Back in the day, the federal government ran the seal business. They brought in wood as fuel for their employees. If it was a hard winter, the employees ran out and burned furniture or whatever they could. Sometimes it wasn't enough," Heaven Ray said.

"The storms in winter are lethal; it's not frozen rain but actual shards of ice blowing first one way then another. It's impossible to walk to the village in such weather."

"We'll be stocked with everything we need."

"The drifts pile high, and the wind changes direction the next day and rearranges the drifts. I get lost in this small village we know so well. Last winter, the sea was frozen as far as we could see."

Heaven Ray saw the frustration on Mark's face and gentled her voice, "We survived. I'm not worried." She pulled out the last of the tinned pork and a large can of peaches from the storage room. "I'll prepare a special meal tonight. This year's final ship from Seattle is due any day.   Planning meals a year at a time is nearly impossible, but I'm determined to learn. Tomorrow, Diann Travis, half Aleut and half white, will teach me how to cure seal meat for the winter. And next week, several varieties of berries should be ripe. If I can learn more about how the Natives prepare for winter, I can supplement our supplies. Dried berries and seal meat are a prized meal in the Pribilofs." Heaven Ray finished the baby blanket and prepared to cast off. "See, it's almost done, and I can cross that off my list."

"One blue baby blanket does not mean we're prepared. I worry about you."

"I have a skein of pink yarn," She laughed, "I'll be prepared either way."

"You need to take this seriously." He ran his hand over his hair and reached for the coffee pot resting on the back of the oil-burning stove. He refilled his cup and offered to refill hers.

She shook her head and picked up two letters from the side table. "Your folks will come soon after the baby's born and bring everything it needs."

He chuckled despite his worry. "Mom'll bring enough to outfit every home in the village with an up-to-date nursery."

"And my parents will be here before that."

"What if there are complications? What if the baby comes during the winter? The ships can't get through, and the infrequent flights from Anchorage are usually canceled due to heavy fog."

"I'm a nurse and am taking excellent care of myself."

"But to have a baby on this tiny island in the middle of nowhere..." Mark paced the small combination kitchen and living room.

"Babushka will be here. She has delivered every baby in St. Paul for decades. Mom's a nurse. Dad's a doctor in case anything goes wrong, which it won't."

Mark rubbed the back of his neck. "That's another thing, where are we going to put everyone? There is only one bedroom, and how do you know your folks will arrive before the baby comes?"

"They will be on the first ship in the spring."

"It would be much easier if you would leave now and stay with your folks in Kodiak."

"And then?"

"And then stay there for a good six or seven months until it's safe for the little one to travel." Mark sat and pulled his boots on.

"Mark, don't fuss. Everything is fine."

"We'll talk again later. I need to prepare the lessons for tomorrow. I'll be at the school for a couple of hours. You'll be okay?"

"I'll have supper waiting."

He pulled on his jacket and hat. "Please reconsider, my love," he said as he kissed the top of her head and left.

The winter months were not as severe as everyone expected, and since break up was a week ago, they eagerly awaited the first ship of spring.

A sharp pain had Heaven Ray doubling over. She put her hand over her swollen belly and grasped the table's edge to steady herself. The pain subsided after a minute. She made a pot of tea and prayed. *Please, God, don't let this be the beginning of something serious.* She pulled her old nurses' manuals from the trunk at the foot of the bed and reread the sections about pregnancy and all the possible complications. Her anxiety mounted with each paragraph. Finally, she slammed the books shut. *Mom always said not to dig up in doubt what I planted in faith. I was convinced staying here through the winter was right. I trust You to keep the baby safe. I will not fear.*

The baby was not due for another six weeks. She picked up her notebook and scanned the lists written there. Everything must be perfect before her parents arrived, although they wouldn't care if the house was dusty and the meals simple. In fact, her mother said not to worry about a thing. They weren't coming as guests. Heaven Ray pulled her letter from its envelope and read:

...and don't overtax yourself preparing for our arrival. Your father has declared himself the 'chief cook and bottle washer,' as well as doctor, father, and grandpa. His medical bag is packed and ready. I'm insisting he leaves the baseball mitt and ball at home. You'd think after delivering so many babies, he would know the little one wouldn't be playing baseball for many years. He's so excited he can't think! Men!

By the way, Angel is enjoying a visit with her aunt and uncle in Ninilchik. I can't believe it took almost two years to find them. I sometimes wonder if she will decide to stay with them. I pray Bozhe's best for her, even if that means leaving me.

See you soon,
Love, Mom.

Heaven Ray doubled over again with the same pain. It had come and gone throughout the day. She put on her heavy coat, gloves, and scarf. Even though the sun shone, the sharp wind pierced through her. She bent over twice with those frightful cramps during her trek to the village. She smiled and waved at everyone as she continued past the Russian church to the dwelling of an old woman known only as Babushka—grandmother.

"I'm afraid the baby will come early," Heaven Ray shed her coat and settled at the small table. Babushka poured the tea and placed a small plate of smoked salmon on the table.

"It is good bilik. You eat."

"Bilik? What kind of smoked fish is that?"

"Very old recipe from the Russian Czar. The best."

Heaven Ray thanked her but said she couldn't eat a thing.

Babushka placed her hands on Heaven Ray's belly and said, "He wants to enter this world."

"I'm not due for another six weeks."

"They come when they are ready." She shook her head and narrowed her eyes. "He is active, yes?"

"I'm not ready."

"You say it is not your time? You are sure?"

Heaven wrapped her arms around her belly, her eyes full of unshed tears. "He needs to stay within me a little longer. I was hoping you had some herbs that I could take."

Babushka pulled a sealskin pouch from a small metal tin and gave it to her. "Make a tea with a few leaves, not too many. The tea will tell the little one he is not welcome in the world just yet. Drink it only once a day, not more than seven days."

"Thank you, Babushka. We have much to learn from Native

medicine. Once the baby is born and things settle down, I would like you to teach me if you are willing."

"I am." Babushka grinned, showing her missing teeth, and said, "It is a boy child, strong and determined."

Heaven Ray shrugged into her coat and held the sealskin pouch close to her heart.

With much prayer and a little bit of anxiety, she brewed the tea and took it regularly for the prescribed seven days. The baby settled, and together they waited. She decided not to burden Mark with this little episode.

"Goodbye, Mom. I wish you could stay longer." Heaven Ray sniffed and hugged her mother as they stood on the black sand shore.

"I do too," Haven Ray said, "But I'm sure Mark's parents are on their way, and there is so little room. We will be back often."

"What do you think of your future baseball player?" Mark asked his father-in-law.

He laughed, shook Mark's hand, and said, "The most beautiful baby I ever saw. Smart, too. He grabbed my finger and looked me in the eye. He knows who his grandpa is."

The farewells would have continued, but the ship blew its horn, and the Native ferrying them in his small boat started the engine and motioned for them to hurry. "The captain's waiting. The tide is turning. He does not like me to give my passengers more time to say goodbye."

"Remember, we'll be back soon," Mom called.

A week later, the grind of a vehicle and the blaring of its horn interrupted their dinner. The overcast skies threw an opaque light over everything but could not dampen Mark's face as he ran out of the house; the awkward limping gait did not slow him. "I can't believe you are here!" He wrapped his folks in a bear hug. Laughing and talking, they entered the small house with arms around each other.

Heaven Ray was also hugged and fussed over. "We didn't expect you so soon."

Natalie hugged her and said, "Your folks called as soon as they had news about the baby, and we hopped aboard a Navy plane as soon as possible. Flying halfway around the world was no burden, not when my grandson was waiting for me! The plane from Anchorage was canceled because of fog, so we begged passage on the cargo ship."

"Flights are often canceled," Mark huffed, "I think this is the foggiest place on earth."

"My folks left a few days ago, and we haven't even unpacked our crates from the ship," Heaven Ray put on a pot of coffee.

"We brought boxes of food and things for the baby. It's all on the beach," Natalie said, "But that's not important. Where's my grandson?"

"Sleeping, which he doesn't do often," Mark said, unaware of his mother's disappointment.

"I'll drive you into the village," Commander Lawson said, "We can pick up whatever you need and all the things on the beach."

"We don't have a car, Heaven Ray said.

The commander laughed and said, "Look out the window."

She pulled back the curtain. "It can't be. Is that your Jeep?"

"It's yours now."

"But how?"

"I don't want you walking to the village store or the post office, especially now that the baby is here."

"When will he wake up?" Natalie asked, "I want to see my first grandchild."

"Let's take a peek," she said, taking Natalie into the only bedroom where the little one slept in a cradle Mark had made out of packing crates.

"Sir?" Mark questioned his father, "The Jeep?"

"As you know, a lot of military equipment was dumped into the ocean after the war. That was not going to happen to my Jeep."

"But, sir, rules and regulations?" Heaven Ray said as she and her mother-in-law returned.

"He's a darling. I can't wait until he wakes up," Natalie beamed.

The commander's eyes twinkled. "I seem to remember a certain nurse telling me Alaskans find a way to get things done and do it despite rules and regs. I admit I don't color outside the lines often, but it was necessary."

Heaven Ray hugged the commander. "That Jeep and I are going to be very good friends."

Natalie elbowed her husband, "I said that little boy is the spitting image of Mark."

"Of course he is. I wouldn't have it any other way."

"You were telling us about the Jeep," Heaven Ray said over her shoulder as she headed toward the stove. "Come, sit at the table. You're just in time for dessert."

"We sailed from Anchorage in a former Navy cargo ship and

were brought ashore in a landing craft. I'd rather see the surplus put to use rather than trashed." The commander rubbed his chin, and his crow's feet crinkled as he laughed, "I must confess that poor old Jeep spent a lot of time in the motor pool at the war's end. Now it's got a new lease on life." He patted Heaven Ray's hand. "I feel better knowing you and the baby will have solid transportation."

"Did it really need to spend time in the motor pool, sir?" Mark asked his father.

The commander slapped his son on the shoulder and winked as he said, "Yes, I think it did. Yeoman Richardson kept it in his garage after the war."

"But he lives in Vermont," Mark exclaimed.

"As soon as we received word about the baby's birth, your father called Elly to have the Jeep flown to Anchorage, where we had it put on the ship. By the way, he's making plans to visit. He says he intends to be the baby's great-godfather."

Mark laughed, "I bet he does."

"Your father will never admit this, but he's an old softie. He told me how you drove that Jeep all over Kodiak chasing a certain pretty nurse who wanted nothing to do with you. That Jeep holds fond memories for him."

The commander's face reddened, "No need to say anything further, Nat."

"And he planned to give it to you as a wedding gift if you ever captured that nurse's heart."

"I'm sorry we deprived you of a wedding," Heaven Ray looked at Mark. They both smiled.

"Nonsense. Elly always said you two would end up together. It was his idea to save the Jeep for you. He made the arrangements after the war since I had been deployed overseas. I should have had your mother keep it in Kodiak."

"Mark?" Natalie said.

"Yes," both Mark's answered, and they all laughed.

"My Mark," Natalie said, "Ask them the baby's name."

The commander shuffled his feet, suddenly at a loss for words. "Did you get my letter?"

Mark poured his parents a cup of coffee. "Yes, sir, if you mean your vow on official naval stationery, signed by Commander Mark Lawson, III, that there would be no interference with the boy's name."

"How did you know he was going to be a boy?" Heaven Ray asked.

The commander's face shone. "The Lawson's haven't birthed a girl in five generations. Anyway, there will be no pressure about his name."

"Thank you, Commander," Mark cleared his throat, "er, Dad."

Heaven Ray stood and pulled a large Bible from the small bookshelf in the corner. "He has a name, and I hope you'll be happy with our choice."

Mark cleared his throat again, looked his father in the eye, turned to the Family Tree page, and placed the Bible before his father. "We named him after two honorable men."

Commander Lawson read from the book, "Bradley Anak Lawson."

Natalie wiped a tear from her eye and kissed her son's cheek. "Your brother would have been so pleased."

Mark waited for his father to speak. The commander took a handkerchief from his pocket, blew his nose, and said, "I'm proud of you, son. I'm proud of the life you've built and the man you have become."

St. Paul, Pribilof Islands,
Spring 1949

Miss Ruth held one-year-old baby Bradley on her knee. "I can talk baby talk in English, Russian, Tlingit, and Yupik, little man. What would you prefer?"

He sucked on his fingers and drooled.

"Yes, I thought so," Miss Ruth babbled, "You are the smartest Lawson ever. Did you know that, my boy?"

Heaven Ray laughed, "I hate to break up your love fest, but this little guy needs to be changed. Can't you smell him?"

"There are some advantages to getting old," Miss Ruth's eyes twinkled as she handed the baby to Heaven Ray.

Mark came in, hung his coat on the peg by the door, removed his shoes, and poured himself a cup of coffee. "I'm glad you're here, Miss Ruth."

"I gathered from your last letter that you had something important to discuss."

Mark poured himself a cup of coffee and refreshed Miss Ruth's cup. He sat across from her at the sailcloth-covered table. "Do you think it's possible the evacuees will ever return to their islands?"

Miss Ruth stared into her coffee cup. She took a bag of lemon drops from her pocket and laid it on the table. "According to what I've heard, Attu and Kiska will never be repopulated. There is too much unexploded ordinance there, and it would cost mil-

279

lions to remove it. Far more than the federal government is willing to spend."

"And the other islands?"

She patted his hand, "There is not much hope. Other than forcing the men here to St. Paul during the war to continue killing the seals for their oil, the government has no interest in undoing what they've done."

"Their plight weighs on me. Something must be done, but what and by whom?" Mark sounded genuinely puzzled.

"What about you?" Miss Ruth asked.

Mark sighed and raised his eyes to Miss Ruth. He rubbed his chin. "I want to go back to school and get my teaching degree, but I also want to learn about how the government works, both federal and territorial. Things can change through legislation."

"It's a start," Miss Ruth said, "But we must change how people think about their Native neighbors. After your schooling, what?"

"I don't know."

"The Lord will reveal it to you in time. And I can put you in touch with various elders and activists. There are rumblings, my boy, within the Alaska Native Brotherhood and Sisterhood. They are determined to reclaim their rights as US citizens and the first inhabitants of this land. They want to revive their culture before it's lost forever."

"The natives are restless, as Daisy Dunton would say," Heaven Ray said as she returned. "Our little man is asleep, but I heard your conversation, and I agree with everything Mark wants to do."

"When am I going to meet this Daisy person?" Miss Ruth asked, "You've talked about her so often."

"You'll meet her soon, and you will like her," Mark laughed,

"I'd like a list of these people. Are they all Natives?"

Miss Ruth pulled pen and paper from her pocketbook and began to write. "Most are Natives. A few are sympathetic whites."

"I'd like to see a school where those who still know the old ways can teach the young ones," Mark said.

Miss Ruth laid down her pen, folded her hands, and began to pray silently. Mark and Heaven Ray bowed their heads and waited. "Amen," she said.

"When the school year ends, I've fulfilled my contract here in St. Paul. I've been accepted to the University of Alaska. But I feel so isolated here. Cut off from the rest of Alaska."

"You have built bridges here, Mark. You can build on that. Even though you are an outsider, you have earned the elders' respect. They are in touch with others."

"I just want to help."

"You must realize it will never be what it was, but it can still be good."

Mark's shoulders slumped, and regret filled his eyes. "I wish…"

Miss Ruth patted his hand. "You have a servant's heart, and that's what you must do. You learned the Navy's hierarchy when you were in the military, and you will need to learn how the Natives wish to proceed. Do not promote yourself."

"Mark would never do that!" Heaven Ray spoke sharper than she intended.

Miss Ruth continued in her soft voice. "Do not offer your advice unless asked."

Mark nodded, "That is wise counsel, Miss Ruth. Thank you."

She turned serious eyes to him and Heaven Ray, "You must realize this endeavor will not be popular among most people or politicians. Progress will be slow. It could take decades, if not the rest of your lives, but I sense Bozhe's will in this."

Mark and Heaven Ray reached for the other's hand.

Miss Ruth said, "I'm proud of you both. The indigenous Alaskans have been held down for centuries, first by the Russians and then by the Americans, but they are hardy and resilient. They will find their way."

"Thank you, Miss Ruth. We will call on you often for advice," Mark kissed her cheek.

"And for prayers," Heaven Ray added.

"Bozhe will lead you. Fair winds and following seas, my dears."

MY MAMA'S MAMA: BOOK 6

FINALLY, FRANELLA

PROLOGUE

Somerview Woman's College
University of Oxford
Oxford, England
1950

The ornate, circular assembly room of the Sheldonian Theatre in the middle of Oxford's medieval city was packed. Students and their proud families squeezed close together on the uncomfortable, tiered wooden benches. The overcast sky outside the 17th-century building filtered the light through its ornate windows. The diffused light illuminated the cupola's superbly painted ceiling, aptly titled <u>Truth Descending on the Arts and Sciences</u>.

The culmination of many years of hard work and honest endeavor by these proud young men and a few women had been honored and rewarded. These prestigious students had matriculated some years ago and today received their awards and diplomas. Those who achieved the highest academic levels were recommended by their various proctors and had their names sent to the university's sole selection committee. A chosen few were called to speak. One by one, they rose, made their way to the speaker's box, introduced themselves, and read their prepared remarks.

Franella Feddersen, uncomfortable in her black robe with its wide bell-shaped sleeves, felt a trickle of sweat between her shoulder blades. As each honoree rose to speak, Franella became more agitated. Now, it was her turn. The Oxford University DPhi (Doctor of Philosophy) robe with its blue lining and red border rustled as she stood. Because Franella had achieved the pinnacle of achievement, her gown was marked by broad velvet panels down the front and three chevrons on the sleeves. The tassel hanging from her academic mortarboard swayed with every bob of her head.

The last to speak, Franella approached the speaker's box with leaden feet and a heavy heart. She felt the pain of the past, and it overshadowed her present accomplishments—doctorates in literature and philosophy.

She looked around the horseshoe shaped room but didn't see him. He said he'd be here, that they both would. Behind her, the row of Oxford's deans, proctors, and other dignitaries, in their solemn attire and frowning faces, sat stiff and unapproving. She was an American and a woman, and even though several of her papers had been published in prestigious journals, those who had voted against her showed their disdain by refusing to look her way.

She tapped the microphone, breathed deeply, and cleared her throat. She licked her dry lips and opened her mouth. No words came. She tried again. The audience, hushed and expectant, fed her anxiety. Franella felt the familiar shaking start in her fingertips. She fisted her hands on the podium, hoping her fellow students and many professors would not sense her fear. She drew in several gulps of air.

Out of the corner of her eye, she saw Dean Blythe-Smith. He whispered for her to begin through the gap in his front teeth. She gave him a slight shake of her head. Frantically, he motioned for her to continue. Franella stared at his long, thin fingers, flapping like a gull's wing. She bit the inside of her cheek until the metallic tinge of blood increased her anxiety. She pictured herself screaming and tearing her speech into minute pieces and flinging it at the audience. She saw herself as a child, unable to sit still, study, or even read. What was that rambunctious child in tattered overalls doing here wearing this illustrious attire? She belonged in the wilderness of Alaska, not among the spires of Oxford.

She crumpled the pages of her speech and let it fall to the floor. Heart pounding, shoulders squared, and eyes staring straight ahead as if she were wearing blinders, Franella Feddersen marched out of the centuries-old building. She wove her way through the audience, unmindful of their stares and whispered comments. Once outside, she leaned against the entrance door, doubled over, and pressed her hands on her stomach, ignoring the misty drizzle. *Breathe, I just need to breathe.*

The two men seated center right in the twenty-second row had held their breaths as they willed her to continue, then looked at each other in horror when she left.

"I thought she could do it," the middle-aged man in the tweed jacket said.

"I know, Tollers, I did, too. The question is, what do we do now?"

"You're the better speaker. Take over for her. I'll find her and take her to the Baby. We'll meet you there."

"Shouldn't we let Blythe-Smith handle it?"

"I don't think Old Mud and Whiskers is up to it. He looks like one of your skinny marsh-wiggles crawling to the speaker's box, ashen face and bulging eyes. Poor man." Tollers gave his companion a slight shove. "Go on, Jack. Redeem the situation."

Jack laughed, "You're right. He's very marsh-wiggleish, all elbows and knees. I wonder if I was thinking of him when I created that character. But let's say no more. I haven't sent the manuscript to the publisher yet."

"Go on, put the poor man out of his misery."

Dean Bythe-Smith leaned into the microphone as he looked toward Franella's escape route. "Americans!" he sighed, "I'm sure we're all grateful for what they did during the war, but where's their couth, their civility?" He shrugged and sighed. It whistled through the gap in his front teeth. "Can we expect anything different?" The audience did not respond, and he shook his handkerchief and wiped the sweat from his brow, then smiled as he watched the portly professor come forward.

Outside of the ornate building designed by Christopher Wren, the English air was cool, the clouds low and gray, reminding Franella Feddersen of home. She should have never left Port Alexander; she knew that now. What had possessed her to think she could be—*Somebody*? The old feelings of emptiness returned, and she saw the barrenness of her soul. Awash in a vacant sea, the images attacked. She hit her fists on the side of her head, but still, they taunted her. She felt someone pulling her arms down.

"Sorry, I haven't done that in years," she mumbled.

He didn't answer but put his arm around her shoulder. She leaned against him and laid her head on his chest, "Who did I think I was?"

"Why, my dear, you are your own wonderful self."

"Herring Pete said it was the only solution, but he just wanted to get rid of me."

288

He patted her shoulder and led her a few blocks to the taxi stand. She stumbled and would have fallen had he not kept his arm around her. He hailed a taxi and settled the both of them in the back seat. "Who is Herring Pete?" He pulled a large white handkerchief from his vest pocket and mopped her face. She took it and blew her nose.

"I dismantled his still."

"What?"

Franella sniffed, hiccuped, and sniffed again, "He's a horrible, no good man. He added to my misery."

"You'll tell me and Uncle Jack all about it, and we'll find a solution."

Franella turned wide eyes to him and said, "I could never call him—Uncle!"

He chuckled, held his pipe out, "May I?" At her nod, he lit it and chuckled again. "We will keep the uncle part between ourselves, but I know he has a deep affection for you."

"I'm nothing, nobody."

"Come, my dear, I will not hear such talk from you.

As the audience saw the professor rise and approach Dean Blythe-Smith, curious but tentative applause spread throughout the auditorium. Blythe-Smith breathed a sigh of relief, shoved his face into the microphone, and said, "This man needs no introduction." He hurried away, mumbling about classless, uncouth, undependable Americans.

Jack reached for the crumpled paper Franella had dropped. He smoothed and folded it, then put it in his vest pocket. "This is a graduation ceremony you won't soon forget, but not for the reason you think." Some in the audience laughed hesitantly, unsure of his meaning. "I am going to tell you a story, a true story, that begins on an island on the other side of the globe. A cold world of the north, unfamiliar and strange to us, I'm sure."

www.ingramcontent.com/pod-product-compliance
Lightning Source LLC
Chambersburg PA
CBHW051129190726
48290CB00006B/1758